The Tenth Saint

The Tenth Saint

D.J. Niko

MEDALLION
PRESS

Medallion Press, Inc.

Printed in USA

Table of Contents

Published 2012 by Medallion Press, Inc.

The MEDALLION PRESS LOGO
is a registered trademark of Medallion Press, Inc.

Cover design by James Tampa
Edited by Helen A Rosburg and Emily Steele

Names, characters, places, and incidents are the products of the author's imagination or are used fictionally. Any resemblance to actual events, locales, or persons, living or dead, is entirely coincidental.

Typeset in Adobe Garamond Pro
Printed in the United States of America

ISBN# 9781605422459

10 9 8 7 6 5 4 3 2 1
First Edition

For Nicola

In memoriam

One

The camel trod tentatively on a patch of cracked earth. The upper crust shattered underfoot the heavily laden beast like unfired pottery broken into a thousand pieces. The camel driver, a gaunt man shrouded in indigo gauze from head to bare feet, made an urgent clicking sound and hit the animal on its hindquarters with a palm frond whip. The camel took two quick steps in reaction to the insult, then halted, groaning its displeasure. Despite repeated calls from its driver, it was going no farther and that was that.

The man peeled back his headdress to uncover his face. His skin was the color of antelope hide, with deep grooves carved into his forehead and cheek hollows. The sun had taken its toll on him over the fifty years he had walked the desert. He looked like an emaciated octogenarian, tired and beaten down by life, but his eyes, pools of liquid onyx, shone with a spirit full of vigor and wisdom, the kind needed to guide a tribe of nomads through this unforgiving country. He squinted to the sky to confirm the position of the sun. It was as he thought: directly overhead. He appraised the desert around him. All that he surveyed was arid and parched. Parched like the camels and his fellow riders. The midday sun scorched without remorse, and there was no salvation—no water, no shade—in sight.

With one hand, he drew circles in the air to summon the other men. "We will stop here," he told them when they'd gathered round. "The animals are tired. They must have water."

"But, Shaykh, there is no water," said one of the younger men, his narrow eyes full of doubt. "There hasn't been water in many moons."

The leader put his hand on the young man's shoulder. "Then we shall find some, Abu. The desert is our mother. She always provides."

The young man did not talk back to his elder. It was the Bedouin way: trust and obey. The elders had proven themselves as men of great character and honor and, as such, commanded the respect of the goums. Hairan was chief of the tribe, the Bedouins' moral and spiritual leader.

The others stood by the old chief, waiting for direction. Hairan instructed them to make camp and start a fire. Then he summoned the old woman Taneva and asked her to gather some of the womenfolk and walk toward the east in search of water.

Taneva kneeled before the chief in reverence, shrinking into her black woolen robes, the standard dress of Bedouin widows. She was the eldest woman in the tribe and therefore the one who had witnessed the most, including the birth of two generations. Nothing remained of her youth but dignity. Her eyes, ringed in black kohl, smoldered like a half-spent fire. Her receding brown lips were taut with determination. The strands of hair escaping her black veil framed her face like threads of silver tinsel.

Hairan motioned to her to rise and stand as his equal. "There was rain in the east two days ago." He pointed to a pair of high sand dunes. "Behind those dunes is a low valley. Look for the water there."

Taneva bowed and backed away.

Three women accompanied Taneva eastward, the sand hot as a simmering cauldron beneath their bare feet. Balancing earthen jars on their heads, they did not complain but walked on, as their people had done for centuries before them.

For half an hour they endured the discomfort, and they were rewarded for it. Just as Hairan had predicted, a pool of water was inside a hollow in the sand. It wasn't much—barely enough to last the day—and it swarmed with insects. But tomorrow was a new day, and it would bring as much hope as any other. The women kneeled to collect what little water there was, straining it through the gauze of their head veils to purify it.

Driven by a premonition that there was more to find, Taneva left the others and walked toward another depression in the sand. As she came to the edge of the hollow, her gaze fell upon a thing she had never before encountered. She squinted to get a clearer look.

In the sand was a bulge.

She hurried down, raising great plumes of dust with her bare feet. Something was there, indeed. Something unnatural.

She approached the mass and with a desert woman's sense of duty began brushing the sand aside to reveal what lay beneath. Her hand swept over a coarse snarl like the heap of her woolen embroidery threads after a sandstorm. She jerked her hand away, her eyes wide and mouth trembling with dread. Instinctively she looked around for help, but no one was near. With a deep breath, she returned to her task. The women of the desert, like the men, did not turn away from what was put on their path. It was their fate. To walk away would be to defy the powers, which would lead to certain ruin.

Taneva's hand came upon something hard, a protrusion, like bone. With both hands, she made a groove in the sand and dug with new resolve.

The head revealed itself first. The eyes were deep in their sockets, the skin around them purple from impact or pain. The hair was fair of color and short, so crusted with sand it resembled the fleece of a long-dead sheep.

Taneva pushed the rest of the sand aside to uncover the naked body of a man, curled in the fetal position and pale as death. She pressed both hands to her mouth to contain a shriek. Falling to her knees next to the body, she chanted the song of the dying as an offering for the soul of the victim.

That night, Hairan tended to the stranger inside his own tent. By all accounts, the man should have been dead. By some miracle, he wasn't. Hairan himself doubted he would live, for his breathing was shallow, his body battered, and his unconscious state closer to death than slumber. But as a Bedouin, a shaykh, and a medicine man, he was bound to care for the stranger until he had either recovered or given up the fight.

Hairan had put the man on his own mat and covered him with all of his woolen blankets to reverse his plummeting temperature. The stranger's skin was cold and dry to the touch, as if life was slowly departing.

The chief had never seen a man with skin the hue of bleached bone or hair the color of the sun. It did not matter. Whoever the stranger was and wherever he had come from, they were the same, just as man and beast and grain of desert sand were the same.

With the vacillating flame of an oil lamp as his sole guidance, the old man placed some herbs on a stone and rolled them between his fingers. He picked up a pinch and put it to his nose. "Not enough," he muttered and continued crushing until the healing oils of the leaves were released.

When he was satisfied with the consistency and aroma of the paste, he rubbed a handful on the stranger's cheeks, forehead, and lips and another on his chest. The remaining pulp he placed inside the man's hands, closing them in loose fists.

Hairan lifted his own hands to the sky in deference to the powers. "I am a simple man who knows nothing," he chanted softly. "Whatever wisdom has been granted me I gladly share with my pale brother. But he is not mine to save. His fate is known only by the Great Spirit, the keeper of all life."

He curled up on the ground next to the stranger. That would be his bed tonight, cold and inhospitable as it was. Discomfort was not appalling to the Bedouin. It was as much a part of existence in the desert as the beating sun or a camel's foul breath or the endless expanse of dunes gilded by the last streaks of daylight.

Hairan stared at the man who lay battling for his earthly life. With his sharp-angled nose, pale pink lips, long fingers and limbs, and unpigmented hide, he was neither Bedouin nor Arab, nor Jew for that matter.

Taneva walked in with a glass of warm goat's milk. "Will he live?"

The chief shook his head. "Of this I cannot be certain."

"Is he one of those savages from the East, Shaykh?"

"Perhaps. Or perhaps he is from the other side of the Red Sea, a trader. There is no need to ask such questions. All things will be revealed if it is time and if we are ready."

"You are a wise man, Hairan. A generous man."

"I do only what is required of me. We are all one, and we live to serve each other."

She threw her own blanket on Hairan and stroked his hair tenderly in a rare display of affection. Before the other inhabitants of the goums, he was the shaykh and she an old woman. Only when they were alone was she his mother. "Your father would be proud. Good night, my son."

The stranger opened his eyes on the morning of the seventh day. The veil of unconsciousness still weighed heavily on his eyelids, and his body ached so much he could do no more than lie still.

He surveyed his surroundings in the stupor of long slumber, like a bear awakened from hibernation. The walls were thick burlap, the roof held up by a tree trunk in the center of the room. There was no floor. He lay on blankets stretched out on sand. In the far corner was a small bench carved from wood holding some stone implements. At his bedside were an earthen pot, blackened from fire, and a pile of filthy gauze. His blankets were woolen and so heavy he did not have the strength to lift them, but they were beautiful, obviously woven by an artist's hands, with images of stars and scorpions and all-seeing eyes in indigo, saffron, and crimson.

Though he tried to sort out what was happening, his brain was not processing it. The images were unfamiliar. He knew he was inside a tent, but whose, where? Was he in danger? And how had he gotten here? His head ached as he tried to recall the circumstances that had brought him to this place. He could not. He was looking around in frustration, desperate for a clue to spark his memory, when a man ducked in.

The man nodded at him but said nothing. A tight smile crossed his weathered lips, and his face contorted to reveal a network of furrows.

"Who are you?" he croaked in English. "What is this place? Why am I here?"

The chief said something in an incomprehensible

language, dipped gauze in liquid, and wiped his brow.

He started to pull away but lacked the strength to put up a fight.

The chief handed him a small clay pot, pointed to his own lips, and spoke again.

Still bewildered, he turned his head away. "Leave me be, old man. Go tend to your goats or something."

The chief slipped out of the tent in silence.

With eyes closed, he tried to summon a memory. Random images raced through his mind, and it was impossible to make sense of them. He saw faces—faces he did not recognize, their features erased by memory's cruel hand. Metallic voices banged around his head, mocking him with their sinister pitch. There was darkness, then a bright orange light, amorphous and violent, like fire. The image chilled his blood. A woman's voice emerged from behind the darkness. He could not see her face, but her voice was calm and comforting. She spoke a single word: *Gabriel.*

He knew with all certainty that the name was his own, but his memory cheated him of all else. No amount of effort could muster the recollection of who Gabriel was and what he had been.

Two

At high noon, the sub-Saharan sun baked the earth to a brittle dust. The ground was fragile and dry, like old parchment. Every time a shovel crunched into the dirt, the dust rose in great swirls and hung in the air. Sarah Weston took a break from digging and wiped the grime and sweat from her brow. She was exhausted after working since dawn, as she had every morning for the past five months, trying to find something—anything—to confirm her theory that beneath the hot earth and granite lay a royal necropolis the likes of which no archaeologist had discovered intact in this part of the world.

Aksum. The Ethiopian empire that centuries ago was the most powerful kingdom in East Africa and Arabia. The fabled ancestral land of the Queen of Sheba. The home of kings and powerful warriors and untold wealth, all buried in great labyrinths beneath the broken stelae standing like silent eternal soldiers on the foothills of Mount Saint George.

Sarah confirmed her coordinates against the georadar readings. "This has to be the place." She dug her flat-edge shovel into the earth.

This routine was nothing new to her. As an archaeologist with Cambridge University, she had been dispatched on expeditions around the world, from the tombs of Egypt to the Akrotiri site in Santorini to an unknown Mayan city deep in the jungles of Guatemala. In the field, no one would ever guess she was an aristocrat, the only daughter of a British baronet and an American actress as legendary for her beauty as for the vodka and Valium habit that claimed her life.

In spite of the notorious Weston name, Sarah kept her private life private and went to great lengths to stand on equal ground with her crew. She was the first to roll up her sleeves before dawn and the last to hang up her pickaxe at night.

She looked nothing like the debutantes she'd grown up with. She didn't try to tame her cascading blonde curls, tucking them instead into cheap bandanas she bought from the sidewalk merchants. Her figure, as lean and lithe as a greyhound's, she hid under baggy, shabby khakis and tattered Marks & Spencer T-shirts. Her eyes had the color and clarity of glacial ice, but no one would know it because she rarely removed the big black aviators she'd had since grad school. And she made no special effort to remove the dark crescent from the tips of her fingernails. The "noble dirt," as she called it, reminded her of her connection to the earth and to the people who'd walked it before her.

She worked the dig like everyone else, even though she was leading the expedition—the first time in her thirty-five years she had been given that coveted opportunity. She knew better than to get on a high horse; it was too easy to fall or be knocked down—something she had learned from her mother the hard way.

"So frustrating," said Aisha, an exchange student from Al Akhawayn University in Morocco. "It's been, what, five months? You'd think we would hit pay dirt by now."

"Patience, girl," Sarah said without looking up. "This isn't an Indiana Jones movie. The first lesson of archaeology: it always takes longer than you think. Second lesson: no matter how long it takes, you keep at it."

With long, dark fingers, Aisha adjusted her hijab. She sighed with the impatience of youth and nodded toward the mountains beyond the work site. "Do you think there's something out there?"

A light breeze whispered across the parched landscape. Sarah squinted toward the horizon. "I know so."

"Is that your professional opinion or the famous gut feeling archaeologists are supposed to have?"

"Bit of both, I suppose. Look, if it were easy, chances are the site would be looted already. The fact that it's taken us this long to find it is actually a good sign. Whatever's down there has very likely not been seen by human eyes for fifteen-plus centuries. That's a sexy prospect, don't you think?"

"Only a Brit would think that's sexy."

Sarah laughed and patted the girl's shoulder. "Come on. Let's go into town to get some lunch. I'm absolutely famished."

The modern town of Aksum had nothing of its once-great identity. Forgotten by all but the faithful, who kept guard over the churches, and the farmers, who insisted on scratching a living off the arid earth, it stood as a sad reminder of an eminence long lost.

Still, the town claimed forty-seven thousand inhabitants, most of them out and about at midday. The place bustled. The spicy aroma of *wat* cooking emanated from clay courtyards. Old, toothless women, too feeble to cook, sat on benches on the sides of the road, spinning cotton for the looms. Children ran unchecked on the half-paved streets, shrieking their delight as they chased each other with thorny acacia vines. Villagers wearing white cotton robes and the gaunt countenance of poverty loitered in the streets with no other intent than to alleviate their boredom, the kind that is inevitable in a poor, isolated farm town.

Sarah's favorite canteen was Tigrinya, a helter-skelter roadside stand that fed hundreds of Ethiopians at lunchtime. The food was not particularly good, but the energy was priceless. Everybody gathered there to see each other and share the gossip. This day was like any other: nowhere to sit, locals fighting with the cook over the wait for their meals, the stench of hot oil saturating the air, Amharic music blaring from an eighties vintage boom box.

"Try to snag a table," she said to the others. "I'll go order."

She spoke Amharic better than any of her crew. Since childhood she'd had a flair for language, and her ability to pick up foreign tongues in mere months had given her an advantage among archaeologists. She liked to practice on the locals while standing in the lines, engaging the farmers in conversations about the brutal rainless summer and the teenage boys about their foosball strategies. Truth be told, she enjoyed talking with the Africans more than with her own people, whose cannibalistic gossip about one another she found insufferably boring.

Over her shoulder, an Ethiopian man whispered in broken English, "You are the English lady, yes? From the dig in the valley."

She turned to face the stranger. He was tall and lanky, wearing torn Levi's that hit above the ankle, a chain with a silver Menelik coin pendant, and an old Yankees baseball cap. She sized him up as the typical profiteer from these parts who would trade counterfeit antiquities for anything foreign, preferably American. She forced a stiff-lipped smile but did not reply.

"I can help you. I know a place with old things."

"Look, mister—"

"Ejigu." He extended his hand. "Most nice to meet you."

"Look, Ejigu, I mean no disrespect here, but I don't need your help. Thanks all the same."

"Look this." He took two pottery fragments out of his pocket, looking furtively over his shoulder.

Sarah tried to appear indifferent as she examined the shards. One bore faded geometric patterns—diamond panels, stylized vertical lines, small circles with crosses through them—all rendered in ochre. The other was black and white with fluid scrollwork. She ran her finger down the exposed clay of the broken edge. It was smooth, as if it had shattered ages ago and had long since been cured by the earth. Fourth or fifth century, she estimated based on the symbolism. The cross, especially, hinted at the post-Christian Aksumite civilizations prevalent in these parts sometime after 320 CE. "Where did you get this?"

Ejigu was clearly satisfied with himself for piquing her interest. "Is secret," he whispered in pseudoclandestine fashion. "But if English lady wants to know . . ."

He rubbed his forefinger and thumb together in the universal sign for money.

Sarah shook her head and laughed. "No, thanks, my friend. I work for a university. That means I have no money to give you."

Ejigu looked her up and down. "That is a fine watch," he said, pointing to the beat-up Timex on her wrist. "You give me, I take you to find these things."

"You have seen more like this?"

"Oh, yes, lady. Much, much more." He widened his eyes.

Sarah smirked, showing him she believed he was exaggerating. She didn't trust him, but the fragments intrigued her enough to take it a step further.

The big Ethiopian lady at the window bellowed to Sarah to cut the chitchat and place her order.

"Look, I've got to go. If you are serious, meet me here tomorrow. You take me to this site of yours, and if it is all you claim, I promise I will reward you."

They shook on it, and she walked to the order window.

The next afternoon, Sarah waited at Tigrinya. Her proper English upbringing told her to never trust the locals, particularly in a place like Ethiopia, where anything can be bought or sold for the right price. But her American side carried equal weight. When her parents had divorced, she'd moved with her mother to New York and attended boarding school in Connecticut. In that ruthlessly competitive environment, she'd honed her instincts. She'd learned how to size up people and outsmart them at their own games. Those made-in-America street smarts served her well in the field. She certainly was not afraid of Ejigu. She saw him as a small-time operator, a guy out to make a quick buck and move on to the next deal.

Though she doubted this would amount to much, she'd come anyway. Most other archaeologists, certainly her Cambridge colleagues, would never consider pursuing leads from locals, whom they regarded as money-grubbing false prophets. She, on the other hand, had no such prejudices. Though she realized ninety-nine percent of these promises were empty, she had a hunch about the other one percent, and life had taught her to go with her hunches.

Ejigu was on time. Dressed for a trek in the same torn jeans and mud-encrusted Nikes with lime-green shoelaces he'd obviously traded some tourist for, he joined Sarah on a wooden picnic table under a tree, away from the lot of loitering locals.

She lit a cigarette and offered him one. "So," she said with a suspicious tone, "where are we going?" She spoke in Amharic lest she be perceived as a clueless outsider.

Ejigu motioned toward the mountains, north of the valley where her expedition was stationed. "Up there. Not easy to find. You must climb."

She unfolded her portable binoculars to get a closer look. The terrain was rocky and parched, easing up the foothills and culminating in steep cliff faces blown raw by the winds. On one of the distant cliffs stood a flat-roofed stone structure. Sarah couldn't make it out. "What is that building?"

"Dabra Damo. The oldest church in Ethiopia."

She knew the legend of the monastery. It was one of the churches built by the nine saints who spread Christianity in Ethiopia. Abuna Aregawi, one of the nine, had perched his monastery high on a cliff where no common man could reach it. Even the monks who lived there did not have easy access. Each time they left the monastery to fetch water or go on a walking meditation, they had to descend via a braided leather rope dangling down the cliff face and ascend again the same way.

Its exile-like conditions were not accidental; the place was meant to be isolated from the world. Dabra Damo was where important illuminated manuscripts and fantastic religious paintings were housed, and the Ethiopians viewed the place as sacred. Sarah had long wanted to see it but knew it was impossible, for to that day women were not allowed to penetrate its sanctified realm.

"These things I find inside caves on the road to Dabra Damo," Ejigu continued. "It is very rich. Pottery, coins, glass . . ."

"Glass?" She was surprised. According to Aksumite history, glassware was not manufactured in Ethiopia but rather was imported from Egypt and Syria. It was difficult to ship and very expensive and, therefore, used only by the wealthy classes. Such objects could provide clues to the elusive burial site. She was tantalized.

"Yes, colored glass," he said. "Blue, yellow . . . You will see."

There might be something to this after all. "Let's go then." She extinguished her cigarette on the flimsy aluminum ashtray. "I don't have all day."

After a drive north to the foothills, they hiked steadily upward until they reached the high plateau. Sarah didn't need a break, but she stopped to take in the view. Beneath her to the south was the valley of the stelae, where her colleagues were carrying on digging in her absence. In the distance lay the silent ruins of an ancient compound the locals liked to refer to as the palace of the Queen of Sheba even though archaeologists had dated it to the seventh century, long after Sheba's time. The Ethiopians loved their legends, and science would not discourage their belief.

A few hundred meters up from where they were standing were the infamous granite cliffs with their network of caves, some natural, some not. She was eager to explore them before the light diminished.

"The pottery, it is inside a cave at the top of that cliff." Ejigu pointed toward their destination. "Come. This way." He led her over a boulder field to a narrow path leading up the bare cliffside. The trail wound around the edge of the cliff and was barely wide enough for a person to stand on. A precipice on the other side plunged into more rocks.

Accustomed to thinking one move ahead, Sarah calculated in her mind: if she slipped, she could try to arrest her fall by holding on to the gnarled roots of the kosso trees that grew, impossibly, among the stones.

Ejigu negotiated the path with the ease of one who either knew no fear or held life in too little regard. Back against the cliff face, he inched up sideways one foot at a time like a crab.

Sarah followed reluctantly, a new bead of perspiration forming on her brow every time the loose rock and gravel gave way.

"A few more meters," Ejigu announced, flashing a gray-toothed smile. "Almost there."

Sarah took a deep breath and concentrated on her steps. On the final stretch of the path were no handholds. The cliff had been polished smooth by the elements. She fixed her gaze on the horizon. If she looked down, she could lose her footing. She was sweating in earnest now, partly from the heat but mostly from anxiety. Her hands were clammy and slippery against the stone, but she could not wipe them on her bandana, which she'd wrapped around her wrist for exactly such a scenario.

"Lady, do not move." Ejigu spoke softly but was clearly alarmed. "A scorpion. At your feet. Stay still and it will not harm you."

The scorpion climbed on Sarah's boot and made its way up her leg.

She was motionless and calm. She'd spent enough time in remote places to know that if a scorpion sensed motion it would feel threatened and strike. Holding still might fool it into thinking she was actually part of the landscape.

With its tail curled and dangling like a lariat above its head, the wretched black armored creature inched upward, crossing Sarah's abdomen and reaching her bare neck. Her hair stood on end as she felt its pincers brush her skin, then its eight hairy legs tread, one at a time, across her Adam's apple. A strike to the carotid would be fatal.

She weighed her options. She could fling it off with a swift move that would surely throw her off balance and send her down the precipice, or she could do nothing and hope it reciprocated.

Though she was terrified at the prospect of being needled with a deadly dose of neurotoxic poison, she kept her cool. What she could not control was the perspiration trickling down her hairline, following the contours of her face to her jaw. Her heart pumped double time even as the scene unfolded in slow motion. A single drop fell from her chin onto the scorpion's head.

It raised its stinger.

In the split second before it could attack, she jettisoned it from her body with a backhanded snap. She had no time to see where it landed, for the ground crumbled and she slid down the rocky hillside. She grasped at the rock for even a tenuous handhold, but the cliff was too steep and she was falling too fast. A jagged piece of granite gashed the inside of her left arm from bicep to palm, but she was too pumped with adrenaline to feel any pain.

She looked over her shoulder to check the terrain between her and the rocky escarpment coming toward her with unnerving speed. She spotted the blackened, hole-riddled branch of an ancient kosso tree, reached toward it, and managed to grab a patch of leaves. Gravity did not allow her to keep hold, but the motion slowed her and threw her center just enough to put her on a collision course with the tree's elaborate branch structure.

It worked. Her fall was broken, at least enough for her to regain control. Now she could negotiate the rocks and make it down to the escarpment in one piece.

Ejigu yelled from the top of the cliff. "Lady, stay there. I'm coming down."

"No. It's too dangerous."

It was of no use. Ejigu scrambled down with all the agility of a mountain goat.

In the meantime, she edged down the rock face until she was within safe jumping distance. She let go of the roots and jumped to the ledge, landing on her side like a sack of stones. The final fall knocked the wind from her lungs. For a moment, she thought she was dying.

Slowly air was restored to her lungs, and she surveyed the damage. Her ripped clothes were stained with fresh blood, her ribs ached from the impact, and her left arm was dripping blood onto the stones. She needed stitches. Worse yet, the pain had dug in. Her forearm throbbed so violently she could feel it in the tips of her fingers.

She tried to move, but it hurt too much. She thought it wiser to lean against the rocks and wait for Ejigu. She feared her injuries would keep her from going forward with the dig. *Bloody fool,* her inner voice scolded, *you know better than this.*

Ejigu reached the escarpment with astonishing speed. His competence on the hostile terrain eased Sarah's mind a little, and she allowed herself the faint hope of making it out of there before nightfall.

"Are you okay, lady?" He winced. "You look very bad."

"Flattery will get you nowhere," she said, letting him help her to her feet. "You might have told me we would need climbing equipment."

"Sorry, sorry."

Sarah untied the bandana from her wrist and held it tightly against the wound. When the bleeding was under control, she leaned into a pile of rocks to steady herself and summon the strength for the downhill trek. Even in her rattled state, she could not help but admire the symmetry of the structure. The stones before her were neatly stacked, as if they had been wedged into the cliffside by nature's stonemasons. But there was something odd about the orderly pattern. She looked closer but could not wrap her mind around it. She didn't know if she was delirious with pain and seeing things, but behind a jumble of roots was what looked like an etching in the stone, a rough outline of the Coptic cross, perhaps, or some variation.

She looked behind her at Ejigu, who was throwing pebbles into the void. She turned to the etching, slipping her hand behind the roots to access the surface of the stone. She ran her fingers inside the grooves of the symbol. It was ragged, worn by time and the elements. Her heartbeat quickened.

Ejigu clapped to get her attention. "Hello? We have to go soon. The sun will disappear."

He was right. The sun was starting its descent behind the mountain. It would be dark before long, and they still had a good two hours' hike ahead.

She followed him down, cursing her curiosity every agonizing step of the way.

That night, after paying an after-hours visit to the town doctor and returning to camp with a host of painkillers, Sarah sat at her laptop and sketched the symbol from memory. Now she wasn't so sure it was a Coptic cross. Unlike the crux ansata, the symbolic cross of the Coptic Christian church, this had two circles, one inside the other, with a cross dissecting the inner circle in four equal parts. The staff of power, the vertical line extending down from the center of the circle, was broken. Sarah wasn't sure if that was intentional or due to the erosion of what could have been hundreds of years. She referred to her online encyclopedia of symbols but found nothing exactly like it.

As much as she enjoyed figuring things out on her own, she had no choice but to consult the symbologists at Cambridge. She scanned her sketch and e-mailed it to Stanley Simon, the head of the archaeology department at the university.

Professor:

Found this symbol etched into a cliff face en route to

Dabra Damo. Variation of the Coptic cross—or is it? In the same vicinity: a pile of rocks a little too perfectly arranged. My instinct says it's man-made. Plan to explore more tomorrow. Your thoughts.

S. W.

Under the influence of painkillers, Sarah slept soundly until 5:30 the next morning. When her phone rang, she was disoriented and had no clue where she was. Instinctively she picked up and regarded her phone as if it were an extraterrestrial object. Regaining her faculties, she focused on the caller ID: Stanley Simon. With a start, she realized she was still in Aksum and had slept an hour later than normal. "Professor," she croaked. "I assume you got my e-mail."

"You sound dreadful." The voice on the other end was gruff and curmudgeonly, the professor's usual tone when he was displeased. "Have you only now woken up?"

"It's a long story. Had a bit of trouble yesterday."

"I'm not sure I want to know. What were you doing on the high cliffs anyway? The funerary chamber is in the valley. Or have you forgotten?"

"No, sir. I mean . . . This was a bit of a detour. I was looking into a lead."

"A detour? A lead?" His voice cracked. "Sarah, need I remind you what you have been sent to Aksum to do? Do you realize you have been at it five months and already spent a half million sterling of UNESCO grant money? A lot of people are getting anxious over this expedition. They want to see results. I cannot continue to make excuses for you, particularly whilst you amble along, pursuing random leads from dubious sources."

"It isn't like that. I saw the artifacts. They were authentic. I thought it was worth a couple of hours of my time to go check it out."

"Young lady, you may not realize this, but we are in hot water with our funder right now. UNESCO are getting very impatient. They want to send a consultant."

"I beg your pardon?"

"You heard me. They have dispatched Daniel Madigan to Aksum. He should be arriving in a week's time."

Daniel Madigan—she knew that name. "Do you mean the preening American? Isn't he busy starring in some documentary or other?"

"Whether you approve or not, Dr. Madigan is one of the leading scholars of the Saudi Arabian region. In fact, he's at the Empty Quarter now with a group from King Saud University, and they are making excellent progress . . . unlike some."

She recalled reading reports about the cultural anthropologist's work at Qaryat al-Fau, the ancient city hidden beneath the Arabian sands. The project had earned him worldwide renown, not least of all because he had produced and starred in an IMAX film about his research. "Fine. I'll play along. But if he shows up with a film crew, I'm out of here."

"Sarah, I beg of you, don't embarrass the university. I know it's hard for you to understand, but there is rather a lot at stake here."

Simon's condescending tone grated on Sarah's nerves. She tried her best to ignore it. "Professor? I don't suppose you checked into that symbol I sent you."

"Of course I checked into it. The boys at divinity don't believe it's a crux ansata at all. They were firm about that. The Coptic cross has but one circle. A double circle such as this holds no theological symbolism. Concentric circle ideograms have been found on prehistoric cliff paintings in the Sahara, but those were pagan symbols."

"But what of the cross? Surely that has some religious significance. Especially considering its proximity to the monastery."

Simon huffed. "Sarah, take my advice and let that go. You have your hands full with your current task. There is no time for detours. Do you understand?"

She understood perfectly, but there was no denying her intrigue. She hung up, annoyed that after all those years, the professor still treated her like a child. He'd known her since she was one—he and her father, Sir Richard Weston, had been childhood pals, university classmates, and explorers in the high Himalayan regions—but that didn't give him the right to belittle her.

As friendly as he was with her father, Simon had never warmed to Sarah. He saw her as a bit of a maverick, really. So when he'd insisted she lead the Aksum expedition, going against the conventional wisdom that demanded a more seasoned, preferably male, professional at the helm of a project so grave, she was more stunned than anyone. She'd wondered if her father had anything to do with it but kept her reservations to herself. She did not want to tamper with whatever alchemy had brought her the opportunity she'd wanted for so long.

She splashed water on her face and changed the dressing on her stitched arm. Her curiosity would one day be her downfall, but she could not contain herself.

She heard a knock at the door.

"Sarah? It's Aisha. Are you all right? The crew has been waiting an hour for instructions."

Sarah opened the door.

Like a bewildered gazelle, the girl looked at her leader's wounded arm.

"I'm quite all right. Tell the crew to carry on digging east of the AB stele. Then fetch Dennis and Marcus and gather the rope and carabiners. We are going for a little walk."

Three

In the lab, Sarah recorded metal tools and coins the crew had unearthed the day before. A car horn tore through the stillness of the summer morning. It could mean only one thing. Leave it to an American to announce his arrival in such a crass manner.

She looked out the window, watching as Daniel Madigan stepped out of a beat-up, blue Land Cruiser. He looked just like he did in his documentaries: a rugged, square-jawed figure in dusty khaki shorts and a faded T-shirt from an old Smiths concert. A snake tattoo wrapped around his left bicep. His hair, which brushed the nape of his neck, was a jumble of loose chestnut waves with strokes of gray at the temples hinting at his fortysomething years. Darkened to a tobacco shade by the Arabian sun and sporting the lean muscular physique of someone who worked outdoors, he looked like a middle-aged rock star. He reached into the back of the Land Cruiser and pulled out two army-green duffels and an aluminum computer case. He was staying awhile.

She walked outside to meet him, locking the door to the lab behind her. "Hello, Dr. Madigan. Welcome to Aksum."

"I see you know who I am," he said in a southern drawl. "I'm not sure if that's good or bad."

She managed a tense smile. "Well. You need no introduction. Your reputation precedes you."

His gaze traveled slowly down her body. "As does yours. You are Lord Weston's daughter, aren't you?"

She cringed. She hated when people referred to her as Lord Weston's daughter, as if she had no value of her own. The comparison to her bigger-than-life father, a titled aristocrat and member of the British Parliament's House of Lords, followed her everywhere, even on this dusty mountaintop in remotest Africa. She tried not to show her outrage. "You know my father," she said with false politeness.

"We met last year at the fund-raiser for Medecins Sans Frontières." He butchered the French with his Tennessee accent. "Dreadful evening. If it weren't for your father, I would have left after the foie gras. That guy's one hell of a storyteller."

"I'm sure you have rather a lot in common," she

said, masterfully disguising her sarcasm.

"Two men with a passion for exploration never run out of things to say. In fact, I was at his place in Belgravia for a dinner party just before leaving for the desert. I'm surprised he didn't tell you about it."

"My father and I haven't spoken for an absolute age. I've been rather busy with my own projects. Now, then, is this your first time in Ethiopia?"

"Oh, heavens no. I spent a lot of time in Africa back in the eighties, researching in the Olduvai Gorge for my postdoctoral studies. I went back and forth between Ethiopia and Tanzania for the better part of a year. Then I hung out in Addis with some local skull diggers for a couple of months. We traveled up here for the hell of it. You know, sightseeing."

"Really? That surprises me. There's a deep connection between the ancient Aksumites and the people of Arabia. I should think that would be of interest to you, Dr. Madigan."

"It is. But it wasn't at the time. And for God's sake, call me Danny."

"Very well." She nodded toward one of the porters, a slight African with bare feet and a loose white gauze turban. "Soto will show you to your quarters. When you get settled, come meet me in the lab so I can brief you on our status."

He flashed a confident smile. "You're the boss, lady."

Daniel turned up at the lab an hour later. Sarah was annoyed he'd taken the time to shower and change into a clean army-green T-shirt. In his place, she would have dropped her bags on the bed and left the room before the door had time to close. He hadn't bothered to shave, though, leaving the dark stubble on his jawline.

"So UNESCO hired you to consult with us." She made no special effort to hide her reservations about the whole affair.

"It's more like I was on my way back to the States from Saudi Arabia and they asked me to stop by, since I was in the area and all."

"You make it sound like a social visit."

"We can think of it that way if you'd like." He studied her pensively. "You don't seem real happy to see me."

"Why do you say that?"

"Don't know. The fact that you are standing there with your arms and legs crossed. Your defensive tone of voice. The lightning bolts in your eyes."

She dismissed his suspicions with a scoff. "You're quite wrong."

"Am I?"

Sarah uncrossed her arms. She was not in the

mood for a spar. “How much have you been told about our expedition?”

“Let’s see. You’ve been here five months, twelve days. You have been taking ground-penetrating radar and electrotomographic readings, which indicate that there is a vast chamber, likely funerary, deep beneath the surface of the eastern stelae field. Your dig has uncovered some small objects—metal items, spearheads, coins, lithic fragments, that sort of thing—but you have not yet located an entrance. And because of that, a lot of people are getting antsy. Is that pretty much the size of it?”

“Pretty much.” She walked to the table on which the objects were arranged for measurement and recording. “We have dated these to the fourth, fifth, and sixth centuries. Before Aksum’s demise. We are assuming the necropolis beneath the eastern field is of the same period. The fact that it is so vast and deep suggests it could be the burial ground of royalty or the wealthy ruling classes, so it could be a rather exciting find.”

“So what’s the plan?”

“We dig every day. Start before dawn, work until it gets too hot, take a break for lunch, and finish around dusk. I’ve got a crew on the site now. They’re making quite good progress.”

“And you?”

“I usually dig with them. But today I have to slip

away for a couple of hours. Have to go into town for a few things."

"I can go with you."

"No, no, really, do stay here and familiarize yourself with the project."

"Whatever you want. I'll be on my way, then." At the door, he turned around. "By the way, how did you get that nasty gash on your arm?"

"Accident. I"—she stumbled on her words—"scraped it on some rocks." Not a lie but not the whole truth either. He was the last person she would talk to about her encounter at the cliffs of Dabra Damo.

From the doorway, she watched Daniel get into the Land Cruiser and drive toward the dig site. When she was sure he was out of view, she grabbed her backpack, locked up the lab, and jumped into her jeep.

It had become a daily routine, this afternoon jaunt to the cliffs. She'd spent the first few mornings in town recruiting hands to build the elaborate wood scaffolding that enabled her to reach the escarpment without negotiating steep stone faces and scorpion-riddled gravel paths. She had put about a dozen locals to work under the supervision of her structural engineers, and together they'd constructed the elaborate wooden structure in record time. With the scaffold built, she and a couple of her most trusted colleagues had set about the task of moving the stones stacked next to the mysterious symbol.

"Hello, gang," she called as she reached the final rung of the scaffold. "Any luck today?"

Dennis, one of the most senior members of the expedition and an archaeologist with whom she'd collaborated in Zimbabwe, was sitting on a pile of stones the crew had dislodged. His round face was pink from the sun and heat. With the corner of his T-shirt, he wiped the sweat off his glasses. "We're gettin' there," he said in an East End accent. "Go on, then. Have a look."

She approached the area where they'd removed the stones and put her hand on the small opening. "Cool air." She was surprised. "There's got to be a cave back there."

"Too right. And my guess is this little rock formation here—"

"Did not happen naturally," she finished, excited. She could only imagine what lay behind the stones. But something was there. "Let's concentrate on this portion of the structure. I want us to remove only enough rocks to make a vertical corridor one of us can fit through for the recon. Then we can decide how to proceed."

"Shouldn't take too long. This is the weakest part of the structure. The stone practically crumbles."

Sarah and her crew went to work removing the

rocks the rest of that afternoon, breaking them with pickaxes and dislodging them carefully by hand, until a narrow vertical shaft had been cut into the rock. Sarah shone her flashlight inside. She saw only rock, possibly the walls of a cave, but she couldn't be sure. "I'm going for it. Aisha, rope me in."

Aisha looked about her. "Where's the rope?"

"Oh, bugger. I left it in the jeep. Right. Back in a flash."

She negotiated the scaffolding to the base of the cliff and ran the half mile to the jeep, parked off the nearest road. Daylight was dwindling fast. She rummaged through the trunk and cab, looking beneath maps and tools and loose sheets of random notes. She found the rope on the floorboard between the front seats. That explained why she'd accidentally left it behind.

"So this is what you do when you go into town."

The voice behind her startled her so much she hit her head on the roll bar.

"Sorry," Daniel said. "Should've knocked."

"Are you following me?"

"Yes, I am. I figure you're lying to me, so this evens the score."

"Look, I'm in a hurry." She brushed past him.

"I don't think so," he called behind her. "I suggest you offer me an explanation. Unless you'd like me to give my own version to Dr. Simon and your funders."

"Bastard," she intoned behind clenched teeth. She had little patience for overbearing, self-important men.

"You're treating me like the enemy. Has it occurred to you that I'm here to help?"

She turned to him. "Well, help me by going back to the dig."

He nodded at the scaffolding. "What's up there? Or do I need to climb up and see for myself?"

"This has nothing to do with you. It's a little side project."

"A side project? With expedition crew and resources? Do you even have the proper permits to be here?"

"For your information, our permits cover a twenty-mile radius from the valley of the stelae. So, as you can see, we're perfectly within our rights to be here."

"So this is why your project has been so delayed."

She sighed in frustration and threw the rope to the ground. "Damn it, Madigan. What do you want from me?"

"The truth would be nice."

"Fine. I see I have no choice but to tell you and wait for you to crucify me."

He walked toward her, stopping a few inches short. He spoke calmly, but a warning was in his eyes. "Don't jump to conclusions, wildcat. You don't know anything about me."

She edged back, studying his face. She couldn't

tell whether he was friend or foe, but he'd backed her into a corner and she had no choice but to come clean. "A couple of weeks ago, I came up here with one of the locals. He was taking me to see some caves with pottery fragments. Said he'd seen some glass, maybe even some jewelry. I slipped from the path and fell down that cliff, landing on the escarpment."

"Let me guess. That's how you hurt your arm."

She nodded. "I saw the oddest thing. An ideogram that looked like a Coptic cross etched into the stone next to a pile of rocks. I e-mailed Dr. Simon right away. He told me off, saying I should be concentrating on finding the entrance to the necropolis because UNESCO are growing impatient and, as you well know, they pull the strings."

"But you defied him anyway."

"Don't make it sound so criminal. I know something's up there. I'm an archaeologist. I can't look the other way. I have to trust my instincts."

He smiled. "And I suppose you think I can't relate to that."

"I don't know what to think. As you pointed out earlier, I know nothing about you. Except what I see on TV." She couldn't resist the dig.

"What were you doing with the rope?"

"We have removed some rocks and exposed a shaft—an entrance to what I think is a cave. I was planning to go in." She looked at the sky. "Oh, what's the use? We've lost too much light already." She radioed her crew to instruct them to wrap up for the day.

Daniel walked with Sarah to the jeep and helped her pack the equipment. "You know, I'm something of an expert on caves. Spent a good chunk of my career exploring them in the Empty Quarter, looking for the ruins of a city. I'd like to come with you tomorrow."

She opened her mouth to protest.

He raised his hand. "I insist. The way I see it, you have no choice but to trust me."

They started at first light. With the rope tied securely around her waist, Sarah shimmied into the tight opening.

Daniel followed. "I knew I shouldn't have had that second piece of toast," he joked, face pressed to the rock.

She was not in the habit of laughing. For better or for worse, she was the serious type. Her colleagues often called her Stony, and she took it as a compliment.

Once inside, they tapped on their headlamps to illuminate the blackness. The light shimmered on the cave walls, casting shadows on the nubby texture of the tubelike chamber. With their hands outstretched, they could touch the ceiling and the walls on both sides. The stone was crumbly and chalky and felt to

Sarah like dried mud, which was curious since the mountains were mostly granitic.

As they ventured farther in, the tunnel narrowed and they had to crouch to half stature, bending at the knees and waist.

The mustiness and putrid sharpness of long-since rotted flesh overwhelmed her. The scent of death. Did someone live here? Or was it merely a long-abandoned animal den?

"Over there . . ." Daniel pointed to a small sphincter-like opening.

"Spot on. That might be the chute we're looking for."

"One way to find out. Let me go first, just in case there's something foul in there."

"I don't think so," she said, pushing him aside. "Last I checked, I was still the leader of this expedition. That means I call the shots."

He didn't press the issue. "Suit yourself. I just didn't want you to think chivalry is dead."

She low-crawled through the opening, propelling herself with her forearms. The stone was cool and rough against her body, and the stench of decay and charred earth grew more fetid the deeper she went. She tried to ignore the urge to gag, but what was harder to ignore was the lack of air. Her lungs seemed compressed with a vise, making every breath an effort.

Behind her, Daniel called, "Well? Do you see

light at the end of the tunnel?"

"No. No light," she returned, her voice strained. "But watch yourself. There's a bit of a turn ahead."

The tunnel swerved to the right, where it became wider. "I think we're reaching a mouth. It seems to open right here."

"Can you see anything?"

"It's pitch black. Wait. What's this?"

"What? What is it?"

"The passage turns downward."

"That's your chute. I've seen those a hundred times, and they can be bad news. Watch yourself."

"It's the only way through. I'm going for it."

"Sarah, I mean it, now. Be very careful."

"What's the worry? We're roped in." She started down the chute. "Here we go. I'll try to rappel down." She descended, holding the rope with one hand and gripping the rock with the other. She used her feet to determine the width of the chute ahead.

When the walls gave way and her feet dangled into the void, she knew she'd reached her destination. "Okay," she yelled, tugging the rope. "Lower me down."

She had no idea how far *down* was or where she would land. It could be water, a festering pit of rats, or a mountain of guano teeming with cockroaches for all she knew.

To her relief, after a short descent, her feet touched

terra firma. She looked about, establishing that she was indeed inside a cave. She ran her hand across the stone. It was unyielding and had coarse edges, consistent with the feel of granite.

"Everything all right down there?" Daniel's voice sounded faint from the top of the chute.

"Something's definitely odd," she yelled. "The stone is very different. I think at one point this cave was sealed."

As Daniel made his way down, she marveled at the natural undulations and striations, the evolution of the land over the eons. Observing changes in the earth's crust was one thing she loved about her work. The stones spoke to her, telling her of order and conflict, light and shadow, life and death.

She inhaled. Definitely charred earth. She moved her light, stopping on a patch of rock blackened by fire. It wasn't particularly unusual. Shepherds and nomads frequently started fires in caves to keep warm—but only when there was good ventilation. This was another clue that the cave had once been open and later intentionally sealed. Question was, why?

She scraped a bit of the singed rock into a bag and continued looking around.

Her gaze stopped on the corner of a wooden box, shuttered with thick iron nails that had oxidized over time.

Daniel detached from the rope. "What have you got?"

She shone her flashlight across the length of her find. "A coffin." She looked up at him. "This isn't a cave. It's a tomb."

"Makes sense. The symbol outside, the pile of rocks. Someone was obviously trying to protect something."

"Or hide it." She ran her hand over the rough wood. A splinter wedged into her palm, and she jerked her hand upward. "Acacia," she said, ignoring the sting. In Aksumite tradition, only paupers and ascetics were buried in acacia coffins. Which of the two lay inside?

"There's something etched on the lid." Daniel kneeled for a closer look. "Say, how's your Ge'ez?"

Sarah had studied the characters of the ancient Ethiopian language that predated Amharic but was by no means an expert. She made an attempt to translate. "I recognize a couple of the words. This means *light*. That is the verb *to be*." She shook her head. "That's all I know, I'm afraid. But it won't be hard to translate."

She pulled a digital camera out of her pocket and photographed the engraving as well as the coffin from several angles. The ghostly blue light of the camera flash bounced off the walls like a lightning storm. She took wide shots of the length and width of the box and zoomed in on every detail from the grain of the wood to the rusted nail heads sealing it shut. As she photographed the latter, she paused and lowered the camera. "This is very odd," she said as much to herself as to Daniel, who was measuring the dimensions of the coffin. She leaned in with a halogen stylus to examine the nails under the light. "Come have a look at this."

Daniel pocketed the tape measure and joined her. "There are holes next to the nails." He sounded surprised.

"Right. Which means this coffin has been opened before."

"Looters."

"Maybe . . ." She was skeptical.

"What are you thinking?"

Her mind traveled to the symbol at the entrance to the cave. She couldn't shake the feeling that the same person who'd opened the coffin had sealed the tomb and inscribed the ideogram into the stone. But the thought hadn't gelled in her mind, so she opted not to mention it at all. Instead, she stated the obvious. "It's just that this is clearly the coffin of someone poor. What's there to loot?"

"Oh, you'd be surprised. Even paupers had some belongings. A knife, a simple metal cross. Even the most mundane object would be of value to these rogues." He pointed his flashlight into the hollows behind the coffin. "I'll bet there's something . . ."

"What?" Sarah snapped to attention, turning her gaze to the spot Daniel's light illuminated. Her jaw dropped, and for a few seconds she forgot to breathe.

The entire inner wall was covered in characters carved into the stone. She went in for a closer look. The symbols were utterly unfamiliar and were haphazardly rendered, as if the author had been in a hurry. Though she couldn't understand a word of the script, she could sense the angst. "I've not seen anything like this," she whispered.

Daniel studied the characters. "This is a type of Semitic script. A dialect of some sort. I've seen similar graffiti in Arabia on grave markers."

"Could it be a religious script?"

"Not likely. It's very simplistic. Look at the way the characters bend down, almost forming a spiral. Religious scripts are usually more sophisticated than this, more formal."

Sarah pulled some onionskin and charcoal out of her backpack and traced the characters.

Daniel laughed, questioning her technique and reminding her that photos would give them a more accurate image of the work, but she wanted a physical, tactile record of the engravings and not photographs alone. It felt more real to her, closer to the intent of the inscriber. It was one of her quirks, and she was unapologetic about it.

"We should get out of here. Air quality is diminishing."

There wasn't enough of an opening for air to circulate through the cave. They had used up most of what little oxygen there had been. It was indeed time to turn back, but Sarah wasn't ready.

"You go ahead. I'm not finished here." She adjusted the brim of her cap and pointed it toward the cave drawings, describing what she was seeing. "Inscriptions occupying eighty percent of inner vestibule wall on north side of cave. Characters possibly consistent with a Semitic script."

"What are you doing?"

She put her index finger on her lips to beg his silence, then pointed to a penlight under the edge of her hat's brim.

"A video camera," he whispered. "Now that's genius."

She reached under the brim again, turning off the camera. "I got tired of lugging around a video camera, so I designed this and had our technology department make it. It's really handy in tight spots or whenever you can't afford the extra weight. It can actually transmit to the Cambridge intranet. Brilliant, isn't it?"

"Do you have a patent on that thing? 'Cause everybody in the business is going to want one. Consider my order placed."

"Here's another one you might like." She raised her left wrist. "See this Timex? It takes a licking and keeps on recording."

"Voice?"

"Yes, indeed. I've had this one forever. Now that I have the camera, I don't use it as much. But I keep it because I never know when I'll need it." She clicked on the upper button three times to arrive at recording mode. The watch face showed a digital screen with the usual recorder options, and she pressed another button to demonstrate how it worked.

"You Brits have all the gadgets." Daniel laughed. "And I thought James Bond was fiction."

She shook her head and turned the camera back on, scanning the cave and its contents to create a visual record. Even as her breathing became labored, she continued working. She always finished what she started, regardless of the conditions. It was the nature of the business: you got what you could the first time because there was never a guarantee of another chance.

She stopped only when she felt light-headed and had to steady herself against the granite wall. If she didn't get out now, she wouldn't be able to muster the strength for the ascent.

"Time to go," Daniel said, clipping her harness to the rope. "I'm not taking no for an answer."

Sarah nodded and pulled herself up through the chute, deliberately hyperventilating to increase the flow of air to her lungs and expel carbon dioxide faster. Her chest felt like it was pinned under a fifty-pound weight as she crawled toward the exit. Though nothing excited her more than being inside a tomb, she was pining for the world outside.

When she finally reached the mouth of the cave, she gasped. Waiting for Daniel to emerge, she slipped the bandana off her head and used it to wipe her eyes, which stung from the sweat and grime.

When she reopened her eyes, she saw a figure on the escarpment—an old man with leathery black skin, robed in white with strips of white gauze wrapped several times around his head. His bare feet were calloused and gnarled, like the trunks of the ancient kosso trees. A plaited leather cross hung around his neck.

"Who are you?" Sarah asked.

The old man's voice was shaky as he spoke in Amharic. "You should not be here. You bring evil to this place."

"We are archaeologists," she said in Amharic. "Scientists. We have permission to be here." She reached in her pocket for a copy of the expedition permit.

"You do not have God's permission. You must leave at once or suffer the consequences. He is watching."

"I beg your pardon. Who is watching?"

But the man did not reward her question with a reply. He spat on the ground where she stood and with surprising agility climbed the cliff. It obviously wasn't the first time he'd made the trek.

Daniel emerged from the opening. "Blasted Brits. Would it kill you to make this opening a little wider?"

Sarah didn't even register what Daniel said. She stared at him vacantly.

"What's wrong?"

"Nothing. There was a man . . ."

Daniel looked around. "What man? Where?"

"Looked like a monk, but I couldn't be sure. He wore a cross and spoke of God."

"What about God?"

"He said we don't have God's permission to be here. That we bring evil to this place and should leave at once."

"Well, we have the permission of the Ethiopian Ministry of Culture. That's as good as God, as far as I'm concerned."

"All the same, I think we've done enough damage for one day. We should get out of here."

At dinner, Sarah was unusually quiet. She had mixed emotions about the find. On the one hand, her veins pulsed with excitement about the sealed tomb and the secrets it potentially held. On the other, she had defied Dr. Simon and the rules of the hallowed institution that employed her. Though fully aware the professor would be outraged, she couldn't stop herself from forging ahead. This was her find, the result of her own intuition and initiative rather than a directive from the establishment. There was value in that, even if the learned men of Cambridge couldn't see it.

After they'd cleared the table and delivered the

dishes to the mess tent, Daniel pulled Sarah aside. "I've got something for you." He held up a pair of tweezers.

She rolled her eyes but offered her palm anyway.

He put on his headlamp as a joke and went to work on the splinter. "You haven't said two words all night," he said as he flaked off epidermis to excavate the piece of acacia beneath. "What's on your mind?"

"Oh, nothing." She jerked her hand. "Hey . . . that hurt."

He grinned mischievously and shrugged. "Sorry. It was an accident."

She had no reason not to tell him. If anything, she needed every ally she could get. Her gut told her Daniel was not one of the corporate yes-men but rather someone who genuinely loved the business; she just hoped she was right. "I translated the Ge'ez text from the lid of the coffin."

He looked up, his golden-brown eyes sparkling under the lamplight. "And?"

"And . . . it was a warning. It said, 'Cursed be he who brings these bones to light.'"

Four

The bones lay on the laboratory table, mocking Sarah. She'd been unable to leave the lab since the crew had excavated the coffin and delivered it four days prior. She had no appetite. She slept on a chair, in fits and starts, and then only when exhaustion was too much to bear. She was interested in nothing but studying the specimen, making some sense of the facts before her. The pelvis indicated the body was that of a man. By the long, narrow shape of the skull, the high cheek structure, the square mandible, the angular nose, and the length of the arm and leg bones, she deduced he was not African. She looked at the measurements again: six feet two inches from crown to heel. Caucasian. Definitely Caucasian. The bones were intact, save for two areas: a broken right wrist and a break in the lower left rib cage. Sarah ran a gloved finger over the wound. The severed bone was sharp, untempered by time or the forces of nature. He must have died in battle or in a conflict of some sort. She imagined a spear had delivered the deathblow, a violent thrust to the chest just below the heart.

Returning her attention to the skull, she touched the curves: the aristocratic cheekbones, the dark hollows where eyes once were, the chin. The state of the teeth disturbed her most. Straight and impossibly intact, they couldn't possibly have belonged to a male of ancient vintage. She had no clue as to the age of the specimen—the radiocarbon dating, which could take weeks, would tell her that—but she deduced from the coffin construction that he dated to the early centuries of the Common Era. The facts contradicted themselves, at least for the time being, driving her mad with curiosity.

"My word, what are you doing here so early?" Daniel's annoyingly chipper voice stirred Sarah from her reverie.

She looked at her watch: four in the morning. "I couldn't sleep. What's your excuse?"

"I'm a serial insomniac. Comes with the territory. Is that tea?"

"That makes two of us." Sarah poured some tea into a mug for him. Her hand trembled, and some of the scalding liquid spilled onto her knuckle. Instinctively, she dropped the mug. She grimaced, more in disapproval of her clumsiness than in reaction to the pain.

"He's not going anywhere, you know," Daniel said, nodding toward the coffin. "You ought to get some sleep."

"I'm quite fine." She immediately regretted sounding so defensive.

He squatted to pick up the broken pieces. "You're not fine. You're exhausted. You couldn't even pour the tea without shattering my favorite mug."

She exhaled. "You're right. It's just that I've been obsessing about our friend. I've been chewing on the facts all night and can't make it rhyme." She walked to the coffin, eyeing the specimen. "What would a white guy be doing in Ethiopia that long ago?" she asked, not necessarily expecting an answer.

"I'm not convinced it was that long ago. The earliest recorded whites in Abyssinia were Roman missionaries traveling to spread the gospel of Christianity. That was, what, fourth or fifth century? The average height of Romans back then was maybe five feet seven. This guy is pretty tall, too tall to be of that era. Besides, look at the dentition." He walked to the coffin and pointed out the upper molars. "See this? That's a filling of some kind. Now, are you willing to tell me a fourth- or fifth-century man had dental work done?"

The observation took Sarah by surprise. The only things she had noticed about the teeth was that they were straight and, quite remarkably, all there. She felt embarrassed and a little annoyed that Daniel had picked up on this detail first.

"Obviously, we won't know for sure until we get the labs back," he continued, "but I'd bet the farm we're looking at a modern man."

"I don't know. What about the warning carved into the coffin? Ge'ez is an ancient language."

"Ah, but it's used to this day by Ethiopian Orthodox holy men for liturgies and study. That inscription was probably carved by someone in the religious community. You said yourself a monk told you to get the hell out of there. That's no coincidence."

"Okay. So the church doesn't want the tomb excavated or the bones exhumed. Why?"

He rubbed the stubbly growth on his jaw. "It wouldn't be the first time the church hid something. My guess is that this is no ordinary tomb, that it holds some ancient secret the monks, including your creepy friend from the mountain, are keeping to themselves. We're the infidels as far as they're concerned. They don't want their precious inscriptions to fall into our hands."

Sarah studied Daniel's face. His eyes glowed amber in the low lamplight, betraying a fierce intelligence. She recognized in him the same zeal for the business that she herself possessed. It impressed her and made her drop her defenses enough to allow that he might just be on her side.

"Speaking of the inscriptions, did you figure out what language we're looking at?"

"It's definitely Semitic, but I can't place the exact dialect. There were so many Semitic dialects spoken in different parts of Arabia over a time span of a thousand or more years. We could be looking at anything. But here's the part I don't get: how did an obscure Semitic language from the other side of the Red Sea end up here? The more I think about it, the more I'm convinced we need Rada Kabede."

"Who's that?"

"A linguistics scholar in Addis. I worked with him on a project in Egypt. Sharp guy. I don't know if he can whip out a speedy translation, but he can at least steer us in the right direction."

"Do you trust him?"

"Do you trust anyone in Africa?" Daniel winked. "I've known Rada for years. My gut says he's one of the good guys."

"Your gut."

"We may be scientists, but there's no substitute for instinct in this business. You know that as well as I do."

Sarah nodded. She didn't disagree; it was just that her instinct told her something else. Still, Daniel's proposition made sense. Any clue would make the trip to Addis worthwhile. Besides, she needed a break from the scenery. "Okay, I'm in."

Through her fog of exhaustion, the road to Addis Ababa looked like an endless ribbon of parched red earth. The monotony of the surroundings and the steady vibration of Daniel's Cruiser had the effect of a sedative. As they drove past the northern shore of Lake Tana, the legendary source of the Blue Nile, she took in the scenery. The mist-cloaked islands floating on lilac-gray waters that stretched toward a liquid infinity reminded her of ethereal watercolor images painted on rice paper. A small fleet of reed boats carried provisions from one shore to another. A dogged fisherman stood on his boat's bow and cast his net, disturbing the stillness of the lake. The serene scene cradled Sarah in beauty, and she surrendered to the weight of sleep.

She woke when her head hit the passenger side window, apparently when the Cruiser hit a particularly hostile pothole. The sky was steel gray and thick with clouds, and the rain pummeled the ground with fury. The streets were flooded by a good six inches of water, as they often were in Ethiopia, thanks to the questionable drainage systems installed by the Italians during the occupation.

"Welcome to Addis," Daniel said. "Lovely day out."

Sarah squinted through the gloom and surveyed the capital. Lining the boulevards were tall concrete buildings of monolithic architecture inspired by the nondescript styles of the Soviet era. Almost all were dirty and begged for repairs, a testament to the local laissez-faire attitude toward possessions. These buildings were there to provide shelter or a place to work for as long as the roof would hold. Maintenance was a waste of precious time that could be used for sipping coffee and gossiping with friends or, better yet, sleeping the boredom away.

The people looked similarly disheveled. Businessmen wore faded navy suits at least one size too big and hanging like a father's clothes on his skinny adolescent son. Women wearing their infants in slings squatted under umbrellas on the sidewalks with trunkfuls of wares spread across old blankets or plastic mats. They sold a hodgepodge of stuff: oranges stacked in neat pyramids, batteries, prewar-era suitcase locks, filter-less green cigarettes tied in tiny bundles, milk biscuits, French comic books, cheap cotton panties.

Daniel parked on the sidewalk, as everyone else did.

In the rain, the two walked several blocks to the Fasil Ghebbi restaurant, where Rada Kabede was to meet them for a late lunch. The traditional eatery was in a dilapidated prewar building in the city's market district. Cracks on the façade indicated seismic activity.

Bullet holes on the exterior walls, begotten from riots, civil wars, or some combination of the two, hinted at the country's tumultuous past, some of it not so distant. Sarah felt camaraderie with this building: battered yet solid enough to remain standing, dignified hints at a noble past.

She and Daniel entered an enormous wooden door mounted at an angle at the corner nearest the main road.

"Welcome to Fasil Ghebbi," said a man dressed in a spotless white *tebeb*, the traditional Ethiopian garb consisting of a tunic, narrow pants, and a scarf tied around the waist. "I believe you are meeting someone, yes?"

"Indeed we are. Lead the way, my friend," Daniel said.

"Follow me." The host bowed and walked through an arched opening framed with swagged red velvet curtains.

The dining room was full of smoke and as loud as the bazaars of Cairo or Istanbul. The cacophony of guffaws, chatter, and clinking glasses was profane to Sarah's ears after the past few hours of relative silence, but the smells of spices and strong tobacco awakened her senses. Exotic places braced her, made her feel alive. Though hers and Daniel's were the only white faces in the place, she was instantly at home and walked across the dining room with the self-assurance of someone who belonged there in that moment.

Rada stood from his place at the low table and lunged toward his old friend, offering an outstretched hand. His lips parted wide to reveal two beautiful rows of white teeth. Rada was in his late thirties, but his taut skin made him look a good ten years younger. He wore glasses with black square rims and thick lenses that made his eyes look like two tiny obsidian marbles. Though he had the look of a serious academician, his manner was that of an excited schoolboy.

The two men gave each other a loose hug, briskly slapping each other's back.

"May I introduce my colleague Sarah Weston?" Daniel's hand rested on her waist as he presented her to Rada.

It felt strange to be touched by him, even if it was an innocent gentlemanly gesture.

"Pleased to meet you, lady. Please"—he waved toward the table—"sit."

They sat on low stools around an ersatz table, a round, hammered metal tray on a cylindrical basket weave base.

Rada held up three fingers to a waiter and turned to Daniel. "Tell me, my friend, what brings you to Ethiopia?"

Daniel shook his head. "Work, I'm afraid. Nothing

more interesting than that."

"Well, if it's anything like our last adventure, it ought to be very interesting indeed."

The waiter returned with three bottles of St. George beer.

Rada rattled off a long order in Amharic and then turned to Sarah. "When we were in Egypt, he took a group of us on a safari to search for the rare Nubian ibex. We were up in the mountains for days, with no sign of the ibex. Suddenly, Daniel here started bellowing—"

"Hey, that was a mating call." Daniel feigned indignation.

Rada doubled over with laughter. He had a rapid-fire, high-pitched laugh that made him sound like a cartoon character. "Right," he managed between shrieks. "And what was that crazy dance all about?"

"Did the ibex come or not?"

"It did; it did. It was the strangest thing I'd ever seen."

"I've always had a way with animals."

The two men laughed and clinked their beer glasses.

"Those were good times," Rada said, shaking his head.

Sarah smiled nervously. "Mr. Kabede, we are here to get your opinion on something. We have this—"

Daniel grabbed her hand under the table and squeezed.

Reluctantly, she kept her thoughts to herself.

A server girl arrived with a pitcher and basin for them to wash their hands tableside. Rada took the soap and lathered up over the basin, flirting shamelessly with the girl.

Daniel leaned toward Sarah. "Sorry to cut you off," he whispered. "Things here happen at a different pace is all. It's very rude to talk business at the table. Just trust me."

She rolled her eyes. She was well aware of the protocol; she just didn't have the patience for it.

For the next two hours, the three talked about everything—world politics, Daniel's adventures in the desert around Qaryat al-Fau, the weather in London—except the inscriptions. They tucked into the injera, a large, sour crepe the waiter had unrolled over their tray table, tearing pieces to use in lieu of utensils to pick up bite-sized portions of spicy stewed chicken, called *doro wat*, lentil salad, spiced goat cheese, and chickpea fritters. The only piece of flatware on the table came with the final course. It was an ivory-handled knife with a curved tip meant to cut slices off a hunk of raw beef, the local delicacy.

After they had their fill, Rada rubbed his hands together and flashed a toothy smile. "Now for some coffee."

Sarah was relieved the meal was almost over and they could cut to the chase.

They moved to another room, where the floor was layered with patches of grass. A woman draped from head to ankle with white cotton gauze shawls sat on the grass. Over a coal fire, she tossed a pan to and fro until the coffee beans inside were roasted. With motions none too swift, she ground them with mortar and pestle. She put the crushed beans in a clay pot with water and let the brew percolate for a good ten minutes. She might as well have poured tar into the tiny china cups; it was that dark and viscous.

Sarah swirled the liquid in her mouth. She expected it to taste like petrol, so she was stunned at the smooth, nutty taste. She upended the cup to show her approval and within moments felt her heart racing from the caffeine. It was just as well. She wouldn't have slept that night anyway.

Afterward, the three walked to Rada's office. The humidity of summer had settled into the concrete city. It was always like this after the rain: sticky and thick enough to leave a mist of raw earth and dust on one's skin. They still spoke nothing of the reason for their visit.

Sarah thought maybe this was a waste of time until, at the office, Rada said, "Tell me, what can I do for you?"

"Very well, old friend," Daniel said. "My colleague and I need your help. We have found something. Some inscriptions—"

"In Aksum?"

"Yes. Inside a tomb."

Rada laced his fingers and put his hands to his mouth.

"We found the tomb in a sealed cave near Dabra Damo. There were no personal effects, only a simple wooden coff—"

"We can't go into too much detail about the project," Sarah interrupted, "as I'm sure you understand. We just need to know if you can translate this language." She tossed a batch of photos onto the desk in front of Rada: close-ups of a portion of the text.

Rada studied the characters and glanced up, obviously excited. "This is an ancient language that no longer exists. I believe it's a variation of Safaitic, a type of Semitic dialect. It was spoken in Arabia about two thousand years ago, by nomads mostly." He fixed his eyes on Sarah, then Daniel. "You said you found this in Aksum?"

Daniel nodded.

"Impossible. That dialect was never spoken here." Rada picked up a magnifying glass for a closer look at the inscriptions. He sat back and slipped into silence, shaking his head.

"I see your wheels turning, old boy," Daniel said. "Tell me what you're thinking."

"This is only a theory, but the nomads of the Syro-Arabian Desert often went to the settlements in the

Negev, or south to Ubar, to trade their livestock. It's not preposterous to think some slipped away from their tribes and made their way west to Egypt and eventually down to Nubia and Aksum in search of better fortune." He looked closer. "Most Safaitic inscriptions that have been found are accounts of nomadic life. The people who spoke these dialects were simple tribal folks, so at the very least this could provide great insight into early goat herding and camel races." He issued another high-pitched laugh.

Daniel chuckled.

Sarah understood the joke was merely a tension breaker, but it annoyed her nonetheless. "Mr. Kabede, can you or can you not help us?"

Daniel opened his mouth, but she quieted him by raising her hand.

Rada shrugged. "I could possibly translate some of this. But the only person who can really help you is the one who holds the stone."

Daniel looked at her. She knew he was thinking the same thing: there had to be a key to translating the ancient languages of the region, the equivalent of Egypt's Rosetta Stone.

"And where is this stone?" Daniel asked.

"It is locked away in the catacombs of a church near Lalibela. Yemrehana Krestos. That's the rumor anyway. Nobody has seen it. It's very closely guarded by the local priests. Like the Ark of the Covenant."

"Mr. Kabede, you said you could translate some of this, yes?" Sarah said. "How long would it take you?"

"Give me a few days to look into it. Very little has been written about this dialect. I'll need to do some research. But I can't promise anything."

Sarah, loath to trust anybody, reluctantly left the photos.

By the time they got to the Hilton, it was eight in the evening. Sarah told Daniel she would see him first thing in the morning for the drive back to Aksum, then retreated to her room. She secured the dead bolt and turned on the light.

On the floor next to her feet lay a white envelope. For a moment she thought about not opening it, figuring it was a notification from the hotel about the next morning's checkout. But the envelope was oddly shaped and the paper thicker than most hotels' stationery.

She tore the envelope open and found a card stamped with the insignia of the Ministry of Culture, beneath which were the words Office of the Director, Antiquities Division. On it was typed a curious message:

Dear Dr. Weston,

Welcome to Addis Ababa. We have some things to discuss which pertain to your project. Please meet me at the Sheraton Addis, penthouse suite, this evening. Come alone.

She couldn't make out the signature but assumed it was the director's. The clandestine nature of the note perplexed her. Why wouldn't the director go through proper channels if he required a meeting? But it would wreck her plans to make an enemy of the Ministry, especially now, since they controlled her permits.

She pulled herself together and went downstairs to summon a cab.

The gates opened, and the driver pulled in to the motor court of Addis' top hotel. Outside the gates, the streets were dirty, the houses crumbling. Beggars populated the sidewalks. Inside was a different story. Sarah couldn't believe the incongruity of the place. It was a shrine to opulence that stood in blatant disregard of its surroundings. Massive fountains were lit in a succession of neon colors, and spouted columns of water danced to Western music piped into underwater speakers.

The lobby was a study in European elegance, with inlaid marble floors, Oriental rugs, and crystal chandeliers hanging from tray ceilings. Fat African patriarchs—

politicians, traders, minor royalty—populated the silk-covered antique sofas, alternately laughing and roaring their opinions behind a blue veil of cigar smoke.

Sarah strode toward the front desk and told the clerk she was meeting someone at the penthouse suite.

"Mr. Matakala has been expecting you, miss." The clerk picked up the phone to announce Sarah's presence, then bowed politely. He showed Sarah to the elevators, inserted a card key, and punched the PH button. When the doors opened, he pointed to the room labeled Presidential Suite.

She stuffed a few birr into the clerk's hand and walked across the hallway to the mahogany double doors.

"Welcome, Dr. Weston," a man dressed in butler's clothes said in perfect English as he held open the door. "We've been expecting you."

The suite was larger than her flat in London and certainly more ornate.

"Please wait here," the man said, pointing to a pair of reproduction Queen Anne chairs in the sitting room. "May I bring you a cold refreshment?"

"No, thank you. But kindly let your master know I am in a bit of a hurry."

"Mr. Matakala will be with you shortly." The butler bowed and took his leave. An echo filled the room as his hard-soled shoes hit the marble floor.

Sarah wondered if her host intended for her to be impressed. She wasn't. She had grown up with the finer things, so luxury never affected her, least of all the gaudy opulence of the nouveaux riches. She was far more impressed by authenticity, in people and in objects.

True to the butler's promise, Andrew Matakala appeared a few minutes later. A slender man who seemed to be in his early forties, he cut a dashing figure, dressed in a smartly tailored pinstripe suit with an Hermès necktie decorated with a pattern of small stirrups and crops. His café au lait skin and fine features—a small, angled nose, thin lips, and high cheekbones—gave him a regal appearance. His straight black hair was parted on the side and neatly slicked back. He looked more Arabic than Ethiopian.

It was rare for African bureaucrats, particularly in a poor country like Ethiopia, to be so highly compensated as to enjoy tailored suits—his was obviously Savile Row—and expensive neckties. The possibility that he engaged in shady side deals crossed her mind, but she didn't let the thought settle.

"Dr. Sarah Weston, at last we meet. Andrew Matakala." He offered his hand, his British accent indicating he had probably been educated abroad. "I'm truly sorry for bringing you here at such an hour. It's very good of you to come."

His manner was a bit too slick for her taste, rather like the pretentious rich foreigners' with whom she had studied at Cambridge. They had always seemed to overcompensate for their lack of Englishness, as if that were a folly. She decided to keep an open mind but play her cards close. "Anything for the Ministry," she said, smiling. "I trust you will tell me what this is about?"

"You Britons always cut to the chase." He straightened his tie. "Very well, then. But rather than tell you, I will show you. Follow me."

Matakala led Sarah to the dining room, where he had set up projection equipment. He opened a laptop and brought up an image of a granite throne, then zoomed in on the inscription. "This is Greek." He turned to her. "But you know that."

"An Aksumite king's throne?" She was intrigued.

"Indeed. This was erected by King Ezana late in the fourth century, toward the end of his reign. He raised several of these throughout the empire, as you well know."

"Ah, yes. The postbattle monuments that paid homage to the gods and told of the king's heroics."

"We Ethiopians like to think of them as our earliest history books. So little is known from that period; these inscriptions are like windows to our past."

"Why are you showing me this particular inscription?"

"It is of consequence to you and your expedition. And of even greater consequence to us."

She crossed her arms. "Go on."

Matakala scrolled up to the beginning of the script and translated it to English. "By the might of the Lord of heaven, who in the sky and on earth holds power over all beings, Ezana, son of Ella Amida, Bisi Halen, king of Aksum, Himyar, Raydan, Saba, Salhin, Tsiyamo, Beja, and of Kasu, king of kings, never defeated by the enemy." He pointed at the screen. "This is a record of the king's battle in Meroë against the Noba people. I won't bore you with all the details." He opened the next image. "This is the part that should be of interest to you. If I may?"

Sarah nodded.

"A terrible Noba warrior dared threaten the king. But it was the will of the Lord of all that I survive and rule the land. My medicine man placed himself between my body and the lance-blade and fell in my place. It was the loss of a fine and brave man. But his sacrifice was not for naught, for my troops killed the enemy and took prisoners and returned home victorious, thanks to the might of the Lord of heaven."

"The Lord of heaven. Ezana was the Christian king," Sarah recalled. She was well versed in Aksumite history but downplayed her knowledge. "I don't understand how this is relevant."

"Patience, Doctor." He called up a different screen, this one showing a stele. "This is from an obelisk erected near your expedition site, on the cliff where Dabra Damo now stands. It says, 'Let it be known that the brave medicine man who was sanctified by the church of the Lord of heaven is laid to rest with the highest honors and privileges for saving the life of King Ezana, king of kings, ruler of Aksum and of the vast empire. May his soul be forgiven and accepted into the kingdom of heaven by the Lord of the land and of heaven and of all things holy. I have raised this gravestone by the power of the Lord of heaven and if anyone defaces it or removes it, let him and his race be removed from the face of the earth.'" Matakala paused and looked at Sarah.

She kept staring at the words. "You say this stele was near our site. Where is it now? I should like to see it."

"It is in private hands, I'm afraid. This was stolen from Ethiopia by bandits many years ago and sold on the black market to a German collector. No one knew where it was until he died and his estate was auctioned. We tried to acquire it but were outbid by an anonymous collector. We managed to get these photos from the auction house."

"I suppose you're going to tell me why you asked me here."

"It's . . . complicated." Matakala seemed to weigh his words. "Are you a person of faith, Doctor?"

"I am a scientist. I believe what I can see, hear, and touch."

"This is a matter of faith. Let me see if I can put it plainly. As you may know, our faith recognizes nine saints—the Tsadkan, or righteous ones. These are the pious men who spread the word of Christianity and built monasteries across our country. But according to Coptic mysticism, there was a tenth saint. We had no proof of this until we saw the inscription on this stele. It's all there, etched in stone: the man to whom the stele refers was made a saint by the Ethiopian church a good century before any of these nine men walked our lands."

Sarah interrupted. "What do you know about this tenth saint?"

"According to legend, he wasn't Ethiopian; he was from the West. That's conjecture, but it's all we know." He leaned forward. "Dr. Weston, we need your help."

Sarah knew what was coming. She gritted her teeth and let him talk.

"We believe what you have found is the tomb of our tenth saint." His gaze hardened. "I cannot emphasize enough the significance of this individual to our religion. We . . ." He raised a loose fist to his lips. "Let me put it another way. As a guest of our government, you have certain rights. No one disputes that. We are prepared to grant you a state-subsidized labor force in order to hasten your excavation of the royal necropolis, but we must insist that this particular find be turned over to the Ministry."

Sarah's face burned, but she spoke calmly. "Presuming I cooperate, what will the Ministry do with it?"

"The saint belongs to the sacred ground of Dabra Damo Mountain. We intend to return him to his gravesite and seal the tomb. We will then turn everything over to the church. Those are the wishes of our bishop, and we are obligated to abide by them."

"And wipe out the historical record," she said with an ironic smile.

"I know this is not the way of the West, Doctor. But it is how things are done in Ethiopia."

"And if I refuse?"

"I don't recommend it. It would be unwise to challenge the powers at play here."

"Mr. Matakala, first of all, I am not challenging anybody. I am completely within my rights to be here." The moment felt surreal, as if someone else were talking through her as she watched the scene unfold. "Secondly, my first and only commitment is to science. My job, if you didn't know, is to research and document ancient history through remains such as these. I don't care if the tomb in question is of Jesus Christ himself. That would not stop me from excavating the truth; it would compel me to do so. You see, Mr. Matakala, just as you believe the devout have a right to keep their holy man buried in silence, I believe the people have a right to know their past. So I'd say it's your will against mine."

"Be careful, Doctor. You don't know whom you're up against."

"Is that a threat?"

"I suggest you give some thought to our request—if you want to continue working in Ethiopia, that is."

Sarah nodded and briskly turned toward the door.

"Oh, Dr. Weston?" Matakala called. "Have you ever seen this?"

Sarah stopped and took a deep breath. She turned to face him.

The ideogram from the burial site filled the projection screen.

Against a tide of emotions, she struggled to keep an expressionless face.

"This is the symbol of an ancient religious brotherhood. Its members will stop at nothing to protect what is theirs."

She fixed her gaze on his.

Matakala closed the laptop. "Around here, people only get one warning. If I were you, I wouldn't squander it."

Five

Days wax and wane, winters give way to spring, and famines claim the lives of the weak, but tribal life persists as it always has, earnestly and without ceremony. The way of the nomad is to accept everything as it comes: there is no anticipation for better days, no longing for the unrequited, no despair for loss. The day-to-day existence is hard enough without such complications. Egoism is a luxury the nomad cannot afford, not when there are goats to milk, sheep to shear, camels to saddle, bread to bake, children to feed, blankets to weave, night skies to interpret, seasons to predict, music to play by the campfire.

Days go by mostly without event; nothing, at least, that would shatter the sacred routine. The men and boys spend every hour of daylight driving the livestock to water and grasses and letting them have their fill, not knowing what tomorrow may bring. Pastures are few and far between in the desert, but the Bedouin knows how to navigate the sands to find errant patches of life or, better yet, full-blown oases where streams flow and plains are fertile and palms are pregnant with dates. They do not linger long, only enough to bolster the strength of the beasts and replenish their own supplies. The law of this inhospitable land is unwritten but commonly respected: every passing tribe consumes modestly, then allows the resources to replenish themselves for those who come next. It has been done this way for centuries, and no one questions it. Greed is a serious infraction in these parts. The shaykh of any tribe that breaks the law is hunted down by the violated and variously humiliated, robbed, or beaten, depending on the extent of his trespass.

The women have their own responsibilities. At dawn, they collect the daily water for cooking, drinking, and washing. They prepare the meal for their goum, as the Bedouin family is called, in the morning and let it sit in covered pots until the men come in from the plains. Depending on the day's bounty, the meal might be as elaborate as mutton stew on the days a sheep is slaughtered or as simple as a watery legume broth mopped up with globs of sticky cornmeal or bread baked in a sand oven. On a good day, the men bring fish they catch in the streams and the women rub them down with crushed cloves and cook them over an open flame.

After the siesta, when everyone naps to escape the punishing heat of the midday sun, the men return to the grazing lands and the women gather in circles to gossip, giggle, and sing as they weave their daughters' dowries. Weaving and embroidery are hardwired into the genetic code of Bedouin women, so much so that it is customary for proud fathers to proclaim that their daughters are born holding needle and thread. Traders offer fancy beads, sacks of pepper, spices, and ivory amulets in exchange for the weavings, but the Bedouin women decline, not because they cannot be parted from their masterpieces but because they are serving a useful purpose, like separating the men's quarters from the women's or keeping the children warm on icy winter nights.

Evenings are special in the desert, a time for the goums to celebrate surviving yet another day on this unforgiving land full of dangers and hardships and interminable solitude. Men and elders, women and children take their places in the circle by the fire, chatting to their neighbors about not much at all until one of the younger men begins the festivities by pounding on a goatskin drum or scratching the strings of the rababa. The others join in one by one. The flutist blows into a clay pipe, releasing the cheerful, simple singsong of the animal herder. The old me n contribute to the percussion by shaking small dried-goatskin casks filled with date pits or seeds. The women are the singers of the group. Sitting together in a chorus of sorts, they sing of the seasons or the day's events or love, their melancholy high-pitched voices piercing the silence of the night like claws of a tigress ripping the flesh of her prey.

Gabriel waited for the blood ink to dry before putting aside the length of dried goat hide that had been presented to him as a gift when he had emerged from the healer's tent. It was symbolic of new life, an offering to show renewal of the flesh. He had been with the tribe many moons, too many to count, spending most of his time in solitude, observing and writing. He knew nothing of the desert, the sky, or these people who huddled by the fire night after night, their faces glowing copper in the blackness. He kept a journal in English, the only language he knew, hoping the recording of his impressions would help him come to an understanding of this place.

It had. What had started as impatience and intolerance of a culture utterly unknown to him had evolved into a sort of compassion. The nomads let him be but never treated him as an outsider. He was always welcome to participate, or not, and tonight was no different.

He felt a hand on his shoulder.

Hairan gestured toward the fire circle as he spoke.

Gabriel didn't have to speak the language to understand the old man wanted him to join the festivities. He was reluctant. "Thank you," he said, waving off the invitation. "I don't think I am up to it. Perhaps another night."

Hairan nodded, but the children had no use for such courtesies. Encouraged by the invitation of the chief, they rose from the campfire and gathered round the stranger. Giggling, they examined his long, pale fingers, his ashen blond hair, knotted and wiry from dryness and neglect, the unruly reddish beard covering his face from the cheekbones down, hiding his milky skin and giving him the gruff cast of an old man. The boys kneeled around Gabriel and lifted up his robes to see what unusual features lurked beneath, whispering their curiosity to one another. One took Gabriel's hand and pulled him toward the group. The other youngsters joined in, expressing their enthusiasm with laughter, until he had no choice but to accept the hospitality of his hosts.

The children led Gabriel near the young men of the tribe, and he took his place among them, awkwardly nodding his greetings. He wrapped his woolen blanket around his body to ward off the chill and tried to get lost in the background. It was impossible. Everyone was aware of his presence. He knew he was as unfamiliar to these people as they were to him. They all stared, not in a threatening manner but in study, as if prolonged exposure to the subject would help them understand his nature.

Gabriel avoided meeting their eyes, staring instead at the belly of the fire. Perhaps the Bedouins did not feel threatened by him, but he wasn't sure he felt the same of them.

How had he ended up amongst these people? He struggled to recall something about his life before, but he could not. Memory was a charlatan, cheating him of something so basic as his identity. It was as if his life had begun on the night he'd woken, tenuously clinging to life, in Hairan's tent. All that came before was a mystery whose veil had yet to be lifted.

He stared at the fire and tried to concentrate. What came to mind was the same jumble of nonsense: faces with no names, unfamiliar places, images ebbing and flowing like the tide of his dreams.

The shrill voice of a woman singing a cappella interrupted his racing thoughts. She carried a tune admirably, her voice rising and falling and reverberating in her throat, floating dreamily in the space between reality and illusion. Everyone was still, transfixed by the chanteuse, as if nothing mattered but her song.

Gabriel was surprised by the reverence for beauty displayed by the people he had dismissed as philistines. A wave of shame washed over him.

The songbird's anthem was the prelude for an entire evening of dance and song. The musicians played with a fervor usually reserved for big events, like the passage to spring or a birth, human or animal. The instruments wailed under the continuous pounding, plucking, and blowing.

The women kneeled before the men and poured wine

from goatskin bladders into small clay cups. Taneva, the eldest of the womenfolk, bowed before Gabriel and poured wine into his cup. The old woman looked at him with the tender eyes of a mother and smiled broadly, revealing the four teeth that clung like stalactites to her purple gums.

Gabriel had no idea who she was, nor that it was she who had excavated him from the eternal sands. He drank. The liquid tasted like vinegar, sour and sharp, but he was parched, so he gulped. He was oblivious to the fact that he was being watched until the young men around him whooped their approval as he upended the cup. He winced at the aftertaste.

Two of the young men pulled Gabriel to his feet and dragged him, in spite of his protests, toward the center of the circle. To the happy beat of a bucolic flute song, the men stomped and rocked and waved their arms skyward, chanting an unintelligible cadence. They prodded him to move as hysterical laughter and good-natured hollers from the crowd ensued. He had no choice but to have fun and let himself be made fun of. He did his best to imitate the other men's movements, but he lacked the grace to improvise a dance to an unfamiliar tune. It was of little consequence to him or to anyone else, for that matter. The idea was to delight in the moment. Eventually, he released his inhibitions and let the music take his feet as he gazed dreamily at the strange and beautiful scene around him.

slipped into primitive backstrap looms fashioned of sticks and rope and sang as they worked, simple tunes about the stars, the plenitude of the oasis, the stubbornness of the animals, the loneliness of the desert. It was a ritual born of necessity, for the women made these textiles for function and warmth, but there was immense beauty in it.

Weaving was an outlet for expressing emotion, and it was evident in the finished piece. If a woman had just taken a husband and was in good spirits, her cloth depicted abstract figures reaching to the sky. Trees laden with fruit symbolized fertility and life. If a woman had recently suffered the loss of a child, her textile somberly depicted stars and scrolls representative of the spirit-sky. Gabriel looked down at his own blanket, examining the characters for the first time. It was an elaborate pattern of scrolls and peaks arranged in concentric circles, which he interpreted as the changing seasons in the desert.

Behind him, a voice spoke. Gabriel turned to see a boy who couldn't have been older than sixteen. He was diminutive in stature, no taller than five feet, his hands and feet as small as a young child's, but didn't seem to be intimidated that Gabriel towered over him. Back straight and chest out, he asserted his presence. He pursed his fleshy lips as if he was considering the odd man before him.

"I don't understand, my friend," Gabriel replied.

The impish boy spoke and placed his hand on his chest. He repeated slowly: "Daaa'ud."

"Da'ud. Pleasure to meet you."

The boy pointed to Gabriel. "Abyan." He said something more and started to walk away but turned back and signaled him to follow.

The sand felt like dried breadcrumbs to Gabriel's naked feet. It was unusually coarse in this part of the desert, where basalt outcroppings protruded from the sand and gravel to give the land a prehistoric appearance. It was just one of many faces of the desert. Day to day and week to week, the terrain changed from vast dustbowl to scattered stone fields to brush plains to fecund oasis. It was this variety that enabled the nomad to subsist, and his survival depended on his knowing the idiosyncrasies of each terrain as he knew the stride of his own camel. But to Gabriel, it was all frustratingly foreign and unpredictable.

Gabriel wondered where the young man was leading him. The Bedouin tents were well out of sight now, and the two of them were threading their way around a basalt labyrinth. These stones, bleached to a chalky gray by the cruel sun of the millennia, had surely seen it all: volcanic eruptions, continental drifts, ice ages, meteor impacts. Now they were headstones in a sandy graveyard, the silent sentinels of some universal secret containing all the wisdom of the ages in their fossilized masses.

Da'ud said something to him, then disappeared behind a monolith and into a cavity in the massive boulder's underbelly.

Gabriel crawled in behind him. It was dark and cool, a welcome reprieve from the punishing heat. The air smelled of ash.

Da'ud proceeded to light a fire with some sticks and dry brush that someone had left in the cave.

A refuge. Gabriel would have never fathomed, had he not seen it with his own eyes, that a place as hostile and bleak as the desert could provide so well for its creatures. Shelter, food, and water were always available for those who knew the desert's curves and caprices and were willing to submit to her rhythms rather than create an order of their own.

Gabriel sat on the cold ground, gathering his knees to his chest. Though his line of sight was limited to a stone wall tentatively illuminated by the anemic fire, their voices bounced and echoed off unseen chambers. Shadows danced around him like the silhouettes of muses, alternately hiding and revealing the texture of the rock.

The young Bedouin stuffed a clay pipe with tobacco and, with a kindly smile revealing his misaligned gray teeth, offered it to his companion. Gabriel used a piece of kindling to light the pipe and drew back, coughing as he inhaled.

"What is this stuff? It's disgusting."

Da'ud howled hysterically.

Gabriel laughed too. He drew back again and feigned his pleasure on the exhale so as to not offend his new friend. He was repelled by the substance, but the act of smoking was comforting.

Da'ud wrapped a piece of gauze around a stick and dipped it into the fire to make a torch. He gestured to Gabriel to follow him as he scooted, using his hands and feet like a monkey, toward the far end of the cave. He held the torch close to the wall.

Remarkably, the rock from the base of the wall to the ceiling was covered with strange drawings and what appeared to be characters of a language, all carved into the stone.

"You can write? You know language?" Gabriel was stunned.

Da'ud pointed to the stick figures accompanying the text, which were lined up in storyboard fashion, and with charadelike gestures proceeded to explain their meaning. He pointed to the figure of a horseman raising a spear and emulated a mean expression.

Gabriel watched intently. Though he understood nothing the boy was saying, he could sense his anger. He read the gesture as the description of an enemy.

Da'ud pointed to another scene, showing the horseman and his men trampling people and tents. His voice grew loud—almost frantic—as he recounted his story. The next figure depicted a man lying on the ground and the horse rearing over his body while a small boy stood nearby. Da'ud wrapped his arms around himself and rocked back and forth, his eyes glistening with tears and his voice full of angst.

Gabriel struggled to comprehend. Was the trampled man a relative? His father, perhaps? Was he the small boy watching the scene unfold?

Da'ud composed himself, and his eyes filled with hatred. He thumped his chest thrice and held up his fists. He pointed to another figure that showed two men fighting hand to hand. He clenched his teeth and ran his hand across his throat, a gesticulation that was unmistakable.

The figures, combined with Da'ud's gestures and wild-eyed delivery, told the story of revenge, the taking of one life to avenge another. The boy before him might have been young but not too young to spill blood for justice. Gabriel was at a loss for words.

Da'ud continued, pointing to another row of figures. His eyes were blank as he told the last part of the story. He pointed to a piece of sharp stone on the ground, picked up the flint, and handed it to Gabriel.

Gabriel protested, but Da'ud's hard expression told Gabriel he'd better acquiesce. He put his hand on the young Bedouin's shoulder. The two exchanged glances, a silent understanding between men. They were not so different after all.

Six

Sarah sat at her desk, staring out the window of her cabin at the ceaseless downpour that had kept her crew inside the past three days. The wet season had finally arrived in Aksum.

Two weeks had passed since their trip to Addis, and she was still trying to make sense of the events. She kept thinking of the inscription on the Ezana throne: *My medicine man placed himself between my body and the lance-blade and fell in my place.* The king's narrative was consistent with the wound on the entombed man's rib cage. Could this be the tenth saint? Was that why the warning was etched on the coffin?

She had spent the time indoors researching the battle at Meroë, hoping for any clue about the king's medicine man, but had found nothing. The only evidence of his existence, as far as she could tell, was what Matakala had shown her.

The brotherhood to which Matakala had alluded also weighed on her mind. She and Daniel had both placed calls to colleagues at Cambridge, Rutgers, and elsewhere, but the responses had come back empty. Either this sect was extremely well guarded or it didn't exist at all. She hoped for the latter.

She picked up a letter from among her pile of papers. It was from Matakala, on official Ministry of Culture letterhead, and had arrived by certified post shortly after their return to Aksum.

Dear Dr. Weston,

I enjoyed our meeting the other night and look forward to a mutually cooperative relationship.

I trust you have had the time to evaluate my proposal. Please call my office in the next forty-eight hours with your reply.

Most sincerely,
Andrew Matakala

The deadline had come and gone, and she hadn't answered. She was determined to stand her ground, whatever the consequences. Still, she wanted to know more about her adversary. She poured herself a glass of Ethiopian *tej* and drew back on her harsh Rothman cigarette. Technically, she'd quit two years ago, but she needed whatever help she could muster.

"Weston here." The voice was a source of both comfort and angst.

"Hello, Daddy." She drew the smoke deep into her lungs and exhaled.

"Darling, are you smoking? Don't tell me you're so weak willed you've gone back."

Sarah felt the pang but brushed it aside. "Not now, Daddy. I need your help. There's someone I want you to check out for me. A man by the name of Andrew Matakala. I need to know who he is, where he was educated . . . whatever you can tell me about him."

"Is this your new beau, darling?"

"I'm being serious. It's someone I ran into in Addis. He works for the Ministry of Culture, but there's something about him I don't trust."

"Oh, Sarah, are you sure you're not being paranoid? This isn't your overactive imagination speaking, is it?"

There he went again, dismissing her as if she were a child. She regretted calling him. "Listen, if it's a big deal, forget about it. I'll get the information some other way."

"Let me see what I can do. But it will take some time. I have an agenda full of meetings, you know, and then there's all the travel: Brussels, Dubai, Tokyo.

I will try to get to it between things."

Between things.

She heard a rap on her door. Matakala's warning came to mind: *You don't know whom you're up against.*

"Fair enough. Must run; someone's at the door." She hung up hastily.

Another knock.

"Sarah, it's me."

Relieved to hear Daniel's voice, she opened the door to find her colleague standing in the rain. Drops trickled down his forehead like tiny rivers, skirting his thick black brows and outlining the contours of his face as they fell to the ground. He was pale as the morning fog, his jaw tightly closed.

She let him in and went to a cupboard to fetch some towels. "You don't look good."

He stared at her blankly, his eyes completely devoid of their usual luster.

His silence made her stomach tighten. "Danny? What is it?" She touched his forearm.

He was silent for a long moment, then looked at the ceiling and exhaled loudly. "Rada is dead."

"What?" She had expected him to say he had some bad news from abroad, that he had to leave the camp at once—anything but this. "No." She sat motionless.

"His secretary called me. She found him this morning. It must have happened late last night.

She left at ten o'clock, and he was still at the office. Apparently someone broke in sometime after that and planted three bullets in his chest. Damn it to hell."

Sarah dropped her forehead to her hands.

"His secretary thinks it was a robbery. Said the place was ransacked when she got there. She found him on the floor, bleeding on a pile of papers."

Sarah sat up. "A robbery? That's bollocks."

"It sure as hell wasn't a robbery. Rada was onto something, and somebody was trying to silence him."

"How do you know this?"

"When the secretary left last night, Rada gave her a sealed envelope addressed to me. He told her it was some documents I was expecting and to courier it to me first thing in the morning. She did it on her way to the office, before she found him. What do you want to bet these documents had something to do with the inscriptions?"

"Did the secretary know anything about it?"

"No, she had no idea. He didn't confide in her."

Sarah walked to the window and watched the rain, like needles of molten silver, pelt the ground in the light of the full moon. Her thoughts lingered on her conversation with Matakala. What if . . . ?

She turned to Daniel. "I can't help but think of what Matakala said about this Coptic brotherhood. That they would stop at nothing to protect what is theirs. If there is any truth to that—"

"There's no way to know, but something tells me the truth will reveal itself sooner than we think. And we'll be caught smack in the middle of it like Rada was."

Sarah studied Daniel's face. Behind the veil of ire lurked anguish, maybe even guilt.

"I'm sorry about Rada. I know he was your chap. But don't blame yourself, Danny. This is not your fault." She tried to sound sympathetic, but her tone was awkward, all wrong for the situation.

He gave her a bitter smile, stood, and walked to the door.

The thought crossed her mind that neither of them was safe tonight, but she didn't want to reveal her vulnerability.

Instead of asking him to stay, she bade him good night and bolted the door behind him.

Seven

The tribe stayed in the basalt lands to wait out the winter. Though the days were never cold, the night temperatures often plummeted below freezing and the tribesmen took refuge in the caves. Gabriel sat with a few men near a fire, shivering though wrapped in two woolen blankets. His mood was somber. Earlier he had witnessed the passing of one of the elders, a frail old creature whose heart had succumbed to the cold. It affected him more than he would have expected, watching life flee like that. But the Bedouins were unfazed by the hardships winter brought, regarding it as an inescapable part of life that they were powerless to change. Their good-natured chatter and the earthy scent of pipe smoke lulled him to sleep.

In his dreams, he could not escape the persistence of his fragmented memory. He was in a big hall, in front of a sea of people. There must have been hundreds, thousands maybe. He could not tell what he was wearing, except that he wore spectacles that kept sliding down the steep angle of his nose. His words were garbled and senseless. The only intelligible thing was a young woman's question: "But what of the Mediterranean Sea? Haven't we learned from those mistakes?"

He turned restlessly in the throes of tortured sleep. Dreams kept coming, some incoherent, others painfully real. In one he saw himself inside a steel tube that barely fit around his body. It was cold, but he was drenched in sweat and clearly frightened. He felt claustrophobic, desperate to get out, but couldn't move his arms enough to push on the steel walls and find an exit. A cold liquid rose from the bottom of the tube, covering his feet, his knees, his thighs, his navel. His lower extremities felt numb. He screamed for help, but no sound came from his mouth. There was only the pained, terrified expression of a man on the edge of unspeakable doom. The liquid reached his bottom lip.

He awoke gasping and was comforted to see the crumple of his tattered Bedouin blankets and the feeble remains of the night's fire. The more he tried to concentrate on making sense of the images, the more they eluded him, taunted him, made a fool of him.

Hot with anger, he stormed out of the cave and ran aimlessly across the desert until the cold sobered him and he fell to his knees, too exhausted to care.

The pieces of the puzzle that was Gabriel's life were coming together, albeit in helter-skelter fashion. Judging by his frustration with the laborious life in the desert, he was sure that at home, wherever home was, things happened at a much faster pace.

He couldn't surmise what year it was. The nomads knew the passing of the seasons and counted the moons of their own lives, knowing, for example, that a person had lived through eighteen summers or another was born forty moons after the passing of spring, but there was no broader concept of a place in time.

As Gabriel learned enough of the language to communicate on a basic level, he unraveled the mystery of his new home. The tribesmen didn't call it by name. They simply called it the desert as if there wasn't another desert in the world. What they did know was that there were twin rivers passing through the sands, that there were fertile slivers of land to the north and west, and that traders passed through these parts as they made their way from the east toward the sea to the west.

Arabia. How he'd ended up there, half buried in a sandy grave and left for dead, remained ambiguous, gnawing on his consciousness day and night.

Every passing month chipped away at Gabriel's impatience, and he eventually became more resigned to the inevitable. A man knows deep in his bones when to give in and go with the flow. As the Bedouins liked to say, the answers came when they were ready to come, to those who were ready to receive them. Fighting the natural course of things would be counterproductive, even destructive. He recalled the explanation Hairan had once offered when the two of them were sitting by the banks of a stream in an oasis, washing their robes.

"Do you see those two rocks?" Hairan pointed to a round, smooth stone beneath the surface of the flowing water. Then he pointed to another, one whose crown was above the surface. The water parted as it hit the stone, flowing around and past it. That stone was slighter and had sharper edges. "The first rock submits to the water. It does not fight the current. That's why it is whole. The second rock stands against the current, but it doesn't change anything. The water still flows as it always has; it just takes a different course. But the rock itself is eroded. Soon there will be nothing left of it."

Gabriel was humbled by the statement. A man like Hairan might not have seen much of the world outside these expanses of sand, but his wisdom ran far deeper than that of those who called themselves civilized men.

Gabriel liked spending time with Hairan. He saw kindness in the old chief's ebony eyes and an uncommon calm in his manner. Nothing ruffled him, not even painful memories.

Gabriel had asked him one night why he did not have a wife and children.

"I had a wife," Hairan said, a wistful smile crossing his lips. "Ain. Her beauty was more radiant than the evening star."

Gabriel was certain by Hairan's use of the past tense that Ain was no longer living. "What happened to her?"

"She passed to the other realm. It was her destiny."

Gabriel respected the silence.

"Ain became pregnant on the night of our wedding. There was much joy in the goums. The men slaughtered a lamb and cooked it on a spit. Everyone ate and drank and danced to celebrate the arrival of the shaykh's heir. I was very happy. It gave me great pleasure to see Ain with child. My child."

"You loved her."

"More than the grasses love the water. She was destined for me. I had seen it in a vision once. I was walking through a lush orchard. I tried to pull the fruit off the branches but couldn't. Then Ain appeared from behind a tree and handed me the juiciest orange in the orchard. I knew then she was the woman I would marry."

"And she had a good pregnancy?"

"She did not. She was sick all the time and could

not eat, could not sleep. Her pains came early. The elder women tried to save the child, my son, but he was already dead. There was nothing they could do."

"I'm so sorry." Gabriel felt his heart beat in his throat. He felt genuine empathy for the man, as if he had been in that place himself.

"It was not meant to be. Things always happen the way they should."

"And Ain?"

"She died from grief some moons later. She wept every day. I could not console her. She stopped eating and drinking. She lost the will to live. All she wanted, she said, was to be with her son. So she went to him." Hairan sighed and trained his eyes on the evening star.

Gabriel closed his eyes and lowered his head, uncertain why the story sounded so familiar.

Gabriel was by nature an analytical man. What the nomads knew by instinct, he knew by mathematical exactitude. His mind dwelled in the realm of reason and order. On a steaming summer day, his logic told him a sandstorm might be approaching. He could tell this by the temperature of the air and ground and the direction from which the rare breezes came. The air was so dry breathing felt like a gasp for oxygen in a fire, the sand so hot it could not be traversed even by those with the most calloused feet. He knew, before the Bedouins themselves knew, what would happen: in nature's inimitable way of attempting to achieve balance, the heat would distribute itself upward and outward by organizing convection currents. If the heat was intense enough and the currents strong enough, a fierce wind would be formed and move mass quantities of sand with no regard for anything or anyone in its way.

Gabriel went to Hairan to relay his suspicions. He bowed his head and pointed his eyes toward the ground. "Shaykh, it has not rained in months. The air is still and hotter than I have ever seen it. The camels are restless. I fear great walls of sand are coming."

"And how is it," he said with a harsh tone, "that a man who has never lived in the desert knows so much?"

Though he had been there almost a year, he was still considered a visitor. "I humble myself to your wisdom and that of your tribesmen. I do not know the desert like you do, but this I know. I am certain of it."

"Abyan." Hairan used the name Da'ud had given Gabriel. Everyone had adopted the epithet. "I believe you are sincere, but you have to respect the knowledge of the people who live and die by this desert." In an apparent show of courtesy, he made an unusual concession. "I will call the council of elders together this evening. You may state your concerns before everyone. Then the elders will make a decision, and you must abide by that decision whether you agree with it or not."

No sooner had Gabriel agreed than he began to regret it. How could he possibly explain it to the elders? They spoke a different language, literally and figuratively. None of the ruminations of his mind would make sense to them. He couldn't write down mathematical formulas or explain concepts like the interaction between ground heat and the atmosphere. They looked at the weather like their ancestors always had: intuitively. They knew rain was coming when they saw the scarabs burrowing in the sand. They knew the weather would get cooler when birds started flying south in great numbers. And they knew sandstorms were coming when they saw smoke on the horizon.

There was no smoke this night. The sky was clear, its indigo cloak illuminated by a dazzling, perfectly round moon. The elders were gathered in the communal tent, smoking their pipes and recounting stories from the past when Gabriel entered.

The room fell silent.

He worried everyone already knew what he was about to say and, worse, had prejudged him. He shook off his momentary desire to make for the door and stood firmly before them.

Hairan addressed his tribesmen in the authoritative tone his rank demanded. "Abyan has something to say to us. Listen carefully. His is a warning. Warnings are never to be taken lightly."

Gabriel spoke in a combination of Bedouin dialect and hand gestures. "Brothers, friends. I am but a stranger to these lands and bow to your wisdom. I claim no authority over this council, but I humbly ask you to heed what I am about to say. I have cause to suspect a great wall of sand is heading in our direction as soon as midday tomorrow. The people must prepare for this now."

"You realize this is a grave matter," one elder said. "Why should we believe you?"

"Have you seen a vision?" another said.

"No, no visions. Just fact. The desert is too hot. Even the animals feel it." Gabriel struggled to disguise his frustration. "It will rise up and revolt to bring itself back to a balanced state."

"Tomorrow we ride for the oasis," one of Hairan's top lieutenants said. "If we take cover as you are suggesting, we will miss our turn in the fertile lands. This would be devastating for our people and for the animals."

"But not taking cover would be far worse. You could lose lives and property. It would be a major setback for the tribe."

The elders whispered among themselves, clearly weighing both sides of the equation.

As the deliberations became more heated, Hairan clapped to call for quiet. He turned to Gabriel. "You must take your leave now. We will discuss this matter in private, and we will inform you of our decision. Please . . . go."

With a sense of foreboding, Gabriel exited the tent. He had been hopeful that the elders would be more reasonable, that when faced with the prospect of death and destruction, they would choose the safe route even if doing so wasn't convenient. Now he wasn't so sure.

They seemed to be divided, clearly unconvinced a random white man could have any knowledge of things they had learned through the wisdom of their ancestors. His kind had no jurisdiction here.

When Hairan finally walked out of the tent, his old eyes screwed up, Gabriel could tell what the verdict was.

"I will lead the caravan to the oasis tomorrow. We have no supplies, no water. If we do not go, we will surely suffer the consequences."

Gabriel clutched his unruly blond hair, now so long it dusted his shoulders. "This is madness. I can see what's happening here. I am not one of you, so you summarily dismiss me. You would rather risk lives than believe a white man. Is that it?"

"This isn't about you, Abyan. What I believe is that the people's livelihood is at stake. Their very survival. I will not put them in the way of peril."

"And yet peril is exactly what you will face."

"We have been through countless sandstorms and survived. We are not afraid."

He pointed at the chief, fully aware it was a sign of disrespect. "You are being foolish. You will regret this."

"When I asked you to present your case to the council, I also said you had to accept their decision. It shows bad character to go back on your word."

Gabriel looked away, insulted. Hairan might as well have slapped him.

The chief softened his tone. "All will be well. You will see."

Gabriel did not reward him with a reply or even a look in the eye.

Hairan turned and walked to his tent.

Da'ud signaled to Gabriel to come sit with him and his cronies by the fire. Handing him a pipe of tobacco, the young man said, "You look pale, Abyan. What has happened to you?"

"I don't belong here, my friend. No matter how much I know or how I try to help, I will never be accepted. We both know that."

"You are different from us. You do things a certain way, and we do them another way. That is not a bad thing."

"Says who?"

"Our covenant. We believe no man is greater than another. Your knowledge and beliefs have a place in your society. We respect that. And you must respect our way of looking at the world."

"You are too young to be talking like this."

Da'ud laughed. "I'm not so young. I'm getting married before the next full moon. You will dance at my wedding, no?"

"You? Married?" Gabriel feigned shock. "Of course. I wouldn't miss it. Besides, who else will pick you up when you drink too much of that camel-piss wine?"

Da'ud pointed to the pipe in Gabriel's hand. "Or smoke too much of this camel dung."

"Camel dung? That's what I've been smoking all this time?" He took another puff. "Rather good."

The two men laughed and shared a smoke. But even that lighthearted moment couldn't lift Gabriel's sense of dread.

It was the next evening when Gabriel saw the umber haze on the horizon. He had known with all his conviction this moment would arrive, though some part of him wished the elders had been right to dismiss him. He would sooner suffer the humiliation of a mistake than the full wrath of the desert wind. The caravan was still en route to the oasis, making use of all available light. The most they could hope for now was a swift, painless gale.

Hairan rode next to Gabriel. "It appears your

predictions were true." He turned to the caravan and spoke at the top of his voice. "We will make camp here. Tie down the camels and fill some sandbags. Make haste. A storm comes our way."

The Bedouins scrambled to fill sandbags, which would act as weights to hold down tents and supplies. This part of the desert was nothing but sculpted dunes. No trees, no shrubs, nothing to impede the wind. It was the worst possible scenario. He surveyed the tribesmen. None of them looked agitated. They just went about their preparations as they would any typical day's chores. Two women even made a fire for tea, anticipating that the storm was still a couple of hours away.

Within an hour, the storm had gotten closer and appeared far more ominous. A rolling mushroom cloud of dust glowing orange in the twilight grew out of the ground. Rolling toward them, it engulfed more sand and swelled until it eclipsed the sky. The equivalent of a tsunami on land, the sixty-foot wall of angry sand thundered forward in a fierce bid to stomp these helpless people into oblivion.

The hiss of the advancing cloud drowned out the tribesmen's voices and the camels' wails.

The warm rush of fear-tinged adrenaline filled Gabriel's senses. He had seen nature's fury before, in another time, another place—and though the details of his past were still sketchy, he knew that what he'd seen was much worse than anything an angry desert could muster, for it had been brought forth by the most sinister workings of men.

He wrapped his headdress tightly around his face, taking care not to leave even a hairline opening through which the sand could enter. It was time to take shelter. Through the indigo gauze of his veil, he looked for the others. Some were hunkering down behind a dune inside a perimeter of blankets tied together. The women were huddled inside a tent, trying to quiet their howling children, for whom there was no comfort. One tiny boy, choking with the dust already thick in the air, bolted out of the tent, falling as he ran up a dune to escape the madness. His mother screamed hysterically after him.

Gabriel bade her stay in the tent and ran after the boy himself. "Come here, you little devil," he shouted in English, unable under stress to recall any Bedouin words. "You will die. Do you hear me? You will die!"

He was surprised how fast the toddler could run, his feet accustomed to the sinking sands of the desert.

Gabriel struggled for air. The tempest was almost upon them. "Stop, damn you. Stop right now, or you will kill us both."

The ground had gone dark in the cloud's shadow. Gabriel looked over his shoulder and saw the massive wall of sand approach with violent speed. Any second now it would swallow them. He resisted the urge to panic and turned back to the boy. The little one was on all fours, crying and coughing so hard vomit spewed from his mouth. Gabriel fell on top of him, sheltering his tiny body with his arms as the apocalyptic cloud swept over.

The next few minutes or hours—Gabriel wasn't sure—were endless. He felt as if he were in a tomb deep underground, unable to breathe or hear or see. His senses were prisoners of the eternal dust. All he could feel were the frenzied grains of sand whipping his hunched back with no remorse. The feeling was akin to being dragged by a truck across a gritty dirt road. Sure his back was raw and bleeding, he tried to transcend the pain by making sense of what was happening.

It is the way of nature to seek balance. Balance is necessary for all living things. Out of calamity comes balance and order. He kept repeating the mantra in his mind, but he was not strong enough to believe it. His thoughts turned to doom. His mind's eye was flooded with images of darkness and fire, vicious clouds of smoke from which there was no escape, people lying dead at his feet, trees as black and brittle as spent charcoal. He saw the pale blue eyes of a boy staring at him vacantly, frozen in death. He gritted his teeth to prevent the sobs from spewing forth, and his mouth filled with the metallic taste of sand granules scraping at his teeth and gums like coarse sandpaper. The sobs came anyway, then the screams of despair, then nothing.

The next thing he felt was a stick poking his ribs.

"Abyan. Abyan." The voice of Hairan was muffled, as if he were talking from behind a glass wall.

Gabriel rose slowly, pounds of sand rolling off his head and body. He ripped his headdress off his face and gasped for air.

Day was breaking.

"I must have passed out." He suddenly remembered his tiny companion. "The boy." Alarmed by his own caliginous thoughts, he clawed at the sand. "Where is the boy?"

"He is with his mother. She is very grateful that you saved his life."

"And the others?"

Hairan fell silent. A vague mist covered his ebony eyes.

Gabriel looked down at the makeshift camp and saw very little commotion. The women's tent had been ripped to shreds. Bits of burlap attached to tent posts fluttered in a weak breeze. What was left of the fabric was strewn here and yonder. The men's protective barrier of blankets, rickety to begin with, had vanished, probably swallowed by the voracious monster of dust. He heard crying—but not ordinary crying.

These were the rhythmic lamentations of a requiem. His heart sank.

"The desert takes what she wants," Hairan said.

The two men walked down the dune to survey the damage. Gabriel felt sick. Men pulled out bodies from sandy graves and checked them for signs of life. Those not breathing were laid in a pile to receive a proper burial later. A dozen or so were in the pile already. A young woman fell to her knees and with her hands muffled a heart-wrenching scream.

"Her beloved," said one of the men, scraping the cocktail of sand and sweat off his face. "Dead."

When they ripped the veil from the young man's face, Gabriel realized it was Da'ud. His skin had the sickening gray pallor of departed life. He had suffocated like the others. Gabriel fell to his knees and heaved, nothing issuing from his throat but a thread of slimy saliva. He was utterly spent, physically and emotionally.

Damn you, Hairan. Damn you and your council of fools. None of this had to happen. These people did not have to die. He wanted to bellow his anger at Hairan but thought better of it. He knew a scene like that would only make things worse for these people, who had their own grief to deal with. Instead, he joined the other men in their grim task of searching for the dead.

The mass burial took place in the afternoon,

when the bodies were returned to the earth and covered with a thin film of sand. Over time, the shifting desert would engulf her sons and daughters. Their flesh would feed the scarabs, ants, and scorpions; their bones would calcify the sands. The burial was without ceremony. Loved ones simply left a pile of the deceased's clothes at the head of the grave, a symbol of letting go and an offering to passersby in need. Nothing was wasted in the desert, least of all tears.

Gabriel sat alone for the rest of the evening, grieving in his own way. He smoked Da'ud's pipe, which the young man's betrothed had given Gabriel at the burial.

"You shared this pipe," she had said. "It belongs with you now."

His anger had subsided and been replaced by a profound sense of despair. The world he'd found was as cruel as the one he'd left.

Hairan sat next to him. "I am sorry, Abyan. Sorry for your loss."

"What do you know of my loss?"

"I can see it in your expression. You are different."

"Well, saying good-bye to friends will do that to a man." Gabriel made no attempt to mask his bitterness.

"I do not understand your anger. Da'ud, your friend, would not have understood it. It is the way of all life. Death comes to all living things. We do not will when it comes. It happens according to the plan."

Tears obscured Gabriel's vision, his emotion equal parts frustration and grief. How could he explain to this simple nomad that there was no plan, that man and man alone created destiny? He knew he could not penetrate the armor of faith that enshrouded the desert dweller. He wiped his eyes haphazardly with his palms, took a deep breath, and stared at the sky, wondering if he would ever find peace.

Hairan invaded the silence. "We could not foresee that the sandstorm would be catastrophic. And yet you knew. How?"

Gabriel sighed and spoke in a softer tone. "I cannot explain it to you, Shaykh. The things I know are my own burden."

Hairan put a gentle arm around his shoulder. "You remember who you are, don't you?"

"Yes. And I wish I didn't."

Eight

My friend Daniel,

It is my humble duty to inform you the inscriptions you have found are not what I thought them to be—that is, an innocuous account of nomadic life. There is a message here, a warning perhaps, though without the benefit of the full text I cannot give you but a partial explanation. The passage you left with me translates thus:

Great tongues of fire will cover the land.
The tainted air will feed the flames.
Smoke will rise to the heavens with a terrible fury
Until all life is devoured and there is nothing
But the eternal silence.

Something strange is at work here. When I consulted my sources at Yemrehana Krestos, they were reluctant to discuss it. They demanded to know where the inscriptions were found and who else knew about them. I told them nothing, of course. I have never known these peaceful men to be so unsettled.

I caution you and Sarah to be vigilant. It seems these are murky waters you are treading.

Best wishes,
Rada Kabede

After reading the letter, Sarah was more convinced than ever that the tenth saint lay prostrate before her. In silence she surveyed the skeleton, fixing her gaze on his severed rib cage. *The eternal silence. Death.* Could he have been describing his own fatal moment? Could he have foreseen it before he fell to the lance-blade? Perhaps he was a prophet of some sort. That could explain his sanctity.

To complicate matters, the report from the radiocarbon dating lab arrived in her in-box sometime during the night. For the most part, it was consistent with her suspicions, but some things still didn't make sense.

When her phone rang, she already knew who it was. She was certain Professor Simon, whom the lab had copied on the report, would want to discuss the curious nature of the findings.

She answered cheerfully. "Professor, did you receive—"

"Are you alone?"

"I'm in the lab. There is no one else here. Is something wrong?"

"Listen very carefully, Sarah. I had a call from the Minister of Culture today. Apparently, your expedition has been the subject of discussion in very high circles. It seems there has been a little too much attention on the Cambridge project, thanks to this Mr. Kabede's murder. Yesterday, investigators went through his office and found certain objects that connect him to you. There were files in his computer marked *Aksum Expedition*. They contained only notes, but that was enough to rouse their suspicions. Then they snooped around and got eyewitness reports of his dining with you and Daniel Madigan. The final blow came when his secretary confessed that on the night before his death Mr. Kabede handed her a letter to courier over to Dr. Madigan."

Sarah went numb.

"Sarah? Are you there?"

It was as though an invisible hand had gripped her throat. "I'm here," she whispered.

"Where is this letter?"

"I have it. It arrived this morning."

"Well? What does it say?"

Sarah read the contents to the professor.

"It is just as I thought—bad news." His voice

shook. "Why you insist on defying authority, I will never know. Now hear this, Sarah. You must turn this letter over to the police. Surely they are on their way as we speak."

"I don't think that's a good idea. It will only make matters worse."

"No. What will make matters worse is your lack of cooperation. The expedition is already in hot water, and not cooperating would jeopardize the delicate diplomatic relationship between Ethiopia and England, to say nothing of Cambridge and UNESCO."

"Professor, you don't understand. This letter will be ammunition in their hands. They have been looking for an excuse to shutter the Cave I Tomb. This could be it."

"That tomb is the least of my worries. Our predicament, young lady, is much worse than that. The Ministry want everything turned over to the government. They are pulling our permits until further notice."

Her worst fear had come true. "What?"

"You heard me. We must shut down operations. I want you to send the crew home, effective immediately. We will then make arrangements to have artifacts already excavated shipped to the national museum in Addis, where they will be studied by an Ethiopian team."

"This is bollocks! They have absolutely nothing to warrant shutting us down. The fact that we consulted

Rada does not make us guilty of his murder. We have done nothing wrong."

"Well, sneaking around on unofficial business with an Ethiopian linguist who turns up dead a few days later certainly does not look good, does it?"

"But what of the cave? Abandoning it now would leave the site vulnerable to looters—or worse." She raised her voice. "We can't afford to have these inscriptions fall into the wrong hands."

"That's the Ethiopian government's concern now. They will be guarding the site until it can be reopened."

"Dr. Simon, please. You must convince the Ministry we are the best stewards of this site. The thugs who killed Kabede will return. The inscriptions are what they're after. Do you really think the Ethiopians will protect it when they can be bought and sold for a handful of birr?"

"That is quite enough. The decision is final. Now, I expect you to stay no longer than is needed to wrap things up. Is that clear?"

"And if I don't?"

"If I were you, I would do exactly as told. There is more at stake here than just this expedition." He cleared his throat. "The regents were not in support of sending someone so young and inexperienced on this project. It was I who insisted you were ready. Now I look like a fool, and they are demanding your removal.

There are rumblings about . . . pulling you away from fieldwork altogether. I cannot defend you anymore. But if you play your cards right and come back to England, perhaps your father can intervene on your behalf."

"My father?" Sarah's voice broke. "I am not some little girl who needs to be rescued. I have done nothing wrong, and I will prove it. I will clear my name in my own way." She slammed down the phone and let out a scream.

Matakala had gotten what he'd wanted after all. *I suggest you give some thought to our request—if you want to continue working in Ethiopia, that is.* When she had not rewarded his request to turn the tenth saint over to the church, clearly he'd taken it upon himself to teach her a painful lesson.

Still, she had no regrets. She would have done nothing differently.

Except one thing.

She reread the letter several times, memorizing the lines Rada had translated.

Then she held it above her lighter and set it aflame.

When the police came, she told them the letter had been shredded along with some other documents. She "hadn't realized it was a piece of evidence—sorry." But it was "nothing of note," merely a "progress report on a routine translation."

Daniel corroborated her story.

The police didn't believe it, but they couldn't prove otherwise.

Packing never had been easy for Sarah. It reminded her of the day she had helped pack her mother's belongings to donate to the charity shop. Now, as then, she saw it as a barbaric act, this cold jettisoning of objects, each of which was attached to a memory, as if they'd never meant a thing.

As she arranged the artifacts and tools and journals, she knew in her scientist's mind she should not be attached to her work; she should let go the minute an object was excavated and move on.

If only it were so simple. In this burial ground lay answers to questions she had never asked, forgotten lives in whose footsteps she had never walked. She had failed Cambridge, failed her crew, failed her father. Worst of all, she had failed the man who in death lay waiting for his message to be found, only to have it fall into bureaucratic oblivion. The question remaining was whether she would fail herself.

Aisha, the last of the crew to leave, walked into the lab, her hair wrapped in a bandana like Sarah's, her raven eyes misty. "I'm so sorry. I know this must be very hard for you."

"Don't be silly, girl." Sarah tried to sound cheerful. "This is only a temporary measure. We will reassemble, I promise you. And when we do, I'll come looking for you. You have been my absolute right hand."

The two hugged and kissed, and Aisha wiped away a tear as she strapped on her backpack. She opened the heavy door of the lab and let the sunlight into the darkened room. She waved as she walked outside, then descended the hill to the bus stop.

Sarah would miss the crew, miss Aksum. She stared at the rows and rows of wooden boxes, lined up like coffins waiting for the undertaker, and broke down.

Sarah and Daniel were the only ones left at camp. The night before they were to hand the project over to the Ethiopians, Daniel showed up at her door with a bottle of Glen Garioch 21 Year Old and two glasses. He flashed a sly grin and held up the goods. "May I come in?"

She'd just walked out of the shower and thrown on a crumpled T-shirt and jean shorts. She untangled her wet curls with her fingers. "I see you found the good stuff. I was saving it for a celebration, not a funeral."

He sat on the bed and poured the scotch into the glasses. He took in the bouquet. "Aaahh. This stuff is the nectar of the gods. I don't know why I didn't notice it in the canteen sooner." He raised his glass and offered a toast. "To better days."

She tried to smile.

"This isn't easy, is it? To give up, I mean."

She took a long sip of scotch and another to work

up the courage to tell him. "There's something you don't know."

"Oh?"

"A couple of nights ago, I heard from the radiocarbon lab."

"And?"

"And it was mostly as we suspected. The bones and coffin dated to 1600, plus or minus eighty, BP. That would put him somewhere around the fourth century, which is consistent with Ezana's throne. What the lab couldn't figure out were the teeth. They tested the enamel and the substance used for the filling, and they have no idea what it is. They looked at every substance ever used for dental work and came up empty. It's a polymer of unknown makeup and apparently far more advanced than the ones currently used in dentistry. It couldn't have existed then. It doesn't even exist now."

"Christ. Why didn't you tell me?"

"I wanted to. I've just been so . . ."

"Busy?" He finished his drink in a single gulp. "You still don't trust me, do you?"

"If I didn't trust you, I wouldn't have told you at all. But the fact of the matter is I feel like this is my burden. I don't expect anyone to walk this road with me. That includes you."

"There's no road to walk, Sarah. Or have you forgotten the Ethiopians have shut down your expedition?"

She stood and walked to the window, staring at the barren hillside. In the bowels of those hills lay humanity's past and her future. She saw the latter flashing in her mind's eye like images from a silent film. Standing before an assembly of archaeology students, pointing to a giant screen as she delivered her lecture. Attending one dinner after another, debating the fine points of Mesopotamian stone carvings with crotchety old men. Presenting a case for support to yet another scientific foundation. Was this the future she wanted? Over the past days, she'd been asking herself this very thing. She could take the safe route, eschewing fieldwork for the path of academia, or she could take the biggest gamble of her life.

She turned to Daniel. "You remember what you once told me about instinct? That there's no substitute for it in this business?"

He looked at her without expression.

"Everything in my bones tells me this is one of the biggest finds of our times. That this man holds answers to questions we dare not ask. I have spent my entire career digging for something like this. Not just another artifact that fills in some blanks but something that could illuminate a fundamental truth. Whatever is inscribed in that rock is big enough for someone to kill for, which means something priceless could be destroyed. Knowing that and walking away would make me a traitor to everything I believe." She considered not telling him, but someone needed to know in case the unthinkable happened. "Danny, I am not getting on the plane tomorrow. I am not going back to England."

"Are you crazy?" He threw up his hands. "You can't stay here. If you don't think you're a target, you're not as smart as I thought."

"They will not find me. I've already made arrangements." She stopped herself, studied Daniel's eyes for any trace of insincerity, and found none. "I will carry on with or without Cambridge's blessing."

"What are you talking about? How do you intend to—wait a minute. No."

"Save it, Danny. My mind is made up."

"Damn it, Sarah. You heard what Rada said that night. The stone is guarded. What makes you think those monks will receive you with open arms?"

"This." She pulled a stack of photographs out of her bag and fanned them on the bed like a deck of cards. They're close-ups of every section of the cave wall. "I have something the Christians have wanted for centuries. The teachings of the tenth saint."

"How do you know?"

"After I read Rada's letter, I was haunted by the reaction of the monks. I couldn't shake the feeling they knew something. So I slipped out late one night and drove to Yemrehana Krestos. I met with the abbot. I told him about the tomb and the inscriptions, and he perked straight up. It turns out there really was a tenth saint, according to the Coptic mystical texts. The abbot believes the saint was buried with some significant teachings the church has wanted to get its hands on for centuries. I told him I would give him access to the inscriptions if his scholars would help me translate them. You see, we each have what the other wants. So he offered me asylum, and I offered him the chance to rewrite history."

Daniel huffed. "This is crazy. Don't you get it? You could be walking straight into the maw of the beast. Don't you find it odd that as soon as Rada consulted the monks someone showed up at his office with a sawed-off shotgun? Have you considered that perhaps someone within the monastery tipped off the assassins?"

"Listen to me, Danny. Rada's assassins got exactly what they wanted: to close down the expedition so they can bury the tenth saint and his inscriptions forever. They don't care about the translation. They want to hide the evidence."

"Fine. Let's pretend you're right. Let's say those thugs don't find and kill you. Even if you do translate the inscriptions, you will be held in insubordination. Your career as an archaeologist will be over. Why put yourself in such a corner?"

"Look, I appreciate your concern, but don't waste your breath trying to talk me out of it. The wheels are already in motion. I will leave tomorrow at first light."

"Why are you doing this? What are you trying to prove?" He paused. "There are easier ways for a daughter to earn her father's respect."

Her cheeks flushed. "This has nothing to do with my father."

"The hell it doesn't."

"Fuck off, Madigan. You don't know anything about me, so spare me your psychobabble. Save it for your tawdry television audience."

Daniel opened his mouth to say something but stopped himself and raised his hands in a sign of truce. "We've said enough. I don't want to make an enemy of you. Let's just part right now before we really hurt each other."

"Fine." She walked to her bed and started stuffing clothes inside her backpack, keeping her back turned to him. She was shaking and didn't want his last impression of her to be one of weakness.

Without a good-bye, he walked out and slammed the door.

Nine

The jeep clattered up the mountain along a pothole-strewn, red clay road leading to the second Jerusalem, as Lalibela was known among Ethiopia's Orthodox Christians. Sarah was excited but apprehensive. The stone that held the key to the inscriptions would soon be within her grasp—and with it, the opportunity to decipher one of history's great puzzles. But she wasn't naïve enough to believe it would be without cost.

She would trust no one. She was perfectly alone, exactly as she wanted to be, yet she felt numb with dread. She missed Daniel, though she was loath to admit it. If only she'd been able to utter the word. *Stay.*

She cursed her impenetrable arrogance, her precious invincibility. It was a Weston trait, a birthright handed down like the trust fund or the thirties Phantom she didn't want. She saw it for what it was—a window dressing on an empty store—but had not yet found the courage to let it go.

She rounded the final corner and came to the roof of an eight thousand–foot–high mountain, where thirteen rock-hewn churches were carved deep into the earth. She parked and walked to the edge of a chasm, marveling at the monument standing in its midst. Carved of a single hunk of stone in the perfectly symmetrical shape of the cross, the church descended hundreds of meters into the bowels of the arid mountain. Its intricate keyhole windows, pedimented doorways, and platform steps gave it the appearance of an ancient fortress meant to protect the spiritual riches of the kingdom. Sarah stood in awe of this feat of twelfth-century architecture and smiled as she recalled the popular legend that Lalibela's churches were carved by angels.

Yemrehana Krestos, one of the lesser known of Lalibela's rock churches, was a few miles from the main complex, situated within a cave above an isolated village in the highlands. Sarah recognized in the church's intricate façade an allegiance to the Aksumite school of architecture. A series of horizontal reveals carved across the width of the exterior gave the building a three-dimensional quality. The thicker slabs were painted white, while the reveals were left the natural brick-red color of the local stone. Keyhole windows were ornamented with crosses—a curious combination of Coptic Christianity and Arabic influence. The only resemblance Yemrehana Krestos bore to Lalibela's other churches was that it was made wholly of stone.

Sarah returned to the jeep and parked in a thickly wooded area away from prying eyes. She wasn't taking any chances.

She strapped on her backpack, in which she had placed a few bare necessities and her travel documents, and continued up the terraced mountainside on foot. Save for the distant hum of cicadas, the mountain was utterly silent. The crisp, vaguely floral scent of juniper laced the air, and the midday sun warmed her face. As she approached the entrance of Yemrehana Krestos, she felt a strange serenity. She didn't question it. Instead, she stood in reverence before the main doorway and let the feeling settle within.

She entered the church through a side door, as she had been instructed to do. "I'm looking for Father Giorgis," she told one of the young acolytes. "He is expecting me."

The boy surveyed her from head to toe, his contempt for a woman in their midst apparent. He addressed her coldly. "Wait here."

For all its magnificent detail, the church was dark and gloomy inside. Its small windows admitted scant light, as if any more would make the brothers long for something brighter and warmer than these damp confines. The walls and ceiling were decorated with paintings of saints and biblical scenes, hardly visible in the shadows. Four columns linked by arches delineated the nave and drew the eye to the domed sanctuary. The space was the essence of simplicity, designed not to impress but to grant spiritual wings to the devout.

A figure emerged from the stone altar. He wore dirty white linen robes and a white turban and clutched a wooden rosary. His face was weathered from the years and the elements, his curly beard more white than black. Still, his gaze was placid, as if he had found redemption from life's suffering. "Miss Sarah," the abbot said, "it is good to see you again."

Father Giorgis led Sarah down a narrow stone corridor lit dimly by makeshift torches—tree branches wrapped with linen dipped in kerosene. As they walked past, the flames shuddered. A trail of soot stretched to the ceiling.

Sarah realized they were heading into the heart of the cave. The damp air chilled her.

There were turns everywhere, dark passages leading to unseen corners. A maze. The place had been built to hide something. The interconnecting corridors were so identical that if she got lost, finding her way out would be nearly impossible. She tried to banish the disturbing thought and concentrate on keeping pace with Father Giorgis' hurried footsteps. After what seemed like miles, they came to a wooden door painted with Christian saints and angels. Sarah, impressed by the exquisite depiction of the Resurrection, vowed to study the iconography one day when time was on her side.

With an iron key, Father Giorgis unlocked the door and led his guest into a chamber of tiny stone cells resembling a prison more than sleeping quarters. "Come." He motioned. "This is where you will stay."

Sarah's and the abbot's footsteps echoed down the corridor. The cells were empty and rife with cobwebs, as though the place hadn't been inhabited for years. They stopped at a room no bigger than the interior of a compact car. There was just enough space for a modest cot and a washbasin.

"No one is on this side of the compound. The monks sleep elsewhere. We take oaths of celibacy, and . . ."

Sarah spared him the awkward speech and threw her backpack on the cot. "This will be just fine. You are very generous to allow me to stay here as your guest."

"You have brought us something important to our faith. You were sent by God. For this you are most welcome."

The next day, Sarah met the church's leading scholar. Father Giorgis had described Brother Apostolos as a gifted linguist and a man of unwavering piety. Because of his flawless character, Apostolos had been selected above all other monks to guard the stone.

When she saw him in the courtyard, Sarah recognized him immediately. He was a diminutive young man whose eyes radiated serenity, but his prematurely furrowed face suggested a life of trials and sorrows. Bony fingers and delicate wrists protruded from the white robes draped several times around his slight body, covering everything except his face and hands. In one fist he carried a staff topped with a wooden cross and in the other a red umbrella with tattered yellow fringe. The monk treaded lightly on the ground, almost floating above it. He was so delicate it seemed a swift breeze could have carried him upward.

He stopped within ten feet of her and spoke softly in Amharic, eyes fixed on the ground. "Father Giorgis sent for me." His speech was as spare as his appearance.

Sarah sensed a great distance between them, both physical and psychic. Still, she was intrigued by the fragile creature to whom something so grave had been entrusted. "I have come for the stone," she replied in his native language.

"I speak English," he said, still avoiding her eyes. Father Giorgis had said Apostolos had devoted his life since boyhood to the study of obscure dialects and ancient tongues, but he'd mentioned nothing about English. She was relieved that they could communicate in her mother tongue, even though communicating didn't seem to be his forté.

Apostolos started toward the entrance to the labyrinth.

Sarah followed, determined this time to make some sense of the twists of the maze. In an attempt to commit the route to memory, she counted the corridors before each turn but couldn't keep track of the many detours. Using her archaeologist's instinct, she tried instead to find landmarks: a groove in the stone, patterns in the soot left behind by the torches, anything. Finally, she turned to her own finely tuned senses. As the corridors got narrower and darker, the scant air smelled of ash. She knew the sensation well: they were venturing deep into the darkness of the granite mountain. The chamber closed in around them like a sepulcher, the damp coolness radiating from the stone.

Without warning, her silent guide stopped and fumbled in the dark corner for a lantern, igniting it with an old Bic lighter. The anemic flame cast a golden halo around him, and he looked like one of the saints in the old Coptic icons.

He walked forward into a round vestibule with three heavily carved wooden doors. He chose the one on the right and inserted an iron object shaped like a horseshoe into two notches until the object became a handle, which he turned. The heavy gate groaned as he pulled it toward him. He held the lantern in front of him, faintly illuminating the contents of the chamber. "This is what you seek. The Sheba Stone."

For a few seconds, Sarah forgot to breathe. Her eyes were riveted to the enormous stele inscribed with linguistic characters completely foreign to her. In her years as an archaeologist she had been in the presence of many monuments, but this was quite extraordinary. It was the single missing link to so many of antiquity's mysteries. Her heart leapt. She had made the right move to come here. In a near trance state, as if a different force were willing her, she walked to the monolith and instinctively raised her hand to touch it.

"Stop!" The monk's clear, loud voice seemed out of character for his gentle nature.

She remained motionless, like a child who had just been admonished by a strict parent.

"I'm sorry," Apostolos said, his voice soft again. "Human hands must never touch the stone. It is sacred." He fixed his gaze on hers.

For the first time, she noticed the monk's emerald-green eyes, which sparkled with the intensity of the gem itself. The words he spoke next rattled her.

"It will help you only if you have faith. If you do not, it will destroy you."

Ten

Gabriel and Hairan squatted shoulder to shoulder in front of the cooking fire as the mud-brown brew simmered in the iron cauldron. The steam rising from the pot carried a medicinal smell to Gabriel's nose, his cue that the potion was done. He dipped a clay spoon into the pot and brought a sample to his chapped lips.

"It is finished, Shaykh," he said in perfect Bedouin patois, which he had mastered after years in the desert.

The chief squinted his raven eyes and nodded his satisfaction. "Very good, Abyan. You are ready."

"I've been studying under you for many years. It's about time, don't you think?" Gabriel put an arm around his mentor and friend, and the two men roared with laughter. Then the chief's young apprentice poured some of the tea into a stone bowl, added a few drops of camel's milk, and walked out of the tent.

It was to be his first test as a novice apothecary. A young girl had developed a nasty case of chickenpox—or birdworm, as the Bedouins called it—with a fever and spots covering ninety percent of her tiny body. She had scratched the spots so much that they had suppurated, making her look like a leper. As a result, the parents had tied the girl's hands with camel-hair rope, which had left her wrists raw and bloody. There was no question the child was suffering.

Gabriel dabbed her open welts with lemon balm, which soothed the itch and pain almost immediately. He bade her drink his special concoction, a tea of rosemary, licorice, and hyssop meant to treat her fever.

He turned to her parents. "When the Evenstar appears in the sky, she will be better. But she must stay in the tent until her sores disappear."

The mother looked puzzled. "But she has chores. She must tend to them."

"Any child with birdworm must remain in isolation. She must particularly avoid the pregnant women of the tribe. If she were to touch one, that woman could lose her baby or even her life."

"How do you know this?"

Gabriel could not speak of scientific proof, for it was a foreign concept to these people. He could only tell stories or conjure images and hope they could somehow relate. "Do you remember two years ago when Mehoud's bride, Mela, died suddenly in her sixth month of pregnancy?"

The young couple nodded in unison.

"Mela's son had birdworm, and he infected her. I saw Mela's body after she died. There were sores inside her mouth. Like these." He opened their daughter's mouth and motioned to them to look inside.

The mother looked alarmed. "Will our girl die?"

Gabriel smiled and tousled the child's hair. "No, my friends. Children are very resilient. But you must do as I say to keep others out of danger."

It didn't take long before the knowledge Gabriel had imparted to the young couple reached all the goums. That night after supper, the tribesmen showed their appreciation for Gabriel's lifesaving revelation with a fire circle in his honor. Telling stories by the fire was one of the most sacred activities to the desert dwellers, reserved for nights of celebration and tribute. Gabriel knew how important this rite was, and he felt humbled to be at the center of it. In the six years he'd spent among the Bedouins, a fire circle had never been dedicated to one man. He felt the simple people's appreciation and respect in the depths of his being and was grateful.

The drummer pounded a soft beat on a square goatskin drum painted with stars and moons to symbolize the night, for playing the storyteller's drum was strictly a nighttime ritual. Anyone who had a story to share was draped with the ceremonial blanket and given eager audience.

A beautiful young woman named Banu shared a story about the scorpion and the elephant. She had told it before, and the children whooped with delight when she started. As she went on about the scorpion king who was outwitted by a cunning baby elephant, Gabriel found his thoughts traveling to another realm.

Mesmerized by Banu's silken black locks and café au lait eyes sparkling by the firelight, he thought of the woman he loved. Calcedony. Speaking her name was like tasting honey. In his battered mind, she was the most splendid creature walking the planet. It had been long years since he'd last seen her, but his memory of her burned like the Bedouin fires: her hair falling around her face like ribbons of black satin; her slender, sharply angled nose; those eyes, the clearest sapphires suspended in almond-shaped pools; her laughter as playful as a child's.

He still remembered the day they'd met, though it seemed several lifetimes had passed since. They were in the isles of Greece one summer. It had been raining, a freak storm from out of nowhere. Quite happily she stood in the warm downpour. While everyone else sought cover under the eaves of the ancient stone houses, she walked along the cobbled path she'd chosen. Gabriel was so taken by the metaphor in that lyrical moment he felt compelled to approach her. There he stood, next to her in the drizzle, his heart singing with the freedom he felt in that fleeting moment. They spent the rest of the summer together, frolicking in the Mediterranean, debating the true meaning of the word *love* in Plato's *Symposium*, drinking wine out of a copper jug, growing into passionate lovers. As autumn's first breaths cooled the air, he asked Calcedony to warm him that winter and every winter of his life. She followed him home, and they built a life that lasted almost seven years, until the fateful day when all their dreams were swallowed by an impenetrable cloud of smoke.

As Banu's story came to an end, Gabriel felt a dull ache in his bones. No matter how he tried to change his life, to tell himself he had found his place in this strange new world, the plain truth was that he lamented the loss of everything he'd held dear. More than anything, he missed Calcedony—her abandon, the way she could cut through the nonsense to find truth, her calm and peaceful spirit even in the face of a thousand sorrows.

And he missed their son. The pain of that loss had a relentless grip on his heart. Many nights he sat awake, tormented by the tiny laughter of the boy in whom he had placed all his faith for the future. Other nights the boy would come to Gabriel in his dreams, as alive as if he had never died in the fire. Those nights he woke to the sound of his own sobbing, cursing the weakness that would not relinquish him from his grief.

"Abyan's turn . . . Abyan's turn," exclaimed Banu, laughing as she draped Gabriel with the ceremonial blanket. Everyone, young and old, cheered wildly. In all those years, the pale stranger had never told a story in the fire circle. Now that his language skills had come along, it was time for his debut. He didn't fight being the center of attention, as he had during his early days with the tribe. He felt less self-conscious now, less like an outsider. He puffed on his pipe, which he'd kept all those years since Da'ud's death and which had become almost an extension of his being. He brushed the tangles of long, wavy hair away from his face so that the children could see his expressions, paramount to the art of storytelling, and began.

"This is a story about the tree of life. It was a lone tree in the middle of the desert, with a trunk the size of a camel's hump and more branches than a palm tree has dates. Its leaves were shiny green and leathery as Hairan's skin." He reveled in the nomads' innocent laughter at his joke. At long last, he shared their humor, which made him feel more connected to them. He waited for the laughter to subside. "This tree bore the most succulent, tastiest fruit known to man. It gave its fruit freely to everyone who passed by, even to the animals and birds, sustaining all life in the desert. It required very little in return. It was nurtured by the sands and the sun and the nutrients in the air and the water from the rains. The scarabs gnawed on its roots, and their saliva became food. The monkeys swinging from its branches fertilized the soil, and their waste became food. The worms slithered on the leaves, and their silk became food. All the creatures worked as one to make sure the tree of life lived on, for it would in turn feed and shelter the others.

"One day, a passing tribe of men came upon the tree and stopped to get their fill of its delicious fruit. As he sat beneath the canopy to avoid the sun, their leader got an idea. Since the tree was so wide and always provided fruit and shade, they would claim it as their own. They could slaughter the animals that frolicked in its branches for food. They could make wine out of its flowers. They could puncture its trunk and let the water run so they would never thirst. Why should they take the long road across the desert, always searching for food and water, when everything they needed was right there? They decided to colonize the tree of life.

"Years passed. The tribe still lived under the shade of the tree, only they had created an entire village. They stopped dwelling in the desert because it was so much easier to take from the tree. Every winter, they would cut more and more of its living branches so they could make fires. They plucked the leaves and used them to make roofs for their houses. In the summer, when the air was hot and the creatures were thirsty, they made gash after gash in the trunk so they could extract every drop of water. Each spring, they would pick all the fruit to sell to passersby, instead of letting them take what they needed as they had always done in the past. That way they amassed chickens and goats and oranges and grain. They were rich and fat and had everything they ever needed, even bird's milk. But one day the sun burned hotter than any other. In all their years dwelling in the desert, the tribesmen had never known such heat. It burned hotter every day, as if the sun were coming down from the sky and scorching them with its rays. The branches had been plucked of their leaves, so the tree could not provide shade. Without shade, the ground grew so hot the water beneath the tree's roots dried up. The tree could no longer make fruit or provide water for the tribe. Its branches became the color of ash. Its trunk withered. Livestock perished. Locusts swept in and ravaged the tribe's grain reserves. The people died of thirst and hunger. And still the heat would not relent. It got so bad the tree of life, dry and barren as it was, caught fire. The tribesmen panicked.

They scattered like ants in a flood, leaving the tree to burn to the ground. They disappeared in the heat waves of a mirage and were never seen again. And the tree and all the creatures it sheltered and sustained were no more."

Without the traditional Western expectation of a happy ending, the Bedouins cheered for Gabriel. He could tell it wasn't the story itself they liked but rather the telling of it. To his delight, he had kept them engaged and, when he'd occasionally flubbed up a word, amused.

They pushed and taunted him in a loving, playful way, and Gabriel reciprocated in a show of appreciation and acceptance. As the frolicking quieted down, he noticed Hairan in the distance, sitting alone and silently observing the spectacle with a smile.

If only the old man knew how much he'd taught his young acolyte.

The night before the tribe reached the camel festival, spirits were high. The goums had been traveling for several fortnights to reach Ubar, where tribes from all corners of the Syro-Arabian Desert gathered once a year to trade their animals and goods. Gabriel had heard that Ubar was a prosperous place, the land of milk and honey, full of fascinating strangers with exotic habits. He knew it was a highlight for the Bedouins, the just reward for the hardships they had to endure the rest of the year. They were so close—only a few kilometers away—that Gabriel could practically smell the myrrh and taste the plump dates reportedly lining the streets. In anticipation, the Bedouins sat around the campfire, drumming and toasting with palm wine.

But Gabriel was not in the mood to celebrate. His intuition had been telling him for some time that forces in the universe were stirring. He'd sat in solitude night after night searching for answers. On this night, a full moon floated like gossamer in a filmy sky. An opportunity for enlightenment and change, the Bedouins always said. The prospect filled Gabriel with hope. He was sitting in waking meditation, studying the sky and stars for omens, when Hairan approached. Gabriel looked at the old man without any hint of surprise, almost as if he'd been expecting him.

"Come with me, Abyan. It is time."

Without the desire to know what it was time for, Gabriel followed his teacher to the eastern edge of camp, noting that the choice of location was not random. In the Bedouin tradition, the east was the source of all life and everything sacred. It was also where leaders looked for direction and wise men sought guidance.

Hairan stopped on a sand dune and invited Gabriel to sit opposite him. The shaykh pulled out of his sack a gourd and a mortar. In silence, he removed the top of the gourd and poured a dark liquid onto the sand.

Even by the full moonlight, Gabriel could not recognize the substance, but he was all too familiar with its strong smell. Blood. He hypothesized that it was from an antelope the men had killed for food a few days back, for the Bedouins did not make blood sacrifices. In fact, in all the years he had traveled with the tribe, he had never seen blood used—not in daily life, not in ceremony. His logic told him he should be uneasy, but his heart was surprisingly calm. He trusted these people, trusted Hairan. Whatever was about to happen, he accepted as part of the order.

Hairan kneaded the blood into the sand, making a thick paste. Chanting softly in a tongue Gabriel could not comprehend, the old man smeared the paste over Gabriel's eyes, then his own. With all thoughts of the West tucked in some inaccessible corner of his mind, Gabriel surrendered to the rite. The night wasn't cold, but his skin was like goose flesh and he trembled. He could feel his forehead, now beset with the lines of hardship and advancing age, tighten as he tried to concentrate. The sweet, sharp smell of burning resin crystals filled the air. The smoke was thick, heavy. Gabriel let it fill his nose, his lungs. He felt weightless. The chill on his skin was replaced with a flush that warmed his face and weighed down his eyes. He began to drift, though not quite to sleep. It was a state he had never entered before. His mind's eye was a gray screen, a hollow womb.

Then, suddenly, faces. Covered with black cloth, all but the eyes. Marching somberly, without purpose, without direction. Strangers, one after another, appearing and vanishing like souls departing. Except for one woman, who stood motionless before him. A gust of wind ripped the veil from her face. She was pale, ghostlike. She lifted her eyes, and he came face-to-face with those sapphires he knew so well. The woman wore Calcedony's face but had the detached demeanor of a wraith. She lifted a cloaked arm, pointing toward something.

A city on a mountain. A kingdom in the clouds. He walked toward it, knowing not where his feet took him. Treacherous steps led him up a vertical slope, and he clawed his way to the top. There he came to a stone gate, inscribed in the Bedouin dialect with these words: "Men's fate is written in stone, but they have gouged out their eyes and cannot see."

Everything went white.

Gabriel awoke in the fetal position, his skin burning and covered with sweat.

Hairan sat in lotus posture opposite him, his manner as calm as the sea on a summer day.

Gabriel wiped the sweat and blood-mud from his

face, trying to make sense of what he had just experienced.

"You must go, my friend." Hairan's voice was like a velvet blanket, gentler and more peaceful than Gabriel had ever heard it.

"Go . . . where?" Gabriel began to fear he had done or said something in his trance state that had offended Hairan and the tribe.

"Go . . . to the city in the mountains."

Gabriel looked at him wild-eyed. He could not utter a word. How did he know?

Hairan continued. "She calls you to the great kingdom. It is what you must do. What you carry inside, you must take there. And there you shall leave it."

A violent sob left Gabriel's throat. His face was twisted with the kind of pain no potion could heal. Hairan's words hadn't even registered on his consciousness. His thoughts were populated with images of his one true love.

"Is she there? Tell me, for the love of everything you hold dear. Where is she?"

"No," Hairan whispered. "She is not there. She dwells in a different world, which you will never enter."

The chief's words cut to Gabriel's core. He knew in his deepest heart it was true: he would never see Calcedony again. He dropped his head to his knees and sobbed.

Hairan was as unyielding as a hunk of stone. "Do

not despair, Abyan. Your quest is bigger than her, bigger than you. You have been chosen to take the rare journey. Now is not the time for tears; it is the time for courage." He repeated: "What you carry inside, you must take to the great kingdom. And there you shall leave it."

Drained, Gabriel composed himself and let the weight of Hairan's statement settle over him. "I don't want to leave the tribe. My place is here now."

"There is nothing left for you here. You must go. You must walk through the stone gate."

"How do you know about the city in the mountains, the stone gate?"

"I have seen what you have seen. That is how I know this is your fate."

The two men exchanged a lingering glance. There were no more secrets. Gabriel knew what he had to do. At last, he was at peace.

That night on the top of the dune, Gabriel slept alone under the stars.

By daybreak, he was gone.

Eleven

Translating the inscriptions using the Sheba Stone was a far more complicated business than Sarah had imagined. The obelisk-shaped monolith, which stood ten feet tall and six feet wide, was inscribed from top to bottom with writings that apparently praised the life and rule of the Queen of Sheba. Six different dialects from the region were used in the inscriptions, but they weren't organized according to any method familiar to Sarah. A single passage might contain as many as four dialects, perhaps in an effort to encrypt the texts or to have parts of the passage read by certain tribes and not others. Whatever the motivation, the system was infuriating to Sarah, who, though more than two weeks into the process, was getting nowhere.

Day and night she sat next to the Sheba Stone, staring, bewildered, at the text and trying to ascertain some sort of pattern. She was far from a breakthrough and questioned what she was even doing there. For all her talent for language, she felt out of her league.

She stared at the stone blankly, debating whether to leave everything with the church and go back to London, maybe try to salvage what was left of her career. And if she couldn't do that, she could always go to America, where blemishes on one's reputation were far more easily forgiven.

As attractive as it sounded to be rid of this mess and start over, however, she couldn't do it. The same force that had propelled her from the moment she'd found the tomb was still at work, pushing her to take the next step despite her trepidation.

She needed Apostolos' help, but he was as elusive as a leopard in daylight. Whether he was purposely avoiding her or was consumed by his own work, she did not know. But she could not do this without him, so finally she decided to seek him out.

One morning she found him in the courtyard, filling the birdbaths with water and sprinkling crumbs from bread he had tucked into his robes. On a stone bench he sat so placidly Sarah could not bring herself to invade his peace. Instead, she watched him from the opposite corner of the courtyard. Under his fringed umbrella, he wrote into a notebook, periodically looking up as if for inspiration.

She waited a long while before finally approaching.

"Good day. I see you like to write."

Flustered by her sudden presence, he hurriedly closed his notebook and slipped it into the folds of his garment. "It is nothing."

She sat next to him. "I have been meaning to seek your counsel. You are the only one who holds the knowledge I need."

He looked into the sun, squinting. "Others have sought this knowledge in the past. They were not to be trusted."

"I am not them."

"The word of the tenth saint is sacred. It is not to fall into the wrong hands."

She spoke softly and slowly. "I know how important he is to your faith. I respect that. But what if his message is important to all of mankind? Should the knowledge remain with few when it can help many?"

Apostolos fell silent. He looked down and fidgeted with the rosary beads wrapped around his bony wrist. Sarah recognized his unwillingness to take the conversation any further and decided to let him be. She could not push him, for she needed him to be an ally. She would have to find another way to gain his trust.

The rest of the day she scribbled thoughts in her notebook, but her mind was clouded. She hadn't slept well in days, working from early morning until she could no longer stay awake. Exhausted, she rested her head on the table and fell asleep before suppertime.

She awoke before dawn the next morning, still in the same position but covered with a blanket. A bowl of millet rested on top of her papers. She looked for her notes, certain they had been under her hand when she'd fallen asleep. She found only a paper with two words written in English: Mother Sea.

The monk had left her a clue, and though it made no sense, she saw it as a good sign. He was trying to communicate with her, but clearly it had to be on his terms.

In the days that followed, Sarah wasted no more time. She set aside her Western notions of reasoning and negotiating and relied on her instincts instead. Apostolos' distrust of people was painfully obvious. If it was solitude he needed in order to express himself, then she would give it to him. Instead of confronting him in person, she wrote him letters.

Most humble and wise monk,

Today I took a walk outside. The land seems parched, in need of rain. The red clay is brittle underfoot and the birds' bath is dry but for a few drops. Still, a swallow persists, determined to escape the heat.

I feel like that swallow sometimes. Looking for drops in a barren place. Waiting for the deluge.

I bid you good day.
Sarah

At first the letters were part of the strategy. If she showed vulnerability, perhaps he would be more likely to help. But as he replied, in perfectly eloquent English, Sarah found herself taken by the way he looked at the world.

The swallow is a restless bird. He is forever hunting for drops but never waits for the rain. He goes in search of it. His salvation is never at hand, tortured soul. It is always somewhere else, thousands of miles away, where the rooftops look different and day is night. Some say it is the fulfillment, others the curse, of his destiny.

And yet the flight of the swallow is a most wondrous thing. To look upon his black wings, lustrous as Oriental silk, in perfect harmony with the wind, is to know grace.

His words were like poetry—lyrical, raw, human, yet devoid of self. The letter didn't contain a signature, not even so much as a name. It was merely an exchange of observations and ideas, none of which he needed to possess or claim as his own. Sarah was grateful for that window into the soul of the monk with emerald eyes, and for the first time she saw him as an individual rather than a pawn in this complicated game she was playing. She wasn't accustomed to taking interest in the hearts of people. Her work and her pedigree didn't make such allowances. There never was time for it. Maybe it was Apostolos' gentle presence, maybe the safety of the stone womb that cradled her, or maybe the sweet solitude she hadn't known since childhood, but she felt expanded, at peace. Though a sea of questions remained, her horizon was in focus. It was only a matter of navigating the waters.

Sitting on her cot in the cold stone chamber, Sarah reread the monk's letter. How was it possible he had such insight without ever seeing the world outside of Lalibela? Surely wisdom didn't come from books and introspection alone. She resisted the urge to define the man and allowed herself the luxury of forsaking rationale and letting things flow with the cosmic current. The feeling was unfamiliar and not altogether comfortable, but she forced herself to sit with it. By the waning light of her oil lamp, she wrote the next dispatch.

Most gentle monk,

I admire the swallow for the same reason I envy it: It is free. It knows no country. It carries its home in its breast. It comes and goes with the scent of the warm breeze. It is not the prisoner of expectations or convention or duty. How sweet it must be to know that freedom.

Humbly,
Sarah

Apostolos' reply, delivered the next day, stunned Sarah.

Freedom cannot be labeled nor won nor envied. Only when one doesn't realize what freedom is, is one truly free. The gift of the swallow is its ignorance. Men do not possess such a gift. They are indeed prisoners, but they have the ability to make their shackle their virtue.

But the more dazzling the shackle, the harder it is to escape. Only a pure heart can break free. Some search forever for the door to the golden cage that holds them captive without ever realizing that there is no door. But you have awakened to this. You now have only to step outside.

In spite of their short acquaintance and limited exchange, the monk had seen through to her core. Somehow he knew her quest was not for gain or glory but was a personal struggle to step out of the shadows of a gilded but empty world and embrace her own version of truth. She felt a tinge of shame for being so easy to read, an unacceptable trait for women of her class. The unspoken rule was to leave people guessing, to keep emotions in check and desires buried in the deep cavern of the heart. And yet being seen was a liberation of sorts: there was no more need for hiding.

She held the letter to her forehead, at once puzzled

by and grateful for it. Though she had told herself to trust no one, she had no qualms about this man. In her eyes, he was goodness personified.

That night, as she was mulling her reply, another note was slipped under her door. It seemed that just as the monk had won her faith, she had won his.

The man whose writings you seek to interpret was not unlike you. His dying words were his turn at redemption from a heart made dark by the vices of men.

Apostolos knew a lot more than he let on. She needed to confront him to confirm her suspicions. It was late, and the other inhabitants of the monastery were surely asleep, but she could not let this go until morning.

She grabbed a flashlight, threw on her Barbour coat, and started toward the reading room on the other side of the monastery, where Apostolos typically lingered until the late hours. If she hurried, maybe she could catch him before he locked himself in for the night.

The halls were frigid and eerily quiet. Sarah's heart pounded with anticipation, warming her so that she hardly noticed the cold. She hurried through the narrow passageways and mentally constructed the upcoming conversation with the monk. She feared the shy man would shut down and avoid her questions, so she had to approach him with the right words and tone. She could not afford any mistakes.

The twisting corridor looked even more unfamiliar by the feeble lamplight. Damn the interminable darkness. She wished her eyes were more accustomed to the shadows, like the monks' were. They could find their way around the halls without so much as a candle flame. She stumbled on a hard surface and, walking too fast to correct her gait, fell to her hands and knees. The ground was wet, apparently from the humid night air.

She fumbled around for her flashlight. The impact must have shut it off or, worse, broken it. She located it and tried to switch it on, to no avail. She reached for the penlight in her jacket pocket and cast a wan light on her surroundings.

In the distance, she spotted what looked like the great wooden door to the labyrinth.

Her left hand stung from the fall. Turning the light on it to check the extent of the damage, she gasped. The wetness she'd felt when she'd fallen was not humidity at all. It was blood. "Oh, dear God."

She shone the tiny light about her, hands shaking. A pool of blood lay not five feet from where she'd fallen, and the stone floor was streaked with red as far as the entrance to another corridor.

Sarah tried to convince herself there was an innocuous explanation—a wolf, say, had mauled a dog and dragged it into a dark corner to feast on its flesh. But she feared the worst.

Could someone know she was there? Could they know about the stone?

Her lips trembled as she inched toward the wall, crouching in a corner. She searched her pockets for anything to use as a weapon but found nothing. Her heart pounded violently. She drew a few deep breaths and looked for the easiest escape route.

To her right was the labyrinth. Not an option. She'd be a sitting duck in that impossible maze. To her left was the corridor leading to the courtyard. With a bit of luck, she could make her way out and to the jeep.

She crawled in that direction. The place was silent. For a moment, she found herself believing that maybe it was just animals, that she was overreacting.

Then she heard footsteps. The sound was amplified and distorted as it bounced off the stone. She couldn't tell which direction they were coming from, but she was sure they were getting closer.

Before anyone came near enough to see her, she bolted across the dark corridor, focusing on a distant moonbeam shining through a tiny opening in the stone. The outside was not so far away—a couple hundred feet at most. She was running at full stride now, glancing behind periodically to make sure she was not followed. She was getting closer—but not close enough.

Someone jumped out of the shadows in an impact so violent it sent her tumbling. A man whose face she could not see straddled her and twisted her arms as she struggled like a frenzied animal to free herself from his grip.

"Tell me where it is." He spoke in English with a heavy Ethiopian accent. "This is not a game you are qualified to play. Hand the translation over, or you will suffer the same fate as that idiot monk."

Had she landed in a pool of Apostolos' blood? Anger welled, granting her strength she had never known.

"Get off me, you animal," she yelled as she wriggled her trapped knee loose and drove it into his groin. Her attacker fell, groaning, and she seized the opportunity to get away. She ran as fast as she could in the direction of the light, her heart thumping wildly, sweat falling into her eyes.

When she looked behind her, she could see the man's shadow moving in her direction. At the end of the passageway, she turned left, recalling the nearby door leading to the courtyard.

The Ethiopian's footsteps came faster, louder.

She finally located the door, lunged toward it, and twisted the heavy iron handle.

It was locked.

“Damn it!” Hyperventilating, she futilely searched for the keys or another way out.

The footsteps grew even louder.

She stood motionless, almost catatonic, until a hand sealed her mouth.

“Don’t say a word,” a man’s voice whispered. “You must follow me. This is our only hope.”

Sarah nodded.

The man released his grip.

She turned to see the outline of a familiar face in the faint moonlight. “Thank heavens you’re alive.” She wanted to throw her arms around Apostolos, but there was no time. They had seconds to make their escape.

As ever, the monk wasted no words. With a steady hand, he slipped the key into the lock and pushed open the old wooden door. They spilled out into the darkness.

Sarah had never been so glad to breathe the Ethiopian air.

Her joy lasted no more than a few seconds. By the time they had made it to the other end of the courtyard, they were surrounded.

Sarah counted six, maybe seven, men standing in various parts of the courtyard. At least one was armed. A long blade gleamed in the ghostlight. Apostolos was so calm she wondered if he had any notion of the danger facing them.

“There’s an opening on the north side,” she whispered

without taking her eyes off the dark figures. "If we run like mad, we can make it out of here."

"It won't work. You must trust me." He grabbed Sarah's arm and pulled her inside the monastery.

Two of the men launched after them.

"Run," Apostolos cried.

She had no time to question where he was leading her. To her horror, it quickly became evident they were running toward the labyrinth. "Are you mad?" she protested. "We'll never make it out alive."

Apostolos ignored her pleas and ran even faster, bare feet slapping the stone floor.

She had no choice but to follow. With dread filling her, she crossed into the maze of dark stone passages. The weak flames of torches hanging on the walls flickered as they hurried past, casting enough light to illuminate a few feet ahead but not enough to reveal what was around the bend.

Sarah marveled at the robed acolyte's agility maneuvering through the darkened maze. Father Giorgis had told her Apostolos had defected here from another church twenty-odd years ago as a teenage novice. He hadn't left these chambers since, not even for a day. The church had become his sanctuary, and he knew and loved every corner. Tonight Sarah was thankful for it.

She heard the labored breathing and lumbering

footsteps of their pursuers echo through the halls. Glancing back, she saw moving shadows on the far end of the corridor exaggerated by the dim torchlight. "They're on us."

Apostolos stopped suddenly. He said nothing, but there was an undeniable urgency in his gaze. He groped around the wall as if he was looking for something. The approaching men were now in full view and would be upon them within seconds. He pushed on the stones, and a row of iron bars descended from the ceiling just ahead of the men. A trap. The old stone maze obviously was not only a thinking man's game but also a fortress of defense.

Apostolos grabbed Sarah's arm again. She followed him through this turn and that, trusting he was leading them out of this nightmare.

If only it were so easy. One of the men had slid under the descending bars and was still after them, moving through the maze as if he knew its secrets.

The weight of her pursuer toppled her, and the world went dark. She struggled but could not shake her limbs loose from his hold. Desperate, she bit his forearm.

He howled and struck her face.

Her mind reeled from the blow, her attempts at self-defense weakening.

Apostolos lay sprawled on the floor. Was he even

alive? In the tumult of the confrontation, she hadn't fully realized what had happened. She knew only that she would have to summon all her wits to avoid facing the same fate.

The man yanked forcefully at the pouch around her neck containing the photos and her notes. The rope dug into her neck but did not break. With a foul grimace revealing a mouthful of rotting grey teeth, her attacker laughed and pulled out a knife.

Sarah raised her hand in defense, her awkward maneuver landing her palm squarely on the blade.

Just then she saw Apostolos rise. Though his white robes were red with his own blood, he was lucid. He thrust the full force of his body on the man. As the two struggled, the intruder overpowered the wounded monk and pinned him to the wall.

"Run," Apostolos yelled.

Panic and loyalty rooted her where she stood. She couldn't leave Apostolos to an uncertain fate. She looked around desperately for something she could use to give him the advantage.

The torch. She took it out of its iron hanger and, with all her power, swung.

At the moment of impact, the man's head bobbed as if it were not attached to his neck. Sarah knew he would be rendered unconscious but did not anticipate his hair catching on fire. That was a bonus.

She ran to the monk, who had once more saved her life. He clutched his abdomen, blood trickling through his fingers.

"You're hurt."

"It is not deep. Never mind it. He is not dead."

Indeed, the man was starting to stir, regaining consciousness thanks to the flames engulfing his head. He let out a horrific scream and pawed haphazardly at his scorched hair.

The smell of singed flesh sent bile to her throat. "We should have finished him off."

"No." Apostolos' voice was strained. "It is not for us to judge. Come. We don't have much time."

He was stoic, but Sarah could see he was in real pain. His movements were slow, his breathing labored as he tried to rush toward the trap door built into the stone floor centuries ago so the monks could escape persecution from heathen tribes. It was camouflaged well, but Apostolos was not taking any chances. When they lowered themselves into the dark realm of the passageway, he latched it from the inside. His brothers from generations past had thought of everything; they'd had to, for cleverness was their only defense.

He stopped to rest. Blood had saturated the entire front of his robes, and he was pale and weak.

Sarah knew he was understating his injury. "You need help," she said, panic in her voice. "Let me look at this." She opened his robes. A gash stretched diagonally from his navel to his side, blood trickling slowly but persistently. "It could be worse. But if we don't get you stitched up, you could bleed to death. Now tell me the way out of here, and I will carry you."

It was the first time she had seen the monk smile. His expression was so peaceful, so kind she was certain she was in the presence of something far greater than herself. She took his hand and shuddered. It was so cold.

"Allow me to rest a moment," he whispered, "and then we will go." He closed his eyes, and she held his body close to warm him. His chest rose and fell with his shallow breaths.

She had to get him out alive.

He broke the silence with a gasp, fighting to catch his breath.

Sarah's heart sank.

"That's it. We're getting out of here." Her cut palm throbbed as she lifted him to his feet. He was remarkably light, this waif of a man. She put his arm over her shoulder and pressed forward.

"There's only one way out. It leads to the mountain-side, but there is nothing to light our path."

"I'll take the chance."

The path was pitch black, and Sarah had to feel her way around. The monk grew heavier. Though he made a valiant attempt to carry his own weight, he lost his strength and crumpled at Sarah's side.

"Please," she said with a hint of despair in her voice. "Please fight. I need you to fight."

Apostolos reached inside his shredded robes and pulled out a long chain from which hung a key. "This is what you need. This unlocks the secret to the prophecies."

The comment took her by surprise. "The what?"

"The prophecies of Gabriel. The one they call the tenth saint."

"The inscriptions . . . are prophecies?"

"They foretell the final doom that will befall the earth." His voice was weak. "We swore to keep them secret."

Sarah was bewildered by the revelation. "How do you know this? Who's we?"

"Apocryphon," he whispered.

Sarah knew the Greek word. It meant "that which is hidden," though religious scholars interpreted it more as "secret teachings." It was the secret society Matakala had spoken of when they'd first met. Apostolos was obviously a member. She did not push him to explain but caressed his face. It was like touching ice. Life was leaving him. Finally he spoke, his voice barely audible. "Beneath the pulpit of the monastery lies a library of ancient documents . . ."

"What does this key unlock?"

"A vault . . . the prophecies . . . the saint's cross."

"Who else knows about this?" She was afraid of the answer.

"You met him." He touched her wounded hand. "He did this to you."

"The man who attacked us, who stabbed you, was a monk?"

"May God forgive him . . ." Apostolos' skin was gray. His emerald eyes, which had always sparkled with wisdom and light, were now dull. "You must . . . take the relics to Dabra Damo. They will be safe there. Please . . ." His skeletal fingers squeezed her hand as he exhaled his last breath.

Sarah bent over him, her forehead touching his. "I promise."

With a sorrow she'd never known, she wept. It was as if all hope for goodness in the world was lost. She sat with Apostolos, the man who had saved her in so many ways, until her tears dried up.

She slipped the chain off his neck.

She would make good on her promise.

Twelve

By the time Sarah worked her way out of the subterranean tunnel, the sun had already flooded the mountainside with morning light. It was uncharacteristically warm and tomb-quiet, save for the rhythmic twittering of crickets. In spite of the despair seeping into the corners of her being, she summoned her resolve for the trek across the boulders.

She looked down at her throbbing wound. The surrounding skin was red, swollen, and hot, and the gash was weeping fluid. She needed antibiotics.

She climbed, negotiating the rocky ground as swiftly as the injury allowed.

The rocks gave way to a thicket of brittle brush that crackled under her feet. She ascended the mountainside through the waist-high grasses, intentionally rustling the growth to scare off snakes potentially in her path.

The sight of the church in the distance invigorated her. A chill rippled through her as she considered the consequences of the previous night's events. She wondered about Father Giorgis and the other monks, and her heart sank at the possibility that they had not escaped.

As she approached Yemrehana Krestos, it became evident that the authorities had already been notified. Two police jeeps, an ambulance, and a few unmarked cars lined the entrance to the church, their emergency lights throwing a surreal blue hue onto the stones. Scores of villagers gathered, jostling each other for position at the front of the crowd for the best view.

Sarah hoped the presence of emergency units meant someone inside the church was alive and had been able to call for help. She slumped under a tree and monitored the activity as paramedics brought out bodies wrapped in white sheets, one after another, on stretchers, and lined them on the ground. There must have been half a dozen.

Sarah looked to the sky, resisting the urge to scream. She couldn't bear the thought that so many of these gentle, devout men had lost their lives simply because they had offered her asylum.

Her spirits were lifted when she saw a couple of monks being wheeled out on gurneys. They were injured but alive. One of them was apparently unconscious, but the other was waving his arms toward the onlookers, seemingly demanding they go away. His robes were those of the high priest.

The paramedics wheeled him and the other monk into the ambulance, and the vehicle, with lights flashing and a terrible siren wailing, ambled down the dirt path toward the only hospital in Lalibela.

Two survivors.

Sarah clenched her teeth.

But that wasn't the full extent of it. One of the cops was going through a pile of things scattered on the ground. She recognized them immediately as her own belongings: her backpack, emptied to reveal her books, notebooks, jeep key, and a few old clothes.

She had everything of significance—all the photos, translation notes, the correspondence with Apostolos, and the monk's key—in the pouch around her neck. But one thing was missing.

Her passport.

No sooner did she realize she had left it in her backpack than she saw the policeman leafing through it and waving his colleagues over.

"Bloody brilliant," she whispered. So much for getting out of the country.

But her problem was greater than that. The presence of her personal effects would implicate her. Armed with new ammunition since the death of Rada Kabede, the Ethiopian police surely would begin searching for her. At a minimum, her connection to the massacre would hit the local news, which would likely be picked up by the English and possibly international press, imperiling the expedition and throwing her reputation deeper into the gutter.

She had to get to the vault quickly and extract the documents. But the church, now a crime scene, surely would be guarded. She would have to find a way to enter undetected.

Only one person could tell her how.

She remained hidden until well after sundown before making her move. Under cover of night, she had made her way across the backcountry to the hospital. The trek on foot had taken hours, but so much the better. By the time she arrived, it was so late the hospital's corridors were practically empty.

She walked to the unmanned front desk and located the admissions chart. Giorgis' name was preceded by The Holy, the honorific for a man of the cloth, and was followed by the number two hundred twelve. Sarah slipped into the stairwell and up to the second floor.

The abbot lay peacefully sleeping on the rudimentary hospital cot, his dark profile illuminated by the streetlamps outside his window. His head was bandaged almost entirely, and the skin around his left eye was horribly cut, bruised, and swollen. He looked like a boxer who had lost the prize fight.

She sat next to the bed and watched him sleep. How sorry she felt for what had befallen him and his monastery. Nothing she could say or do would ever make up for the calamity she had caused.

Giorgis awoke and looked at Sarah as if he had been expecting her. "You are alive. It is a miracle."

"Father . . . I am so sorry."

"Do not be. You had no evil intent. You were doing a service to the church, to our faith. We are all victims here."

"But this would not have happened had I—"

"No. Do not blame yourself." He hesitated. "Did you see Apostolos?"

"I was the last to see him. He died in my arms." She choked back tears.

Giorgis' eyes clouded. "My good acolyte. At least he won't suffer knowing the intruders destroyed his beloved stone."

Sarah was shocked. "The Sheba Stone was destroyed?"

"Yes. They beat me and left me for dead before taking my keys and entering the sacred chamber. I heard gunfire . . . endless gunfire." A pained expression crossed his face, but he composed himself and continued. "After they had all gone, I used whatever strength was left in me to crawl to the chamber. The door was off its hinges. Inside, the stone was riddled with bullets. The texts were incomprehensible." He looked out the window and sighed. "Such vengeful men."

"What do they want?"

"They know of the inscriptions. They do not want them translated. I do not know the reasons. What does it matter? All is lost now."

"Maybe not all." She looked around the room, then at the door behind her. "Father, I need to know something. How do I enter the library?"

Giorgis looked surprised. "Did Apostolos tell you of it?"

"It was his dying wish that I take something of his, something he kept in a vault."

"Did he give you a key?"

Sarah reached inside her pouch and produced the ancient iron key. "Please. We have no time. They will strike again. They know about the vault. If I don't get to it, they will."

Giorgis nodded. He outlined in detail the route leading to the entrance of the library—a secret that, till this moment, was known by none except the highest ranking officials of the church.

Sarah squeezed his hand and swore she would repay him for the kindness he had shown her.

On her way past the nurses' station, she grabbed

some bandages, iodine, and antibiotics and stuffed them into her coat pockets. So far, so good. She hoped her luck would hold.

The light of dawn found Sarah in an alleyway hidden behind a row of garbage bins. She had crouched there to get a few winks of sleep, which she desperately needed after the ordeal of the last forty-eight hours. She awoke shivering and looked at her watch: six. The day's newspapers would be out by now. She tucked her blonde mane into the hood of her coat and pulled the drawstrings to make a tight seal around her face. She could not afford to be recognized. She walked toward the main street to get a glimpse at the news before the locals started stirring.

Outside the newsagent's kiosk the Ethiopian papers were secured by clothespins on stretches of rope. The *Ethiopian Herald* displayed a huge front-page headline: "Carnage in Lalibela." And beneath it: "Eight dead; English archaeologist missing." Under other circumstances, she might have willingly appeared before the police and cooperated with their investigation. But not now, not here. There was no time, and corruption was rampant. No one could be taken at face value, least of all the officials.

She had to do this alone. The possibility at once

unnerved and excited her. She found a piece of scrap paper in her pouch and sketched a diagram based on her conversation with Father Giorgis. It was a long trek through rough territory to the back entrance of the cave housing the library. She had to move quickly to get there before nightfall.

On the first leg of her journey, she followed a footpath above the main road. The dry brush was high enough to camouflage her, so she walked swiftly and decisively. She had walked miles when the mid-day sun beat down, filling her with a thirst so cruel it was impossible to move on.

Looking down toward the road, she spotted an anemic stream. She'd be exposed, but she was desperate. *Just for a minute*, she told herself and made her way down.

The cold mountain water felt like nectar to her dry mouth, and she drank greedily.

The sound of a car engine startled her. A jeep approached.

She ducked into the brush, hoping her khaki coat would blend with the surroundings, but it was too late. The vehicle stopped, the door opened, and the blood in her veins turned to ice.

She ran as fast as she could in the opposite direction, hoping to get enough of a lead to find another hiding place, but the dry undergrowth cracked with her every step. Behind her, a man shouted, but she could not distinguish his words.

Sarah fell into a thicket of trees and army crawled to a place with plenty of ground cover to camouflage her. If she kept perfectly still and quiet, she might just lose him. She cupped her nose and mouth in both hands, trying to muffle her rapid breaths.

Closing her eyes, she thought about Apostolos, about the tenth saint, about the task before her, and concentrated on the promise she'd made. It was the closest she'd come to prayer since childhood, before she'd rejected religion.

The sound of footsteps broke her meditation. All she could do now was sit still and hope he couldn't see her. If she ran, it would all be over. There was quiet for a few moments, and she let herself believe she had eluded him.

A pair of hands clasped her shoulders, yanking her to her feet, and turning her around.

"Sarah Weston," the man said in that familiar drawl. "I knew it was you."

Sarah never thought she'd be so happy to see Daniel. She fell into his arms. "What are you doing here? I thought you were long gone."

"I've been in Addis, waiting for my visa to be renewed so I could head back to Riyadh. Damn bureaucrats take their sweet time. Anyway, I saw this little article in the *Herald* this morning and figured you needed me." He winked and grinned.

Her body stiffened. "Well, you're wrong. I don't

need you. I'm perfectly fine. You are free to go."

"Not on your life. Not this time."

His words pleased her more than she expected, and she felt a pang of regret. She exhaled and softened her stance. "Look, Danny, I don't blame you for the things you said, for walking out. Anyone sane would have done the same. I mean, look at how badly this has turned out. I'm a fugitive, for heaven's sake."

"Yes, I know. And not a very good one. It's a good thing I spotted you before the cops did." He gestured toward the jeep. "Care for a ride?"

She let out a strained laugh. "As a matter of fact, I would."

"Where are we going anyway?"

"I'll explain on the way. Just—"

"I know. Trust you."

The back entrance to the library was well hidden from the eyes of the world. The abbot had told Sarah it was on the opposite side of the mountain from the entrance to Yemrehana Krestos and that she would have to travel through a tunnel to reach it. What he'd neglected to tell her was how difficult it would be to get there. The slopes looked steep and the terrain impassable, even for two scientists used to conducting their work in such no-man's lands.

At the last outpost of civilization before the

mountains became too inhospitable to inhabit, there was a village of eight mud rondavels with thatched roofs. The gravel road gave way to a dirt path that led to a hillside dotted with meager legume crops.

"Park here," Sarah said. "We'll continue on foot."

Daniel threw a compass, flashlights, some tools, rope, a tape recorder, and a camera into his pack and strapped a water flask across his chest. He checked that his Taurus .38 was loaded and tucked it into his pants.

Sarah had no idea he carried a gun, but a bit of insurance didn't hurt.

The hiking was easy at first. They walked along established paths through terraces where farmers grew chickpeas, a staple of Ethiopian agriculture. The plantings showed signs of stress, indicating impending drought and all the ills that came with it.

The terraces went only a quarter of the way up the mountain. The rest of the journey was far more treacherous. Daniel and Sarah negotiated steep slopes for hours to get to the plateau Giorgis had described. The terrain was a combination of impenetrable brush and dislodging rocks. The thicket was the other enemy. The vegetation was so dense they had to carve a path by ripping dried bushes from their roots and tossing them aside. The process slowed them down considerably, but they persisted, stopping only occasionally to hydrate.

By the time they emerged on the plateau, it was

dusk. The ground was black and gravelly, a combination of granite and volcanic rock, and the vegetation was much more sparse at this elevation. Above them rose raw cliffs, a climber's dream. The exposed rock, stacked in eternal layers, had been torn asunder by the violent earth of prehistory. To the north lay the curious landscape of Lalibela—an unlikely combination of rock-hewn churches, mud huts, and nondescript concrete buildings. The jagged silhouette of the Simien Mountains, glowing lavender in the wolf-light, crowded the horizon.

Sarah caught her breath and looked around the daunting rockscape. "According to the abbot, this is the place. Somewhere around here there's an entrance."

"I imagine the monks haven't made it too easy. If they went to all the trouble to make a secret entrance, it's probably pretty damn well disguised." Daniel studied the sky. It was like an abstract painting, with strokes of alternating lavender and orange and random flecks of crimson and lion-gold. "We have about a half hour before we can't see a thing."

"We'd better get to work then. Father Giorgis said to walk northeast from here and look for a rock shaped like a camel's head. From there, we'll need to descend the cliff until we come to a stream. We should then follow that stream's course for about half a mile, until we see a ledge overhead."

Daniel consulted his compass and nodded toward

their destination. "Northeast."

It was almost nightfall when they spotted the rock. The cliff beneath them looked too steep for a walk down, especially in the encroaching dark. Daniel handed Sarah a headlamp and put on his own. He produced a handful of carabiners and anchors, two harnesses, and a length of fixed rope.

"You travel with this stuff?" She picked up one of the harnesses.

"Always." He grinned, obviously satisfied with himself for being so well prepared. "Now let's get you strapped."

About midway down the rock face, Sarah saw the stream the abbot had described. Illuminated by the waxing moon, it was a vein of liquid silver flowing through an ebony womb. The haunting beauty of the landscape immobilized her, and she hung there, a daughter of this wild land.

Though this was not a difficult descent compared to others she had negotiated, she rappelled slowly, mentally cataloguing the darkening landscape. Considering how much had happened in the past weeks, she was cautiously upbeat, hopeful they would find this mysterious library.

When they reached the bottom of the canyon, they found themselves inside a fortress of cliffs. The face they had just descended looked like flat land compared to the sinister pitch of some of the others. Though the terrain was forbidding, especially under the dark cloak of night, Sarah felt safe and strong. She admitted to herself she appreciated Daniel's company. He was coolheaded and wise to the quirks of the backcountry, a friend in an unfriendly place.

The walk along the stream was the easiest part of the journey. Thanks to a schism in the rock, their path was illuminated by a shaft of moonlight.

For almost two hours they walked, until the ledge appeared. A thin shelf jutting from the sheer cliff face, it was barely big enough for one person to stand on.

Sarah knew it was the right place. She recalled Father Giorgis' description of a pile of rocks stacked like bricks: the entrance to the tunnel leading to the library.

She turned to Daniel. "We'll have to go up one at a time. I'll go first." She took a deep breath and placed her unbandaged hand into one of the holds, then kicked her toe into a crack and pulled herself up.

The climb wasn't too bad, but she took it slower than she normally would have, the faint light and her injury putting her at a disadvantage. When she reached the shelf, about thirty feet above ground level, she had only one option: to grab the ledge and pull herself up.

Small pieces of rock crumbled down the precipice as she strained to hoist herself up to chest level. She gritted her teeth and pressed on, anchoring herself by holding on to the hairline cracks between the rocks. All that remained was to hurl her lower half up to the narrow lip. That was the easy part. Her legs were so long and flexible she was able to lift one knee, then the other, until she had solid purchase.

Standing on that precarious platform was far scarier than anything they had encountered earlier in the trek. One misstep on the narrow ledge would send her tumbling down the rock face. She stood still for a while, summoning all her confidence. Her thoughts turned to Apostolos and his last words.

"This is for you, my dear friend," she said softly and carefully removed one of the stones.

Whoever had devised this system was a genius. The stones had been hewn to interlock perfectly yet still looked natural. Sarah could not help but think the people who had built this had also sealed the tenth saint's tomb; the technique was so similar. With slow, deliberate movements, she removed a handful of the puzzle pieces until she could go no farther. She tried every stone within her reach, but none would budge.

"They won't move," she shouted down to Daniel. "I'm stuck."

"There's probably a combination," Daniel offered. "I've seen this kind of thing before—in funerary chambers in Egypt."

"The abbot said nothing about a combination,"

Sarah said to herself as she felt around for a clue. She tried to pick out unusual shapes in the rock or hidden levers. There was nothing. She tried pushing on rocks to the north, south, east, and west, making the sign of the cross with her movements. When that didn't work, she followed a triangle pattern, the symbol of the divine trinity. Again, nothing. "Come on, Sarah, think."

Her thoughts were interrupted by a momentary flash, a streak of white light in the sky, neither lightning nor a shooting star. It was like nothing she had seen before. At that moment she felt the monk's ice-cold hand in hers. His presence was tangible, encouraging.

Suddenly, she remembered. When they had tried to evade the intruder in the labyrinth, Apostolos had pushed on the stones in a distinct pattern. She didn't realize then but now knew it was the five-pointed star. She mimicked the movements exactly.

The stone gate parted.

"Atta girl," Daniel shouted.

"What are you waiting for? Come on up."

The subterranean tunnel leading to the library was long and unwelcoming. Sarah and Daniel followed a series of stone steps—about a hundred of them, or so it felt—down to a tubelike chamber they could traverse only single file. It reminded Sarah of a prison escape route, which was probably not far from the truth. In any case, it looked like no one had been through in the recent past. Cobwebs hung from the low ceilings, and the moist ground crawled with rats.

Moving slowly, Daniel and Sarah silently made their way through the endless passage. Oxygen was at a premium in the catacomb, and they knew better than to waste what little they had. Many times Sarah wanted to stop, but her commitment to Apostolos and her own hunger for what she might find inside the vault kept her moving forward.

Eventually they came to a fork on the path. They stopped to look around and weigh the options.

Daniel took a coin out of his pocket. "Shall we toss for it?"

"I think we should follow this route." She pointed to the right. "In the portion of the labyrinth leading to the Sheba Stone, we seemed to always be following a series of right turns. It may be random, but my hunch is that this was by design."

"Jesus being the right hand of God?"

"Something like that."

Daniel didn't question Sarah but let her lead the way.

The tunnel grew a bit more spacious, allowing them to quicken their step. It wasn't long before they came to an arched door whose wood planks were held together by rusty iron nails. Sarah parted the cobwebs and turned the handle. "Locked." She tried Apostolos' key, but it was obviously designed for a smaller keyhole.

Daniel tried his own luck. He alternately pulled and pushed at the door, hoping to dislodge any sediment keeping it shuttered. He looked inside the thumb-sized keyhole. "I can actually make out some stone aisles. It looks like a mausoleum in there."

"Must be the place," Sarah said, the excitement adding an octave to her voice.

"Yup. Now if we could only find the keys."

They scoured every corner of the entrance vestibule for potential hiding places.

When they'd run out of options, she shook her head. "The monks wouldn't make it so easy. They probably carry the keys only on their person."

Daniel winked. "Lucky for you, I am an expert lock picker. It's one of my many hidden talents."

"How did you learn that?" She lifted her hands. "Never mind. I don't think I want to know."

"It comes with the territory. The trouble is, you can ruin the lock in the process. Very delicate business." He reached inside his pack for an L-shaped metal gadget and a handful of pokers of varying lengths and thicknesses. "Now, which of these goes in first?"

"Be serious."

"Lighten up. It was a joke."

Daniel wiggled the poker in the keyhole to find

the sweet spot. His expertise at breaking and entering was evident within thirty seconds, which was all it took to pop the lock. The door creaked as if it hadn't been opened in centuries. He shone his flashlight at the church's inner sanctum.

The complex was a maze of stone columns and open shelves built into the cave walls. Parchment codices and books filled every nook. At the far end was a wall of lockers sealed by heavy stone doors. An ancient plank table and two straight-backed wooden armchairs occupied the middle of the room.

"Get a load of this place," he said in a hushed voice that trailed off to a whisper.

Sarah had never seen anything like it. Perhaps a miniature version of the Library of Alexandria, or at least how she imagined it based on the multiple theories she'd researched. Though the place was fairly small—couldn't have been any more than three hundred square feet—there was enough material, much of it probably dating back centuries, to give a scholar an entire life's work. Fighting the urge to thumb through every tome, she focused on the task at hand.

"I think those vaults are what we're after," she said, nodding toward the back wall. She looked at Daniel and twirled the key in her hand. "Shall we try our luck, then?"

She inserted the key in every vault door, but it worked in none of them. She wasn't surprised. If it contained such precious documents, the vault in question was probably not that conspicuous. She groped the perimeter for any sign of a removable stone or rotating wall while Daniel examined the floor. The herringbone-patterned tiles could easily disguise yet another secret passage constructed by monks, veterans at the art of hiding. Both came up empty.

Sarah glanced in every direction. "There has to be something we're overlooking."

"What about behind those?" Daniel pointed to the shelves piled with scrolls and stitch-bound books thick with the dust of the ages.

The two set about gingerly removing each volume and placing it on the table. They emptied shelf after shelf but still no luck.

While they replaced the documents on a low shelf, Daniel stopped. "Check it out. Look at that crack. The wall there looks superficial."

"Spot on. Let's see if it gives way."

He placed the scrolls carefully on the floor beside him, inserted his fingers into the crack in the stone, and pulled the plaster toward him. It gave way too easily, confirming their suspicions. He clawed at it until all the plaster was removed, revealing a small door. With a contented smile, he said, "I'll bet your key works now."

"Why, Dr. Madigan, I do believe you're a genius."

She bit her lip as she inserted the key. When it yielded a satisfying click, she gasped.

This was it. Apostolos' vault.

She reached inside and felt a sculpted metal object. She carefully pulled it out.

A Coptic cross, a simple figure carved of solid gold.

"The crux ansata," she whispered. "The original Coptic cross, begotten from the Egyptian ankh." She recalled Apostolos' mention of the saint's cross. "He must have been buried with this."

"Which explains the extra holes in the coffin. Whoever found him must have taken this out to protect it from looters."

Sarah reached inside the vault again and pulled out a loosely bound, wax-sealed papyrus codex. The fragile paper almost came apart in her hands. She surmised by the quality of the papyrus that the text had been written in the early centuries of the Common Era.

To prevent the transfer of oils from her hands to the paper, she put on a pair of white cotton gloves. "Do you have a magnifying glass in your bag of tricks?"

Daniel reached inside his pack and handed her one.

She took a close look at the impression made by the seal. The ideogram was identical to the one that had marked the entrance to the tenth saint's tomb.

"Take a look." She handed him the glass.

He held the seal next to the Coptic cross. "They're

practically identical. The untrained eye would think they were one and the same. There's obviously some connection."

Sarah pointed at the outer circle of the ideogram. "I can't believe I never saw it before. It's the Greek letter omega. And inside it, the circle divided in four by a perfect cross—the ancient symbol for the lower heaven. Apostolos said the prophecies foretold the final doom that would befall the earth. It all makes sense."

She bowed her head as she prepared to open the codex. She ran her thumb over the intersecting lines that formed the cross on the wax, took a deep breath, and broke the seal. As she turned the yellowed pages, she noted they were handwritten in ancient Greek script, one of the official languages in early Christian Ethiopia. The text was in all capital letters, in the same manner used to inscribe the stelae and thrones erected in the days of the Aksumite empire. Her guess was that it originated between the fourth and sixth centuries of the Common Era. These had to be the earliest, and perhaps the only, interpretations of the original writings. She was in awe.

She carefully opened each page of the codex and photographed it. She removed the first memory card from the camera, placed it in the inner pocket of her trousers, and photographed everything again. She wasn't taking any chances. When she was satisfied with the documentation, she set about translating the text. She was fluent in ancient Greek, so it would not be terribly difficult. She paused to savor the moment and glanced at Daniel.

He was smiling. "This moment is all yours, Sarah Weston. God knows you've earned it."

Thirteen

Gabriel's route took him southwest of Ubar along the edge of the mighty Rub' al Khali desert. He traveled along the beaten path of the frankincense traders but hadn't seen a caravan in some days. In this desolate place, his only company was his faithful camel. He missed the chatter of the women as they kneaded the day's bread, the scent of the embers as he drifted off to sleep each night, the giggles of the children as they chased each other across the sands, the taste of strong bitter tea on his lips. Though he knew he had to move on, he felt the angst of separation from these people, his only friends.

The terrain had been the same for many moons—a great desert ocean stretching in every direction, rippling with waves of high dunes sculpted by the eternal dance of sand and wind. The color changed with each passing hour. Sunrise painted the sands in the electric ochre of raging flames. Late morning brought with it the warm rosy glow of a blushing virgin. In the afternoon the sand took on the hue of a lion's hide. By dusk it turned brick red with long black fingers cast by the waning sun.

As the shadows deepened and the land succumbed to the inevitable darkness, Gabriel wrapped himself in his woolen blanket, which doubled as the camel's saddle, and looked to the horizon for the rising moon. On one occasion, the orb, so close he thought he could touch it, emerged from the peaks of the sand mountains and illuminated the sky as if it were day. As brutal as this place was, it was a breathing, living being that embraced him.

His destination was the kingdom of Sheba. At the westernmost point of Sheba, Hairan had told him, he would find the port city Muza, the very end of Arabia. From there he would board a *baghlah*, a sailing ship that would carry him across the sea to the savage lands. Civilization seemed an eternity away as he walked, kicking up plumes of dust with his every step. After long days of hard travel, his feet had blistered and bloodied inside the sandals he had made long ago from scraps of dried sheep's hide. His indigo robes had become brittle with dirt and dried sweat, and with no way to clean up he smelled like a combination of cured meat and stagnant urine. He had grown accustomed to the stench, as much a part of him as the graying beard grazing his collarbone, the deep lines mapping his tanned face, and the tangles of dirty blond hair well hidden inside his turban.

Gabriel didn't know how many days he had been traveling. Counting was a Western inclination and of little use here, so he'd stopped marking time and let himself rise and fall with the sun and be carried by the simoom that blew hot and dry over the desert. Days and nights dissolved into one another like salt into water, until the morning he crossed the path of the Himyarites.

Gabriel walked past the caravan, where men sat in a circle drinking from small clay cups. He smelled coffee. The men were dark skinned and black bearded, their heads bound tightly with yards of white cotton. They stared at Gabriel with hard frowns, their looks betraying suspicion and anger, but they did not speak.

Gabriel greeted the tribe with a bow. Speaking in the Bedouin dialect, he said, "Hail, brothers. Where do you come from?"

The men looked at each other inquisitively, and one barked out some words that Gabriel did not understand.

There was no mistaking the man's unfriendly attitude. He knew he would have to be careful, for these desert dwellers surely were looking for trouble. He lowered his head and hunched his shoulders, hoping his fellow travelers would interpret it as a gesture of submission and cease to be threatened by him.

The leader spoke. Gabriel picked up the Semitic word for *Roman* along with the contempt these men obviously felt for the white men from the West. Even filthy and weather-beaten, he did not look like one of them. His features and stature betrayed his foreignness. Clearly, that had a different meaning among these people than it had among the Bedouins.

"I mean no harm, wise brothers. I am not Roman. I have lived with Bedouins for many moons. My way is that of the nomad."

One of the men spoke. Then another. The leader waved the other men down and turned to Gabriel, pointing at his camel.

Gabriel read the comment as a provocation but didn't let it show. "He has been my friend through good days and bad."

The leader rose, his bloodshot obsidian eyes staring at Gabriel with contempt. He spat on the ground and spoke gruffly as he attempted to snatch the camel's reins from Gabriel's hands.

It was plain to Gabriel that he could not avoid this confrontation with kindness. "I don't care to part with my camel any more than you care to part with yours."

He straightened his body and looked down at the Himyarite. "Now I will take my leave. Safe travels, brothers."

Leading his camel by its rope reins, he backed away from the group. As he walked toward the west, he could hear laughter and shouts behind him, the crass mockery of hooligans. He quickened his pace, eager to escape an altercation. But he knew his foes wouldn't be satisfied with a peaceful farewell. He heard the shuffle of a djellaba behind him but didn't turn around, hearing Hairan's voice inside his head: *Let what will come, come. Fear is the enemy of men.*

A massive weight hit his back, and he fell to his knees. An arm wrapped around his neck. A fist smashed his temple. A burly Himyarite turned him on his back and held his arms down while another drove a knee into his abdomen. Gabriel gasped for breath. Several fists descended upon his face, punishing him until he slipped out of consciousness.

When Gabriel regained his senses, he was shivering from the pain and loss of blood, his body broken. He tried to stand but fell in breathless agony. He gathered his knees to his chest to warm up. When that didn't work, he dug a pit and dragged his body inside, covering himself up to the chest with sand, as he had seen the Bedouins do on especially cold nights.

The sandy tomb cradled him. For all the burden that lay atop him, he felt surprisingly weightless. He prayed silently. *God, if you have not left me, hear me now. I would rather be dead, dwelling with my beloved and our son in a place that knows not grief nor despair nor the ignorance of men. What hope is there here amid so much hatred? We were fools to think we could change anything. I beg you, let me be taken by sleep and never awaken. Let my body be covered with the eternal sands. Let my flesh nourish the scorpions and my bones calcify the land. And let my spirit escape this prison of consciousness that tortures me like a flesh-eating plague.*

Exhausted from the confrontation and his own conflicting emotions, Gabriel fell into a deep sleep.

When the morning sun beat down on his face, he woke with a start. For a moment, he wondered where he was and how he had come to be there. Then, as the fog of sleep lifted, he recalled everything and regretted that the Himyarites hadn't finished the job. He fought the cruel stabs of pain to rise out of his sandy cocoon.

He felt for gashes on his face and head and realized his nose had been broken, his forehead split open. The wounds were caked with dried blood and sand. A tooth was missing, and his lips were cracked like the flats of the Sahara in the dry season. He looked for his water bladder and saw it was gone, along with everything else—his camel, his possessions, even his makeshift sandals.

Though he trembled with rage, he didn't have the strength to shout. He kicked the sand, but his feet couldn't do the bidding of his brain and he fell gracelessly. His chest heaved, and he sobbed without tears.

Fourteen

By the meager lamplight, Sarah read and re-read the pages of the codex to make sure she was not missing anything. A few words were unfamiliar, but she deduced a rough meaning from their context. Though the language was nebulous, almost cryptic in places, she could tell by the author's urgent, grave tone that this was a warning. She sat back on the rickety chair and crossed her arms.

Daniel broke her concentration. "Enough of this suspense. What does it say?"

She shook her head. "Well, the theory about this being a prophecy is correct. I can say that much. Some of it is downright chilling. And some of it makes no sense at all."

"Read it to me. We can figure it out together."

Sarah read slowly, attempting to find the proper

words in English. The ancient Greek language was so full of nuance and color it didn't always translate easily. English simply wasn't as textured, and the corresponding words often did not exist. She gave it her most valiant effort.

So you may learn what is to come
and change your ways, I write these truths.
I left my destroyed world behind.
I knew I could never return,
But there was nothing to return to.

I am Gabriel, one of three
Who escaped naked but for the truth.
We saw the abominable, the end of ends.
Hear me now: it is coming.

One day that is to come,
Man will become a ravenous lion.
Unable to sate his appetite,
He will gnaw on the bones of his Mother.

He will rape her and dig into her core
Sucking out the black blood that runs through her veins.
She will hemorrhage, but he will leave her to die.
She will plead for mercy
But he, in all his impudence, will laugh at her pain.

But the mighty Mother will rebel.

With her last breath, she will unleash
A cacophony of great storms and pestilence.
But still he will ignore her cries,
In the name of his own divine power.

For when man wants more,
He will be stopped by nothing,
Not decency, not reason, not the wisdom of the ages.
Greed and fear will blind him.

When the air will be fouled by gases
And the life breath will no longer be free,
Man, in his infinite narcissism,
Will assume the role of Creator.

Man will beget a child,
A terrible creation he will unleash on the seas,
And order it to return the life force
To the feeble air.

And the child will obey
Until the day will come
When it must answer only to its own will.
It will join with a foul enemy,

And together they will become the Beast.

The monster will cover the sea
With a blanket of darkness
And bury the fish in watery graves,
And the air will not give life but take it away.

Great tongues of fire will cover the land.
The tainted air will feed the flames.
Smoke will rise to the heavens with a terrible fury
Until all life is devoured and there is nothing
But the eternal silence.

And thus the race of men
Will become extinct.
Take heed, children of God,
For if you can read this, it is not too late.

Sarah looked at Daniel intently, waiting for his reaction.

He was silent.

Tension hung thick in the room.

"The apocalypse," he finally said, breaking the silence, "or some version of it. The first angel sounded, and there followed hail and fire mingled with blood.

And the second angel sounded, and a great mountain burning with fire was cast into the sea: and the creatures which were in the sea and had life died."

"Revelation 8. There is also talk of a beast in Revelation, one that rises up out of the seas—presumably Satan."

"Yes, but something doesn't rhyme with the good book. This Gabriel says he left his destroyed world behind. That he was one of three who escaped . . . as if he was not merely a prophet but a man who had lived through the end of ends, as he calls it. Question is, when did it happen?"

"Something about it sounds awfully modern." She turned the pages. "Look at this part: *he will rape her and dig into her core, sucking out the black blood that runs through her veins.* Doesn't that sound like drilling for oil?"

"Sounds plausible to me," a voice behind them spoke.

Daniel and Sarah turned. An Ethiopian man wearing a woolen balaclava stood at the entrance of an open doorway, a movable wall so well concealed that neither of them had noticed it before. The three holes of the balaclava revealed the man's charred skin, which hung loosely over pink, raw flesh.

Apostolos' murderer.

In one swift motion, Daniel grabbed his revolver and pointed it at the masked man. "Who are you? Speak or I'll put you out of your obvious misery."

"I wouldn't do that, Dr. Madigan."

Daniel turned around.

A second man was in the room.

A pistol pressed the back of Sarah's head.

"Slowly drop your weapon." The man spoke in English.

Sarah looked at Daniel but didn't dare speak.

Daniel dropped his gun. The leader called out to another of his associates, who picked up the gun, made sure it was loaded, and pointed it at Daniel. "I am Mr. Werkneh. I bring the regards of Mr. Matakala. He regrets he couldn't come greet you personally, but you will see him soon enough."

Matakala. Sarah wasn't surprised the director of antiquities was corrupt; she'd suspected it all along. But she hadn't imagined that a government official was the mastermind behind the killings, nor could she fathom his true motives. Her mind raced across a field of possibilities. Had Matakala contracted with a collector for these relics? Was he working for Apocryphon or against them? Was this a matter of faith or greed?

"Turn around." The man prodded Sarah with his weapon.

She turned to face him. The Ethiopian, a short man of husky build, hid his eyes behind mirrored aviator sunglasses. A half-spent cigarette hung from the corner of his fleshy mouth.

She glared at him. "Just answer me this. How did you know about the codex?"

Werkneh laughed. "We have good informants. You see, this is Africa. For the right price, everyone is a traitor." He glanced toward the masked man. "I believe you've met Brehan. Not so long ago, Brehan was the chief acolyte of Brother Apostolos. He was being groomed to succeed him as the guardian of the Sheba Stone and the church's archives . . . the documents in this very library. But he came to realize he could be so much more than a monkey in white robes. He craved the company of women, not men. He liked the idea of driving a Mercedes and drinking beer. The church couldn't do all that for him. Isn't this true?"

Brehan laughed.

Sarah's stomach turned. All it had taken was a fistful of worldly goods and the promise of pleasure for this former disciple of God to sell his soul. He had been entrusted with the secrets of Yemrehana Krestos, down to the hidden entrances to the church's most holy of holies, and he'd bartered them without remorse. She considered how painful it must have been for Apostolos to come face-to-face with his acolyte's betrayal. Even so, he had let Brehan live. He could have easily ended it in the labyrinth, while Brehan had lain defenseless, but that was not his way. She wasn't sure she would have done the same.

Werkneh picked up the codex. "What he didn't know was how to get to this. Apostolos kept that little secret to himself all these years. And yet . . . he told you." He looked her up and down and licked his ample lips. "Tell me, Dr. Weston, how did you get him to trust you? Did you pleasure him in that dark chamber?"

Sarah's face burned, and she instinctively struck Werkneh's face. His glasses crashed to the floor. Snarling, he grabbed Sarah by the throat. The barrel of his gun trembled in his hands as it dug into her forehead.

She didn't struggle but spoke behind clenched teeth. "Go ahead and kill me, you bastard. Or don't you have the guts?"

"It would give me immense pleasure," he hissed, "but Mr. Matakala wants you alive. You can still be of service to him." He waved Brehan over.

The masked monk slipped handcuffs around Daniel's wrists, then Sarah's, and covered their heads with burlap sacks.

The car ride was long and tortuous. The incessant bumps, twists, and turns told Sarah they were in a remote part of the country, well removed from asphalt roads and stoplights: a place where a band of thugs could go about their dirty business undetected. Hours seemed to pass before the car lurched to a stop.

Sarah and Daniel were marched inside. She heard footsteps around the room. A mobile phone rang, and a man answered. She couldn't make out his words.

At last, their hoods were removed.

Sarah's eyes had to adjust to the brightness of the room. Beyond the surrounding bare windows was a remarkably well-maintained rose garden. A mountain range loomed in the distance, but it offered no clue as to where they were. In Ethiopia, mountains always lined the horizon. The room itself was painted white and sparsely furnished. There was a sofa covered loosely in white linen with traditional red embroidery, some floor cushions, and a low tea table. Bookcases, packed to every available square inch with books and overstuffed notebooks, lined the walls. Sarah and Daniel, still handcuffed, were told to wait for "the boss" and left alone.

"So. Your friend Mr. Matakala resurfaces," Daniel said. "Maybe this time he'll tell us what he really wants."

"Would you believe him even if he did? Things are so convoluted here. You can't count on anyone for the truth."

"True, but there's a reason we're here. Maybe he wants to strike a bargain."

"What bargain? He has everything. The codex, the cross, access to the tomb. What can we possibly offer him at this point?"

The door creaked open, and Andrew Matakala walked in, looking dapper in a khaki linen suit with a navy T-shirt underneath. He took a seat on the sofa and crossed his legs, his bony ankles exposed between crisp trouser cuffs and expensive Italian loafers worn without socks. Soft shadows defined the contours of his chiseled face in the afternoon light. He ordered an attendant to bring tea, then addressed them.

"It's good to see you again, Dr. Weston." He turned to Daniel. "And a pleasure to make your acquaintance, Dr. Madigan. I've seen your documentaries on television. Quite intriguing."

"Can't say the same about you," Daniel said. "Why don't you tell me a little about yourself? I like to know who I'm speaking to."

"Very well. I am the director of antiquities for the Ministry—"

"No, pal. I want to know who you really are."

Matakala placed two sugar cubes in his tea and stirred. "Let's just say I work with some very important people. People who stand to suffer from your little project."

For the right price, everyone is a traitor. Sarah resisted the urge to verbalize her anger. It was a dead end. What she needed now was diplomacy. Matakala had kept them alive for a reason. Their only hope was to use that to their advantage.

"Why did you bring us here?" Her tone was calm but firm.

He took a sip of tea, then delicately placed the china cup on its saucer. "It seems you can be useful to me . . . to us. You see, when you didn't leave for England after your expedition was closed, people worried about you. When the news came out that you were in the monastery during that unfortunate siege, why, UNESCO and Cambridge claimed the incident was connected with the Aksum tomb and began demanding answers from the Ministry. Your father, in particular, has been rather up in arms about your sudden disappearance. For some reason, he has been asking a lot of questions about me. He's even sent Scotland Yard agents to Ethiopia—most inconvenient to our mission."

"I sure would like to know what that mission is," Daniel said.

Matakala did not acknowledge his statement but kept his eyes on Sarah. "My offer to you is this. I can let them find you and Dr. Madigan here in the highlands, the victims of a tragic accident. Or I can let you live." He paused and leaned forward. "In order for me to select the latter, you must call Daddy and tell him you are alive and well and to please call off the dogs. Then you will explain to Cambridge that you have discovered the tomb was nothing more than the resting place of a Roman missionary. That the cave inscriptions were merely an account of Christian worship rites and religious battles in fourth-century Aksum. I have taken the liberty of constructing the official translation, which will be authenticated by you on behalf of Cambridge and filed on record with the department of antiquities. Shall I read it to you?"

Sarah was speechless.

"Very well, then." He put on his reading glasses and read aloud.

"In the name of the Father and of the Son and of the Holy Spirit, Sumerius, former merchant, humble monk, unworthy servant of God, in the service of Ezana, king of Aksum and of Raydan and of Saba and of Tsiyamo, king of kings, invincible to his enemies and servant of the Lord Christ, amen.

"I come to Abyssinia from the great empire of Rome, through Constantinople to Nabataea to Persia to the fertile valleys of the Tiger and Euphrates. I am charged by God himself to spread his word to the heathens of Africa, who know not his divine mercy.

"The great King Ezana of the Aksumite Empire has accepted me into his kingdom to teach his subjects about the power and grace of the Almighty. I have erected an Orthodox church on Dabra Maryam, where the men of royal blood may gather to learn the teachings of the Lord Christ.

"The men of Aksum under the leadership of the most excellent King Ezana have been summoned to holy battle at the Kasu. As God is my witness, we will rid the valley of the pestilence of nonbelievers and install the great faith to the heathens that escape our swords. O Lord, your word is our shield, our spear, and our guidance. It is in your name that we pursue our enemies and turn them to dust if they do not repent and bow to your will.

"The men of Aksum fought valiantly and destroyed those in their paths and made prisoners of their enemies. Many of King Ezana's troops were killed in battle in the name of the Father and of the Son and of the Holy Spirit. The losses were devastating but necessary, and those men were martyrs before God.

"This humble servant of God has been speared through the rib and fears the end is near. But the parting is not one of sorrow, for I long to be united with the Creator, the one whose divinity is without question, and whose mercy is greater than the greatest deserts and the vastest skies. Take me swiftly, O Lord, for it is only in your kingdom that I will be redeemed. Amen."

Matakala threw the paper on the tea table in front of Sarah.

She weighed all her possible moves as if she were playing a chess game. Anything she did at this point would likely end in checkmate. Only one move could prevent her from losing, but it was risky and her opponent might well see through it.

She had no choice. "Mr. Matakala, I might be more

inclined to do what you ask if you tell me one thing."

He raised an eyebrow. "You're really in no position to demand anything, Doctor."

"No, I'm not. But I don't get many opportunities to converse with someone like you. All I ask is that we exchange knowledge as one intellectual to another."

He smirked. "Very well. This could be amusing."

"Why does Apocryphon want to keep the prophecies hidden?"

"Simple. It's dangerous knowledge. It has been deemed so since the sixth century, when a holy man named Aregawi found the tenth saint's tomb. If you know your Ethiopian history, and I trust you do, you will know Aregawi was one of the nine saints who spread Christianity. As a Syrian familiar with the dialects of the desert, he translated the inscriptions and saw they were prophecies of the world's last hours. At the time, it was anathema. Just as the church was adamant for so long about keeping the book of Revelation under wraps, they wanted these prophecies safely hidden from common men. If the people believed the end was near, there would be mass chaos." He held a silver strainer above his cup and poured more tea. "So Aregawi removed the cross from the coffin and sealed the tomb. He then formed Apocryphon to keep the secret alive until it was time to release it to the world. He originally hid the codex with his translations in

Dabra Damo, the church he erected near the site of the prophet's tomb. It stayed there several centuries and was moved when Aregawi's last descendants defected and were taken in by the priests of Yemrehana Krestos."

"Apostolos?"

"And his brother."

She was stunned but didn't need an explanation. That was why Apostolos had taken Brehan under his wing. And why he couldn't kill him even in self-defense. She was nauseated by the realization that money and power could pit brother against brother. But there was still something she didn't understand. "You once told me Apocryphon would stop at nothing to protect what is theirs. Why would they destroy what they vowed to defend?"

Matakala smirked. "They didn't."

"Then who did?"

"Someone far more powerful."

"You, obviously."

Her intention was to flatter him. It worked.

"Obviously." Matakala stood and walked to the window, gazing at his roses.

"And these important people you work with?"

"Let's just say my benefactor is the money behind this operation and I'm the brains. He was willing to pay anything for the prophecies. I had the expertise and ingenuity to give him what he wanted . . . using whatever means possible."

Sarah fell silent, trying to process all that she had just heard.

"I don't get it," Daniel said. "What does this guy want with the prophecies? Is it a trophy for his mantle? An ego thing?"

He turned to Daniel. "No, no, Dr. Madigan. It's nothing of the kind. He wishes to see the prophecies destroyed. The information they contain could be misinterpreted. That could be very damaging."

"Damaging to what? Or whom?" Daniel pressed.

"Ah, but that's the million-dollar question, as you Americans say." He laughed and turned to Sarah. "Are you ready to make a phone call?"

"Sarah, no," Daniel said. "He's bluffing. He will never let us out of here alive."

She looked Matakala in the eye. "I think he's a man of his word."

"I said I will let you leave here and I meant it, Dr. Madigan." Matakala handed Sarah the phone. "Whenever you're ready, my dear."

"Don't do it, Sarah."

"No, Danny. I have to believe him. This is our only chance." She took the phone from Matakala's hands.

"Remember, Dr. Weston. Don't try anything foolish. A gun is pointed at your back at this very moment."

Sarah turned around and saw Brehan, indeed

armed, standing behind them.

"All I need to do is give Brehan the signal, and he will shoot to kill."

With shaky hands, Sarah put the phone on speaker and dialed the number of Dr. Simon's private office line.

After the usual seven rings, the familiar gruff voice answered the phone. "Stanley Simon here."

"Hello, Professor. It's Sarah Weston calling."

"Sarah. My word. Where have you been? We've all been worried sick about you. Your father has been searching the whole of Ethiopia for you."

She struggled to keep her voice from breaking. "Everything is jolly good. I have been in good hands. Tell my father I'm dying to come home."

Matakala made circles in the air with his index finger, signaling her to get to the point.

"Listen, Professor, I have some good news. I have translated the inscriptions."

"Have you indeed?"

"I will explain it all when I see you. Suffice it to say we weren't on the right track. Our supposed prophet was indeed a holy man, a missionary by the name of Sumerius." Her eyes darted to Matakala, who nodded his approval. "His writings were merely descriptions of Christian life in fourth-century Aksum. It wasn't the revelation I was hoping for."

"Do go on."

Sarah proceeded to read the fake translation word for word.

"Well. I hate to say I told you so. This makes perfect logical sense. Right, then. When will you be home? We have much to talk about, young lady."

"In a few days' time, I should think."

Simon let out a chuckle. "Prophecies. The tenth saint. You do have an imagination, my girl. Now leave that god-awful place and get back to England."

"Indeed. I do fancy a pint right about now. Good-bye, Professor." Sarah clicked the phone off and let it drop on the table.

Matakala clapped. "An excellent performance. And now for my end of the bargain." He nodded to the masked man. "As I said, I am releasing you. Brehan will drive the two of you away."

"And our belongings?" Daniel said.

Matakala stood to leave the room. "Those have been destroyed, I'm afraid. Anyway, you won't be needing them where you're going. Good-bye, Doctors. It's been a true pleasure."

Sarah turned to Daniel. "What do you suppose he meant by that?" she whispered.

He leaned in. "I told you I don't trust this guy. I don't believe for a minute the monk is driving us to safety."

Brehan motioned them to follow him and led the

way to a battered, dusty Suzuki of eighties vintage. They ducked into the backseat, their hands still bound. Brehan engaged the safety locks on the back doors and slipped into the driver's seat.

"Where are you taking us?" Sarah asked in Amharic.

He turned to face her, and she was revolted by the sight of his singed face peeking through the eye-holes of the mask. His eyes were encircled by charred flaps of skin, and his eyelashes and eyebrows had been burnt off.

"Too many questions," he said with an ugly slur that revealed the extent of his injury, "for a dead woman."

Fifteen

Muza was even more filthy and chaotic than Gabriel had imagined. Bare-chested port hands from the East, their ribs protruding, pushed carts filled with sacks of spices and grain. At the traders' bazaar, veiled women picked through piles of lemons to find the juiciest specimens. Roving merchants, ragged and stinking of sweat and camel dung, haunted the streets vending their "quality" frankincense from the Qarā' Mountains. Miserable souls, some missing eyes, others with lopped-off legs, sat in their own waste and begged for bread. Still, the place was beautiful to Gabriel's eyes.

The last portion of his journey across the desert had been grueling. He was convinced that had it not been for the people in the passing caravan who had taken mercy on him and given him bread and water, he would not have seen this day. Now he had arrived at last, in the port city that only days ago had seemed so far away as to be an illusion. *Muza.* He repeated the name in his mind to assure himself the place was real. Loath to press his luck, he made haste toward the docks to catch the next *baghlah* across the sea. In his rush, he nearly toppled over an old man selling spices. The small pouches, sewn together in rows and draped over the man's arms and around his neck, fell to the ground.

"Sorry," Gabriel instinctively said in English. He caught his gaffe and repeated his apology in the Semitic dialect.

The merchant, his face as dry as old leather, studied the stranger and spoke.

Gabriel didn't understand the words but hoped the man was the friendly sort. He asked, reinforcing with hand gestures, "Which way to the port? To the boats that leave for the west bank of the sea?"

The man grinned, revealing a row of misshapen, decaying teeth. "You know the Bedouin language," he said approvingly and continued in a dialect so close to the nomadic tongue it rang familiar to Gabriel's ears. "You are a long way from the desert. What do you seek in Muza?"

"I am a pilgrim. A nomad like the Bedouins, but I do not belong to their tribe, so I must move on."

"What tribe do you belong to?"

"I know no country, no kin. I strayed into the harsh lands of the Rub' al Khali. I would not be alive if not for the Bedouins. They cared for me and gave me shelter. They were my friends."

"The nomads, they are good people. My ancestors came from the desert. The wandering life is very hard. It makes a boy a man." He waved his hand. "Ah, it was not for me. Me, I like to see people, hear noise. It makes me feel alive."

Gabriel nodded his sympathy for the self-fashioned city dweller. Though city life was a distant memory for him, it was deeply embedded in his consciousness. "I understand you, my friend. Where do you make your home?"

The merchant gestured toward the medina. "In there. I have a bedroll inside the spice shop of my brother. He gives me spices in the morning, and I go find customers." He held up a belt of pouches. "You want pepper? Myrrh? Frankincense? Best in South Arabia."

"No, thank you, my friend. I have no money."

"And how do you plan to take the boat across the sea?"

"I am hoping I can work. Put up sails, clean the deck."

The merchant let out a laugh that made his abdomen quake. "Hope all you want, but if you don't have money, the captain will not take you. You need three drachms. Though for the life of me, I don't know why anybody would pay to make that journey. The sea is swollen this time of year. The wind is coming from the east in great gusts. Some of the boats have capsized. You should stay in Muza for a while and wait for the waters to be calm again."

"You are very wise." Gabriel had no intention of waiting for better weather, but he thought it unnecessary to share his plans with the old man. He did beseech him for one last piece of advice. "Tell me, friend, how can a stranger earn three drachms?"

The merchant scratched his head. "You can try the metalsmith. Maybe he has use for someone to sweep shavings off the floor. But the wages will be paltry. It will take a long time to save the money you need, especially since you will have to spend some of it to eat. You're skin and bones, my friend. And you look like you've been trod upon by a camel."

Gabriel had no idea what he looked like to the old man, so he raised his hand to feel the scars from his encounter with the Himyarites. His brow was cut and covered with dried blood, and his lips were swollen, blistered, and drier than cured meat. A good deal of sand was embedded in the wiry strands of his beard. Suddenly self-conscious, he bowed to the man and turned to walk away.

"Wait," the man called behind him. "My sister-in-law is a very good cook. At least come tonight for a meal."

"I couldn't—"

"Nonsense. It is very rude to refuse the hospitality of an Arab."

That night Gabriel feasted on goat stew and couscous. With the merchant and his brother's family, he sat at a low table draped with embroidered cotton cloth. A fire burning in the hearth warmed them. The walls of the place were made of hay and stone bound by a sand mortar with tiny slits for ventilation. Beneath them, the compacted sandy soil of the arid Arabian lands was covered with trampled kilims in fading shades of indigo and saffron and the deep red of crushed beetles. Everything smelled of rancid goat milk and feces, but it was shelter and for that Gabriel was grateful.

The merchant's brother spoke of his business, complaining that things were not going well. He also complained about the pains and swelling in his joints, and Gabriel was certain he was describing arthritis.

Unsure of the customs in this part of Arabia, Gabriel didn't speak much for fear of saying the wrong thing. He did, however, feel a deep urge to repay these people's kindness. After dinner, he asked the merchant for a pinch of his quality frankincense, a few leaves from the olive tree in the courtyard, and a mortar and pestle.

The man complied, and Gabriel concocted a

paste. “Give this to your brother. Tell him to put it on his aching joints tonight. Tomorrow morning he will feel like a young man.”

The man laughed in disbelief.

The next morning in the town square, Gabriel saw the merchant.

“It is a miracle,” the man said. “You are a healer of the highest order. You and I, we can be rich. I will give you the materials, and you make the stuff. We will sell it and split the profits.”

“I will help you, but I don’t want your money, my friend. It won’t help me where I am going. All I need is three drachms for the boat captain. After that, it is all yours.”

The man agreed.

That afternoon Gabriel went to work smashing leaves and herbs and resins in a stone mortar until the mixture gave off an astringent odor. He knew from Hairan how to test the efficacy of the poultice. “Trust this,” the old chief would always say, tapping his nose. It had taken many tries over the years, but Gabriel had mastered the art of blending the healing herbs. This was one of many muds, rubs, and teas he could make.

As Gabriel cooked up his concoctions, the merchant put his own skills to work, convincing passersby that the answer to their health woes was a rub away—all they had to do was produce a twopenny and relief would be theirs. Before long, they lined up—mothers with scraped-up children, old men hunched over with arthritis—waiting for their turn at liberation from whatever ailed them.

Centuries pass, progress sets in, the world changes, and yet people remain the same, Gabriel thought. *One ounce of hope weighs more than a ton of fortune.*

By the end of the first night, the two had amassed their first drachm. Gabriel happily accepted the merchant's invitation to stay the night in his brother's house in the medina.

Over a meager meal of flatbread and runny lentil gravy, the merchant asked him what had lured him to the savage lands. "White men always know where there are fortunes to be made. Tell me, what riches lie to the west?"

"I know nothing of riches, friend. My reasons for going are not what you think."

"Please, you must tell me." In a conspiratorial tone, he added, "There is a girl in the village . . . I want to make her my wife. But I am a poor man. I have nothing to give her family. I cannot provide for her or any children. But you . . . you are clever. You know the ways to turn dust into gold. I have seen it."

"You give me too much credit." Gabriel laughed.

"I am a simple man, a wanderer. Just as a nomad seeks new pastures when the land dries up, I go in search of knowledge . . . friendship."

"But you have a home, no? A wife?"

"I had a wife and a child. They died. I am alone now. Without them, no place feels like home. This is why I cannot linger anywhere for too long."

The merchant nodded. "We have an old saying in my village: Your shadow is always attached to you. No matter where you go, it follows. You cannot be separated from something that is a part of you."

The two men laughed and said no more of ghosts and shadows and elusive riches. Not that night or any other night. In the weeks that followed, they earned all the drachms they needed, Gabriel for the *baghlah*, the merchant for his impending marriage and another goat. When the first breath of autumn crept into the dawn air, Gabriel quietly slipped out the door.

Sixteen

Brehan had been driving more than three hours through snaking unpaved mountain roads, and the only sign of life was the goat herd grazing on the meager grasses of the hillside. As they ascended the mountain, the road became narrower and coarser until it wasn't a road at all. The path was barely wide enough for one car, with no guardrail to protect against the steep drop down a rocky chasm.

Sarah tried to gauge where they were, but the sameness of the terrain betrayed nothing. They were surrounded by rocky escarpments and stone spires standing on their own like ghosts presiding over this stretch of forsaken country. The Subaru labored over the pothole-strewn red clay path, raising dust so high it nearly wiped out visibility. The crunching of stones beneath the tires drowned out all other noise.

Jostled in the backseat, Sarah and Daniel stoically awaited their fate. Sarah was painfully aware Daniel hadn't looked at her once during the journey. She was certain he couldn't forgive her for throwing Simon off the scent. She wanted to explain but couldn't in the presence of Brehan. What disquieted her most was that she might never have the chance.

Near the top of the mountain, the path disintegrated into a patch of loose gravel.

Brehan stopped the car. "Get out," he barked without bothering to look at them. He tucked a semiautomatic under his arm and marched them down into the canyon.

The sun beat down with soporific heat, and no shadows were cast on the rocky realm. The spires glowed in the early afternoon light, golden fingers reaching toward the turquoise roof of the earth.

With their bound hands throwing them off balance, the prisoners took awkward steps on the descending path. Behind them, Sarah heard the quick steps of their executioner. When they descended to a ledge hanging over the mouth of the deep chasm, he ordered them to walk to the edge.

Sarah winced as she considered his sinister intentions. He would shoot them and let their dead bodies tumble down the canyon, where wolves and bearded vultures would find them. She recognized this as her final, if narrow, window to save their lives.

She spoke in Amharic, not only to endear him but also to ensure there was no misunderstanding. "Brother Brehan, will you grant this doomed soul one last wish?"

"Why should I?" Brehan barked. "Look at me. You did this. Now you pay."

"You are alive. Your brother is dead. You took his life with your own hands. When you were in that labyrinth with your head engulfed in flames, the knife you used to puncture Apostolos' heart lay at his feet. He could so easily have finished it. But he did not. I saw the way he looked at you . . . with the compassion of a true man of God. Even as his own lifeblood trickled from his body, he could not bring himself to harm his own brother. Does that mean nothing to you?"

"You killed him. He put himself in the knife's path to save you." He pointed the gun at her. "Now you will die for your sins."

Sarah let go of every inhibition, every suppressed emotion, every charade of polite society, and spoke. "Money and power will not save you, Brehan. You must believe me. As a monk, you were free. That still is your gift. Do not forsake it for the pleasures of the flesh."

He twitched with discomfort, and she did not relent. "Your brother spared your life because God commanded him to. How can you renounce this

God? Have you no gratitude for the life granted you? Have you no respect for the one who would rather die than forsake you? Enough blood has been spilled. End it, Brehan. Only you have the power. Show Apostolos you are worthy of his sacrifice."

Sarah dropped to her knees and bowed her head. Drops of perspiration fell onto the rock and vanished like raindrops on hot asphalt. For the first time, she resigned herself to death. She was no longer aware of where she was but felt utter peace. Icons from her life flashed in her weary mind's eye: the sun rays filtering through the leaves as she swung under the fig tree in her mother's garden . . . her father putting her on a quarter horse when she was seven . . . her wails of sorrow when she learned of her mother's suicide . . . the sensation of the eternal dust in her hands when she dug for humanity's past even as she tried to escape her own.

A thundering cannonade of gunshots echoed off the canyon walls.

Daniel instinctively cowered to the ground but did not appear hurt. Brehan had either missed or fired the shots in the air.

The monk shouted down at them. "If God wills it, the wolves will find you, and in their jaws you will suffer a slow and miserable death. Your fate is no longer in my hands."

He made his way up the boulders and disappeared over the ridge.

In the ensuing silence, Daniel sat back against a rock and let out a breath. Sweat trickled from his drenched hair into the furrows of his brow and saturated his T-shirt from his neck to his sternum. His eyes moved to and fro, seemingly unable to focus, betraying his agitation.

For her part, Sarah felt surprisingly calm. Her plan was working, at least for the time being. "We got our second chance. I say we make the most of it." She studied the bowl of dust and prehistoric rock for opportunities to escape. "We should get ourselves onto the ridge. Better chance of being seen that way."

"Seen by whom?" His anger was apparent. "The wolves and the jackals? News flash, Sarah: nobody is here. Look around. It's a fucking wasteland." He spat on the ground and groaned.

"Maybe not all is lost. I took a chance back at Matakala's house."

"You can say that again."

"It's not what you think. The reason I called Simon was to give him the SOS."

"What are you talking about?"

"It's something he and my father had put in place ages ago to help each other in times of trouble. Back in the seventies, they had gone stalking for lion in Tanzania—illegally, mind you. A guard for the property owners found my father and detained him at gunpoint. So he radioed his pal Stanley and said the password:

'I do fancy a pint right about now.' It was a benign enough phrase. The guard never suspected it meant he needed to be rescued."

He clenched his jaw and nodded. "That's all well and good, but just knowing we're in trouble doesn't mean they'll find us. Ethiopia is a big place. These mountains are vast and hostile. It would be like looking for an ant in a waterfall."

"Don't forget what Matakala said. Scotland Yard agents are already in Ethiopia looking for us. If Simon does his part, which I'm counting on, they can trace the GPS of where the mobile call came from. That would lead them to this general vicinity."

Daniel shook his head. "That's a lot of *if*s. You do know this is a long shot?"

"I do. But it's the only shot we have. Listen to me, Danny. We can't despair now. It's going to take all our wits to get out of this place."

His voice softened. "I still say this was a gamble."

"Suppose I hadn't rolled the dice. We'd probably be dead already."

He nodded.

They wasted no more time arguing. It was time to move.

By the time they reached the ridge, it was nearly dusk. Their progress up the boulders was slow partly because of their bound hands and partly because of their dwindling energy.

Sarah hadn't eaten a thing in two days, and the relentless heat sapped what little strength remained. At the ridge, she dropped to her knees and exhaled. "I don't know if I can go any farther."

He looked around. "We've got to find some food—before we become food. Surely there's a rabbit or some sort of rodent around here. I'll eat anything at this point."

"And how are you going to kill it, caveman? With your own hands?"

"Remember, I grew up in the backwoods of Tennessee. I can hold my own in the wilderness. I'm going to poke around. You wait here."

"As if I could go anywhere."

She lay on the ground, her face so close to the red earth she could smell the dust of the eons. She gazed at the horizon. Mercifully, the sun was descending behind the ancient spires, casting shadows on the depths of the canyon. Only the tops of the rocks glowed red, like fired iron. The bands of sediment stacked tightly on top of each other like layers of a terrine. Everywhere else the world might have been moving at terminal velocity, but change came to this rocky realm an inch at a time. She liked the thought of that.

She was drifting in the purgatory between sleep and wakefulness when she heard the rustle of firewood. With her eyes still closed, she addressed Daniel. "Are we going to feast on a juicy rat steak? I'd like mine medium rare, please."

"The restaurant was all out of rat. How about roast loin of black chat instead?" He threw two tiny bird carcasses on the ground. "Not much meat on them, but it's the best I could do."

She sat up, stunned. "How the hell did you manage to shoot birds down without a weapon?"

"There was a nest over yonder. These were too young to fly. It was too easy. Their mother will probably hunt me down and peck my eyes out."

Sarah looked at the meager kill. "They'd be great with a spot of truffle oil."

"I knew there was something I forgot to pack," he said, equally deadpan, as he stacked dry sticks for the fire. He split a branch and lay the two pieces side by side, holding them down with rocks on either end. He rubbed pellets of dried goat dung until he exposed the digested grasses, then stuffed it inside the crack between the two branches. With another stick he sawed at a perpendicular angle until he coaxed the first thread of smoke.

Sarah helped by adding dry grass and blowing into the base of the smoke.

The dry wood lit, and Daniel threw the birds directly onto the fire, removing them a minute later to pluck their charred feathers. When all the feathers had burned off, he skewered them on a stick and held them above the flames to roast slowly.

"Voila," he said as he handed Sarah the morsel.

She greedily dug in to the meat and was surprised at the mild taste. She gnawed on the bones, eager for any scrap of nutrition. Afterward, they both lay on the ground and looked at the sky. Thousands of stars and the astral dust swirling around them were visible. Beneath, the dark cliffs undulated like lunar forms forgotten by time. It looked like a snapshot of outer space. Under the monumental panorama, words seemed superfluous.

"Are you worried?" Daniel broke the silence.

She didn't see any need to lie. "A little. What if my father is angry enough to just let me rot in this place?"

"Don't be ridiculous. I'm sure he thinks you were quite valiant to pursue something you believed in. Most people would have abandoned the quest when told to do so. You risked everything for your convictions. Why wouldn't that impress him?"

"You don't know my father. He doesn't impress easily. Not when it comes to me, anyway. I could give him the moon and he'd say, 'What? You couldn't get Venus?'"

"There's no such thing as the perfect daughter, you know."

"Tell him that. I've been wondering what would

be worse—dying here or being rescued and having to face his wrath."

For a few moments, neither of them spoke.

Daniel turned to her. "What was your mother like?"

Sarah didn't expect the question. She didn't speak much about her mother, keeping her memory locked away like antique glass too precious and fragile to handle. As she composed her answer, she felt the familiar knot rise to her throat.

"I'm sorry," Daniel whispered. "That was inconsiderate."

"No," she said, pulling herself together, "it's okay. It's just . . . my mother was my best friend. She was the yin to my father's yang. When he punished me, she would divert my attention with stories of faraway lands and exotic people. And I would imagine myself there, in jungles and deserts, in the company of native people and mythical beasts. To this day, I think her stories are the reason I do what I do." She felt a little embarrassed by her revelation. "I know it sounds corny—"

"Sure as hell does," he said with a chuckle.

"It's funny. She insisted that I play my hand even when I wanted to fold, yet she did not herself have the strength to stay in the game. I'm sure you know all about it."

"Well, the tabloids certainly didn't spare any details."

She cringed at the recollection of her family's private

life splashed all over the gossip media. The press on both sides of the pond had told the story with varying degrees of sensationalism. They wrote about her parents' bitter quarrelling in the months prior to the suicide, even details about the arguments. Somehow reporters knew her parents never could agree on Sarah's education or on money. Her father insisted she receive proper English schooling, while her mother wanted her nearby. Nor could they see eye to eye about money. In the end, Sir Richard cut off his ex-wife, leaving her with no income other than what she earned from her acting jobs, which became scarcer and more insulting as she aged. The combination of his insensitivity and her own lack of self-worth led her to take a bottle full of Valium with a vodka chaser.

Sarah had found her the next morning in the bathtub, her long hair floating amid spent bubbles and her slender, red-tipped fingers still wrapped around a rocks glass.

As those stories became public, Sarah had felt exposed, like everyone's eyes were upon her, judging her for her mother's suicide. *Scandal is always frowned upon in polite society*, her father was in the habit of saying.

Rather than trying to keep up appearances, she had severed herself from that world and walked her own path.

The more solitary, the better.

"It's ancient history." She didn't want Daniel, or anyone for that matter, to pity her. "Tell me about you. What's your family like?"

"What's left of it, you mean? Old man walked out when I was six, so I don't remember much about him. He liked the ladies. Left my mother for a saucy blonde from the West Coast. Never heard from him after that. My mom worked all the time, trying to put food on the table, so my brother and I basically raised ourselves."

"You must be close with your brother."

"Nah. We have nothing in common. He lives in Kentucky, in the backcountry. Works for the electric company, has a bunch of kids. He only calls when he needs money."

"I take it you don't get back home much."

"Not much, no." He sighed. "That's not home for me. No place is, really. I have a small place in Newark, my home base. But I'm basically a wanderer. And a bit of a loner."

At that moment, Sarah felt a deep affection for him. Their backgrounds were as incongruent as the moon and the sun, but life had led them down a similar, solitary path. Their circumstances were different, but she knew they understood each other. "What do you say we get some sleep? We have lots of ground to cover tomorrow."

"You go ahead. I'll keep the fire going. There are wolves out there."

She closed her eyes and listened to the silence of the mountains. Though she couldn't see in the darkness, she could feel his eyes on her. His breath sounded like the ebb and flow of a distant ocean, and warmth radiated from his body. Even here, in this hostile no-man's-land, on the path of unspeakable hidden predators, she felt safe.

The days following Brehan's departure had passed without much progress. As they had every day, Sarah and Daniel started early in the morning when the mountains looked like phantoms, amorphous and cloaked in shadow. The fog was their ally, for it covered the grasses with dew. Even that meager mist was a gift to their parched throats. It was the only water to be had in this arid wasteland, where it hadn't rained in months. The scorched earth of these mountains was one reason foreign armies had stayed out of Ethiopia over centuries of its colonization; the other was the terrain itself, unwelcoming and unforgiving. It was nearly impossible for any creature, save for goats and birds, to negotiate these jagged teeth of rock. One poorly calculated step could send the unfortunate intruder straight into the rocky abyss.

For Sarah and Daniel, the handicap of bound hands and scant food and water made it even more difficult to gain ground. Sarah was beginning to worry they would not be found. Every time she felt the fingers of despair reaching for her throat, she fought to hold on to her ever more tenuous lifeline of hope.

That afternoon, the worst setback came. She felt cramps in her abdomen so severe that she couldn't stand, let alone walk. She knew from experience it wasn't good.

"Dysentery," she said, sweating and weak. "That dodgy water finally caught up to me."

There was alarm in Daniel's eyes. They both knew that, without medical intervention, dysentery was a death sentence. "We'll rest for a couple of days. You're tough. I know you can beat this."

She smiled weakly, her body temperature creeping up as the bug established its presence in her bloodstream. Her mouth was drier than cotton, and her intestines were being twisted by some invisible hand. She had no choice but to rest.

As days passed, she grew weak and gaunt. Dehydrated, her skin shriveled like an old woman's. Her legs could no longer carry her even short distances. She was certain it was the end, and yet among the silent massifs she felt a strange sense of peace. For the first time in her life, she didn't try to make sense of events. There was no real reason to. Their chances of escaping this lonesome wilderness were slim, her chances of survival even slimmer. There was nothing to do but accept that.

When the pain was too intense to bear, she said, "Danny, I need you to hear what I'm saying. I can't make it out of here. You have to go on without me."

"Nonsense. Even if I have to hoist your corpse out of here, I am not leaving you."

"Stop being idealistic about it. I'm asking you for selfish reasons. I want you to get out of here so you can deliver this to UNESCO." She strained to reach into the pocket sewn into the lining of her trousers and pulled out a memory card, letting it drop to the ground.

His eyes widened. "The photos you took in the library? I thought those were lost with everything else."

She laughed. "They never looked inside my trousers. This is our only proof those inscriptions were the prophecies of the tenth saint. Everything else has been destroyed or is in the hands of the enemy."

"I will deliver this to UNESCO with you standing by my side. Look. No principled southern gentleman would abandon a damsel in distress. It's entry number two hundred seven in our code of ethics: never leave a lady to die of diarrhea in a remote mountain."

Smiling, she shook her head.

"Now you wait here. I'm going to see if I can find some firewood and maybe some crickets to eat." He winked at her. "Back in a flash."

Sarah lay on the scant grass and tried to meditate her pain away. In her feverish state, she drifted in and out of consciousness. Her dreams were misshapen but vivid. She saw her father flying on the back of an eagle, swooping in and out of the austere Ethiopian mountains. She stood directly below him waving her arms in a desperate sign of distress, to no avail. He didn't see her and flew away in the other direction. She let out the bloodcurdling cry of the doomed and heard it bounce off the walls of the prehistoric granite amphitheater, amplifying to such a high pitch she covered her ears in horror. In another sequence of images, she saw the scrawny silhouette of a tiny girl. Her white robes flapped like sails in a strong wind, but she stood on a high rock, immoveable, resolute. To Sarah's delirious, impaired mind, it was an omen. She was jarred awake, certain the girl was there.

She saw no one. Not even Daniel.

It felt like ages since he'd left her side. What if he wasn't coming back? Fear gripped her, and she was too weak to fight it. Soaked through with sweat, she trembled as a sudden deep chill penetrated the depths of her flesh and bone. She gathered her knees to her chest to draw on whatever warmth her body would afford her and turned to her side, resting her face on the cool dirt. She heard the squawk of a large bird, some kind of raptor she could not name. It was her last awareness before she passed out.

A roar pierced the silence of the highlands. Through the haze shrouding her vision, Sarah saw the outline of a helicopter hovering above. She lifted her hand feebly, then dropped it.

The violent air current from the rotating blades rushed across her wretched body as the helicopter landed on the plateau.

"You're safe now."

With no small effort, she focused on the man leaning over her.

Daniel wrapped her in a woolen blanket and nodded toward the helicopter. "Scotland Yard. Sir Richard came through after all. Your plan worked, clever girl. It worked better than you know." He lifted her limp body. "Now let's get out of this hellhole."

Seventeen

The *baghlah* arrived in Adulis in the middle of the night. Gabriel had stolen only a few winks of sleep. The air was frigid on the open sea, and the passengers had huddled together for warmth. It made the cold more bearable, to be sure, but sleep was impossible with no personal space, relentless snoring, and the stench of unwashed traveling men.

Gabriel went to the bow and watched the storied port city of Abyssinia approach. He could tell by the bustle of activity, even at such an hour, this place was different from any he'd seen in Arabia. It was prosperous and dynamic and bristled with the promise that any man could be whatever he chose to be if he had the wits and the heart for it. Shivering, he wrapped his blanket tightly around him and inhaled deeply. The air tingled the back of his nose and chilled his throat.

He remembered the feeling from home. It had always reminded him he was alive.

"Don't stand there. Give me a hand," one of the crew shouted as he tossed him a length of rope.

Gabriel resisted the thought that as a paying passenger, he shouldn't have to work on board this ship. The concept was unknown to these people. He said nothing and did what had to be done.

Adulis was remarkably active in the dark of night. Traders negotiated prices for their goods with the local merchants, their voices loud and their tone unassailable. Some men traded gold and ivory; others peddled spices; others sold slaves. The latter practice was particularly appalling to Gabriel, not because he was ignorant of it but because it had never unfolded before his eyes. Strong young lads and beautiful women were displayed on wooden platforms, their ankles bound with iron shackles, while rich Arabians evaluated them for potential servitude. The slaves were serene of countenance and regarded their would-be lords with submissiveness and respect, their fate with acceptance.

After a lifetime of human rights conditioning, Gabriel could not view such a spectacle with tolerance. But as a stranger in this land, he could not make trouble. The notion of freedom and liberation had not hit these shores.

Against his own convictions, he turned away and

kept walking on the road to the mountains whose silhouettes he could barely make out against the starlit sky.

A couple of blocks away, scrawny black men kneeled at the steps of a basalt-hewn church, chanting. He approached the church and inhaled the scent of burning frankincense emanating from the stone halls. The melodic chants of the liturgy, meant to fill the parishioners with the presence of God, floated in the air like a gossamer veil. He recognized a few words of Greek but could tell from the pronunciation it was a bastardized version of the language. He peered inside the structure and saw a priest cloaked in clean white robes, golden embroidered sashes cascading down the front of his dress, as he presided over a blessing ceremony. Behind him were icons of black faces draped with colorful robes and encircled with golden halos, each a protagonist in a biblical scene. On a wooden table sat a filigreed silver cross carved as elaborately as lace. Slim brown beeswax candles burned on a bed of sand. He was surprised to see a Christian ceremony in what he considered heathen lands.

He recalled a few words of the language from that summer he'd spent in the Greek islands, the same summer he'd met Calcedony, and tried his luck on one of the bystanders. Pointing toward the mountains, he asked, "What is there?"

The dark figure nodded but answered in a different

language. Gabriel could not understand a word of it, except for a single name the man kept repeating: "Aksum." That needed no further explanation. Gabriel knew something of the story of the Aksumite kingdom, the great empire connecting Africa and Arabia as a hub for trading between the two continents.

Suddenly the church scene made sense. This was one of the first places beyond the Holy Land to embrace Christianity. He was sketchy on the details but remembered that the religion was brought to those lands by missionary monks and embraced by an Aksumite king who later imposed it on the people. It was sometime in the fourth century, though of the exact dates he was not certain. Still, he knew he was in the ballpark, and that alone was a huge revelation.

For years he had not known where in history's timeline he existed. Knowing where he was and when gave him a point of reference and, as such, an advantage. He waved his thanks to the Adulian and walked toward the mountain.

Gabriel was unsure what awaited him in Aksum, but he had high hopes. He imagined palaces and temples and an air of plenty. People would be civilized there, perhaps even learned. There would be traders and scholars and court ladies draped with beautifully embroidered cloths and gold ornaments. Perhaps the Aksumites would accept him, even listen to what he had to say and preserve it for future generations. His cynical mind, blackened and scarred from loss and despair, slowed him but was not enough to stop him.

When he came to a massive granite obelisk in the road, he knew he was approaching the city. Inscribed in ancient Greek, the language of the Aksumite kings, it must have been a stele of some sort or a monument to an unusually hard-won battle. His knowledge of ancient Greek was limited, but he could make out some words.

I, Ezana king of the Aksumites, son of Ella Amida, servant of Christ the Lord . . . ruler of this kingdom and of all the riches herein and protector of the people. . . . Let those who pass here fear this throne, for it is a symbol of the divine power granted this king by God himself . . .

"King Ezana," Gabriel murmured. "Let's hope he is more tolerant than he is humble."

By nightfall the next day, he reached the ridge above the city and looked upon the ghostly labyrinth of stone structures beneath. He knew this was the place of his dreams, the place Hairan had told him he must come to at all costs. On a hill away from the center was perched an imposing fortress, its granite ramparts illuminated by torchlight. The palace. King Ezana's lair.

Gabriel started to descend into the city. When he heard the howl of wolves, the cacophony of calls surrounding him, he thought better of it. His chances of avoiding an attack in full moonlight were slim. He ducked into a hollow in the granite and was pleased to discover it was the mouth of a cave that cut deep into the mountainside.

A shaft of moonlight faintly illuminated his passage as he crawled inside. The ground was slippery, the air acrid, and he wondered how long before the bats would return from their nocturnal adventures to claim their home. Determining he had until daybreak, he chose a smooth lean-to and passed what was left of the night.

Eighteen

The bedroom of her childhood was just as Sarah remembered. The heavy curtains of Wedgwood blue and yellow chintz were tied back with huge navy silk tassels, framing a picture window toward the west lawn. The morning light shimmered across the Tuscan-style reflecting pool her father had installed as a gift to her mother after a particularly memorable trip to Italy. Her bed was draped in blue and yellow–striped fabric and crowned with a canopy of the same chintz of the curtains, lined with yellow silk gathered to a rosette in the center. The linen sheets, pressed to a perfect knife-edge by the laundry staff, brought back memories of sleeping late on the weekends in the comfort of her crisp, warm cocoon.

She hadn't slept in that bed since her visits home from university. After her mother's death, she had found it too painful to be in Coddington Manor for any length of time. It was full of memories: gardening with Mum on spring mornings, taking long strolls together in the surrounding hillside, watching her cook the Sunday roast as she always insisted on doing despite the cook's protests. For Sarah, the place no longer had the same meaning. Without her mother's warmth, it was a shell of privilege and nothing more.

Sir Richard walked into the room without knocking and approached Sarah's bed. He looked his usual dapper self. Standing at six feet two, he had a slim frame that gave him an aristocratic elegance. His thin, golden-brown hair was parted in the middle and combed back in orderly rows. He wore his tennis whites and his fair face was flushed, indicating he'd just come off the court.

"Well, good morning, young lady." His voice was clear and loud with the standard measure of pomp. "At last you are awake. You've been sleeping the past two days, you know. Gave us quite a scare."

"I feel awful, Daddy." Her words came out coarse and crumpled, as if they had been locked away too long in a trunk of disuse. "What's happened?"

"What's happened is you were on death's door, my girl. You had—well, have, really—a frightful case of dysentery, dehydration, and a nasty lung infection. You're not out of the woods yet." He nodded toward an IV drip she hadn't noticed. "Very powerful antibiotics, those. You'll be on the mend in no time."

Sarah turned her aching head slowly in the direction of the west-facing window. How different the Wiltshire countryside was to the harsh Ethiopian landscape that had become her world. She regretted how wrong things had gone.

"Now suppose you tell me how you got into that sticky situation in the first place."

She felt the weight of his judgment, but it seemed insignificant after all she'd been through. There was no reason to hold anything back. She told him the whole truth, starting with her defection to Yemrehana Krestos and ending with their kidnapping and near execution. Sir Richard listened intently, quietly taking it all in but obviously making mental notes for the interrogation Sarah fully expected. By the time she finished her narration, she was winded.

"Something is not clear. Why would a brilliant archaeologist who's been the star of such a fine institution as Cambridge defy the wishes of her superiors and go off on a wild-goose chase? Please do explain this to me, Sarah, because for the life of me I don't understand."

"I wouldn't expect you to. You never have."

"Well, considering I have just imposed on Her Majesty's government to intervene in Anglo-Ethiopian relations and have enlisted the services of Scotland

Yard agents in order to rescue you from a situation you could have and should have avoided, I would say you owe me at least this."

"You were an explorer once," she said, trying to explain in terms he could understand. "Surely you didn't do it for academic glory or because Her Majesty's government asked you to. You understood there was something finer, something beyond weekend hunts and cocktail chatter, and you went looking for it, fully expecting that no knowledge worth having would come easy. Finding the truth is a journey, a risky one. You taught me that, if only by your actions."

Before he had a chance to reply, his cell phone rang. He picked up, murmured something into the receiver, and quickly hung up. "Urgent business, I'm afraid. I must be off. But do know this conversation is not over."

"I hope not. I've got much more to say to you."

"I've asked Daniel Madigan to come for dinner. He will be driving in from London this afternoon. He has been asking after you every day. If you ask me, the chap seems quite taken by you. You should feel honored."

The thought of Daniel's visit pleased Sarah. She was eager to thank him. Encouraged by the powerful meds, she let herself fall into sleep's embrace.

When Sarah opened her eyes, Daniel was sitting on the edge of her bed. He looked so different now that he had shaven, combed his long locks into a ponytail, and put on respectable clothes. More like a civilized American scholar than the dusty field scientist she had grown accustomed to.

She abruptly sat up. Almost ripping the IV out, she lunged into his arms.

They embraced for a long time.

"You sure look better than you did a week ago," he said.

"Oh, stop it. I look a fright." Suddenly self-conscious, she tried to straighten her wayward curls. "How are you?"

"Happy to be alive. We owe your dad a big debt of gratitude. This was no small rescue operation, apparently."

"I imagine you boys discussed it over gin-tonics already."

He winked. "That's what we boys do. Long story short, they traced the call you placed to Stan Simon and learned the mobile phone was registered to a Mr. Amanuel Abombo, apparently a deliveryman in Addis. They researched Abombo and found that he once had very shady connections to the Chinese mob. Old boy helped them move some weapons illegally, it seems.

The agents informed him he was under arrest for his crimes and his sentence would be far more lenient if he cooperated. He sang like a lark."

"What was his connection to Matakala?"

"There was no direct connection to Matakala. Abombo knew Brehan. Guess he'd lined up some ladies for him during his trips to Addis."

"So they found Brehan?"

"Yes, in northwestern Somalia. Apparently, our friend was running from his demons and trying to start over. So in exchange for amnesty and bodily protection, he gave Scotland Yard a detailed description of where he dropped us. And here we are."

"Where is he now?"

"Under surveillance in Mogadishu. He was reluctant to talk about his superiors. Wanted a new identity, a place in London, and two million quid in exchange for his confession. From what I gathered from your dad, he's likely to get it, too."

"Daddy says you've been in London. What are your plans?"

"I've been thinking about that. My bosses want me to return to Saudi Arabia pronto. We lost one of our key archaeologists, and everyone's out there chasing their tails. Apparently the excavation in al-Fau has yielded a new set of frescoes detailing the tombs of a walled city and they need me to lead the charge."

Reality suddenly stood like a concrete wall in

front of Sarah. Their time together, however intense, had been a brief diversion. Now they would have to tend to old responsibilities and new assignments. Life in the trenches would carry on as it always had. She tried to be stoic about it. "Yes, of course. When will you leave?"

"I've put the trip on hold for a couple of weeks. There's a small matter I must attend to before I go. In ten days, I'm scheduled to speak before the UNESCO archaeological panel in Paris. They want my report on the Aksum expedition." From his pocket, he pulled out the memory card she'd given him when she'd thought she wouldn't make it out of Ethiopia. "I need to know what you want to do about this."

"I know exactly what I want."

"I know you do. But I want you to think about something. That forum will be attended by all of academia, including your colleagues from Cambridge. Word on the street is they're not very happy with you right now. This will only add fuel to their fire. Are you sure you're up to it?"

"I've never been more sure about anything. Gabriel inscribed his message on the rock because he wanted it to be found. I can't let it end with me. I need to be his instrument, to let him talk through me, whatever the consequences."

Daniel looked at her tenderly. "You know something? When I first met you, I thought, here we go.

Another overindulged, undersexed British ice queen who wants to own the world but never will because she's got a chip on her shoulder the size of Kentucky." He shook his head. "Boy, was I wrong about you. You actually have a passion for the work. You follow through on your convictions. That's more than I can say about anyone else in this business."

She tossed back her hair, letting her curls spill over one shoulder, and smiled wickedly. "You really thought I was undersexed?"

"You're darn right I did."

She leaned in and whispered, "You were right."

Their eyes met, and he kissed her. She let herself be swept into the moment, but her father's decisive knock and announcement that supper would be served put a rude end to it.

Sarah slowly pulled away. "You'd better go."

"Guess you won't be joining us, huh?"

"I'm not up to it. Besides, I don't think he cares for my company right now."

He kissed her hand. "You leave Sir Richard to me. I'll see you in Paris."

Nineteen

By the early light of day, the city of Aksum looked astonishingly progressive to Gabriel's weary eyes. The town sprawled for miles, occupying a vast tract stretching from the town center to the distant hillsides. The houses away from town were the most elaborate, constructed with uniform square stones fitted with loose concrete mortar. Doors were made of heavy wood planks held together with iron studs, and windows were covered with shutters to keep out the cold. The wealthy inhabitants of the outer realms lived in compounds, with several buildings clustered together, each dedicated to a different function, such as cooking or washing or sleeping.

Gabriel walked past one such compound on his way to the town's commercial core. Even at the dawn hour, the house was stirring. He saw three slave girls bent over a wood fire, preparing food for the families. The smoke was redolent of juniper, at once sharp and sweet: the smell of the mountains. A young man, possibly one of the sons, stood by the doorway thumbing a string of blue glass beads. He was dressed in immaculate white linen, his shoulders draped with a block-printed cape obviously imported from the lands to the east.

Gabriel tried to avoid his gaze. He knew he looked like a stranger with his overgrown ruddy beard, fair skin, and clothing identifying him with the Arabian peninsula. Wearing indigo to everyone else's white, he stood out like a singular sapphire in a sea of pearls. Where the locals were scrubbed clean and neat of dress, he looked like a beggar. His Bedouin robes were tattered, and his face was black with a combination of grime, sweat, and guano. He smelled like he felt: filthy, beaten, old. He kept his head and gaze low and his arms tucked to appear meek.

The young man called to him.

Gabriel did not comprehend the language. He replied in the Bedouin dialect. "What is this place, kind master?"

The boy twisted his face into a look of contempt and uttered a few more words.

Gabriel did not want a confrontation. He waved and walked away, continuing the trek into the town center. He followed a cobbled path to the inner quarter, where buildings were modest and built so near one could hear the whispers of one's neighbors. The masonry was rough, nothing like the dwellings of the gentry, and roofs were covered with thatch.

The places of worship, however, were impressive. The first building Gabriel came to was a magnificent church carved entirely of stone with keyhole openings for windows and a carved iron door. The structure was almost Byzantine with its clay-tiled dome roof crowned by a simple wooden cross. Its stonemasonry was near flawless and must have taken the craftsmen years to construct, considering their limited tools and resources. He could not resist the urge to go inside. Though he was known to no one and clearly of a different tribe, he suspected Coptic Christians would show tolerance and compassion for all souls, regardless of color or culture.

The church interior was divided into small chambers, each decorated with murals of saints and the Christ, their eyes gleaming in the soft yellow light of the candelabra. The stones were polished smooth and smelled faintly of smoke and incense. Encouraged by the fact that he was alone, Gabriel kneeled before the altar in gratitude that he had come this far. He prayed for nothing, for it was not his custom to pray. He believed in the divine unseen, that which he called God, but he did not tie his faith to an accepted method of worship or to scriptures. He trusted only what he felt, and at that moment he felt the presence of God inside him.

And he felt loss. A dull ache from an old wound

that had never healed right. He inhaled deeply and let the sensation fill him. It wasn't sadness anymore, just an awareness of the impermanent nature of all things. The divine order that his contemporaries had tried at all costs to manipulate and vanquish and that he had come to appreciate only when everything had been stripped from him. He sat with his palms open and pointing in the direction of the sky, ready to receive whatever would come.

The Aksumites were an industrious but fraternal people. They knew prosperity, for trade flourished in their kingdom. Though they could only grow wheat and teff in the granite mountains of the highlands, they had the means to buy what they lacked and the skill to make the rest. The biggest benefit of being at the heart of the world's most important trade route was that they came in contact with Romans, Arabs, Egyptians, and Nabateans and brought away something from each.

Prosperity had carried with it greed and a class system Gabriel had not encountered on the east side of the Red Sea. The nomad societies were different in that regard. They coexisted and respected each other and the laws of the land. In this place, the class societies of the West were taking root and, with them, the conflicts and injustices bred by inequality. But there was also charity. Those with plenty hired and fed those who had nothing. Gabriel didn't know whether to attribute that to the Christian faith these people had embraced, but he was thankful for it.

The local blacksmith, Hallas, took pity on him and let him work at his shop, shoveling iron filings into the cauldrons and hammering molten metal into everything from spears to cooking pots in exchange for a plate of food. More importantly, he taught him enough of the local language that they could communicate.

After a day's hard work, Gabriel sat down to a meal with Hallas and his sons. The blacksmith spooned sticky millet porridge onto a tin plate and topped it with two chunks of overcooked sheep's meat. "It's not as good as my wife made, but it fills the belly." Hallas guffawed. His laughter turned to a nasty cough, likely a side effect of years of inhaling fine iron particles and soot.

"Where's your wife, then?"

Hallas didn't bother to stop chewing before speaking. "Dead. Died when she gave birth to this one." He pointed to his youngest son, a wide-eyed boy of about twelve.

"I'm sorry."

The blacksmith shrugged. "It's life."

At the end of the meal, Hallas offered his new worker a straw bed next to his sons'. Even though it was the warmest bed in town, Gabriel declined politely. He did not want to take advantage of the blacksmith's generosity, and anyway he craved the time alone. He bade his hosts good night and started the long trek up the hillside to the cave that had given him shelter the first night.

When the bats left, rising by the thousands from their granite womb like souls departing, he entered what he had come to know as his sanctuary. Warming himself and meditating by the meager flames of a campfire, he found peace among the stones. Even the wolves' cries had come to feel familiar, like long-lost friends calling him home.

On the long days of winter, Gabriel was most grateful for his work at the smithy. The copious fires of the furnace and the exertion of manipulating molten metal drenched him in sweat while frosty winds howled outside. On one of those dreary days, the messenger of the king came. The crimson-robed captain on horseback summoned Hallas, and the blacksmith kneeled before the noble visitor.

Without dismounting, the captain delivered his decree. "Now hear this. Ezana, king of kings, most pious and just ruler of Aksum, calls upon the blacksmith Hallas to forge armor for five thousand men who have been called to war. It must take no longer than the end of winter to complete this task, for on the first day of spring the king and his army ride for Meroë to battle the great enemy to the north. You will make the archetype of this armor and bring it to the palace. If it pleases the king, you will be paid two gold coins and, when the king returns from war victorious, twenty more." He raised his right arm to the sky. "Praise be to God. Long live the king."

"Long live the king," Hallas repeated. "This humble servant of the king is honored to be appointed with so important a task and pledges to serve His Lordship dutifully."

The captain rode toward the palace, and Hallas whooped with delight. His sons gathered round and lifted him off his feet in congratulations.

Gabriel observed them, smiling. Twenty gold coins was a lot of money, enough for Hallas to retire and his sons to marry very well.

Hallas proclaimed an end to the workday and ordered his younger son to fetch wine and tobacco, two luxuries reserved for only the most important occasions. The blacksmith beckoned Gabriel to join them in celebration of their fortune.

"Tonight, we drink to the king," Hallas said. "The great and generous Ezana has smiled upon us."

"To the king," his sons said in unison.

Gabriel raised his glass. "And to the man who won the king's favor."

It pleased him to see the three men in such high

spirits. They were simpleminded and honest, never complaining about a brutal day's work. They accepted their lot in life, never challenging or detesting it. And now, it seemed, they were rewarded for every ounce of hard labor and every iron filing they had swallowed in the line of duty.

Hallas gulped his wine until the glass was empty. "Gabriel, my friend, you will help us, and for this you will be paid not only in food but in gold."

"I am happy to help you, friend, but you need not pay me. Keep it for your family."

"I insist. If you do not accept, you are no longer in my employ."

Gabriel laughed at the dramatic proclamation and accepted the pipe from the eldest son. The tobacco was sweet and smooth, but it made him nostalgic for the camel dung he'd once smoked with Da'ud. He exhaled the smoke skyward as an offering. *May you know peace, old friend.*

A fortnight later, the armor and weapons were ready and Hallas prepared the horses for the ride to the palace. Gabriel carried the pieces to the stables and helped Hallas tie them down to the saddles. There were swords, long and short, spears, helmets, body armor, and shields of varying sizes. All told, they loaded four horses, one for each of them.

The horses' hooves clopped rhythmically on the cobblestones as the four rode to the fortress on the rock at the edge of the city. The many trees lining the stone path were barren and covered in snow, but the brisk air carried the scent of renewal.

"Whoa there." Hallas, who was leading the line, called to his fellow riders to halt their horses.

They had reached the palace gates. A massive wooden door as tall as four men swung open, and the guards bade them pass into the courtyard.

Gabriel had never entered the realm of a king before, for in his time there were no kings, only men who bought or stole power. In fact, he found the entire concept rather tiresome and the idea of bowing before a mortal man offensive to his Western sensibilities. But this was not his world to judge, so he reminded himself to observe silently and follow the others' lead.

When the king entered the chambers, all bowed so deeply their hair brushed the floor. Gabriel shrank as best he could, trying to blend with the Aksumites as much as his strange appearance would allow. His facial hair, now matted beyond any hope of untangling, and the permanent soot on his hands and face helped—but anyone who took a second look would know he was foreign. His goal was to stay in the background.

King Ezana was a giant of a man, dressed in indigo and red robes draped elaborately around his considerable shoulders and cinched at the waist with a thick belt of leather from which dangled the incisors of lions. Around his neck he wore a golden Coptic cross the size of a man's palm. His head was covered with a tall fez whose wide crown was draped with chains of silver and gold. His skin was dark as night, his features chiseled and fine as a Roman's, his cheekbones high, jaw strong, nose curved like a raptor's, and eyes fierce with ambition. But his most distinct characteristic was his canine teeth, both made of solid gold. The king cut an imposing figure. Despite his contempt for royalty, Gabriel found himself in awe of the raw power manifest in the absolute ruler of these people.

Ezana sat on the throne at the far end of the chamber and stared stone-faced at the assembly of panoply that had been laid before him. A lanky man with shaven head and military dress approached the throne and sifted through the armor, scrutinizing its quality so he could properly advise the king.

Gabriel looked at Hallas and his sons. All three wore the look of dread, as if at any moment the king would approach and give them ten lashings for presenting His Divine Majesty with such inconsequential rubbish.

No such thing happened. Ezana listened to all the criticism of his advisor—"the swords aren't heavy enough, the helmets are weak at the base"—but didn't deliver his own verdict until he walked to the equipment and examined it himself. He swung the swords with the skill of an accomplished warrior and checked their blades with a leather-gloved hand. He inspected every shin guard, every helmet, and the point of every spear before laying down his decision.

"Our enemies in Meroë ought to fear us," he bellowed. "The men of Aksum ride to battle at first snowmelt. And victory will be ours, God willing. This fine armor will serve us well." He called to his advisor. "Laloum, compensate these men for their trouble."

Hallas and his sons beamed with relief. It was a dream come true for them, and it pleased Gabriel to know their lives' efforts would finally be rewarded. But the happy scene did not last long.

A lady of the court burst through the door in tears. "My lord, come quickly. It's Aria . . . She was chasing birds and fell into the fountain. She's not breathing."

"The king's youngest daughter," Hallas whispered to Gabriel. He crossed himself. "God protect her."

Ezana and his guards and advisors exited the chamber in haste. Gabriel, Hallas, and the boys followed.

As the king made for his daughter's bedside, Laloum organized the troops. He instructed one of the guards to ride double-time into town to fetch a doctor, asked a group of court ladies to ready smelling salts and compresses, and ordered another group to pray and chant for the girl's recovery.

Gabriel knew he shouldn't intervene, but he couldn't stand by when a child's life was in danger. He knew his skill was greater than these people imagined and that he had a shot at saving her life. If she had drowned, every minute was valuable. By the time a doctor got there, all could be lost.

"I am a medic," he told Laloum. "I can help the child."

Hallas shook his head, horrified. "No, no, no. Gabriel, you should not do this. Leave it to those who know."

Gabriel waved him off and steeled his voice. "Please, Excellency. I beg you. Let me try. I lost a son once. I cannot bear this to happen to another father."

Laloum stared at him with cold raven eyes, his jaw tight with distrust. "If you are lying, God help me, I will kill you with my own hands."

Gabriel lowered his head. "Please, for the love of God. I must go to the child."

Laloum gestured for Gabriel to follow him.

In the bedchamber, the queen was hysterical over the girl's limp body. A coterie of women were running about like mad, opening windows to let in cold air, fanning the child and loosening her clothes.

Laloum ran to the king's side and relayed Gabriel's proposition. The king nodded, and the advisor led Gabriel to the girl.

The girl's chest wasn't moving. Gabriel checked

her mouth for breathing. Nothing. When he put his ear to her chest, he heard only the rapid thump of his own heartbeat. The girl's heart had stopped. He gestured to everyone to make room.

Though it had been years since he had last tried to resuscitate, he remembered just what to do. He gently pumped the ball of his palm on her chest until the water had been expelled, then tilted her head back and blew air into her lungs. Begging God to give him the power to save the girl, he thought of his own son, lying lifeless in his arms as the raging fires filled their home with smoke. He repeated the motions until he thought he heard a faint heartbeat and, encouraged, kept at it.

The town doctor arrived, rushing to little Aria's side and ordering the stranger away, but Gabriel continued, convinced he was breaking through. The doctor, however, would have none of it and pushed Gabriel to the ground.

At the sound of his body hitting the floor, the girl half opened her eyes.

Everyone looked at her, astonished. The queen let out a squeal and threw her arms around her daughter. The ladies of the court crossed themselves and directed their eyes toward the ceiling.

"She is well," the doctor proclaimed, as if he had restored her life. "Aria lives."

The king walked to Gabriel, who still lay on the

floor on his side, and offered his hand. Gabriel took it and let Ezana pull him to his feet. The two men's eyes met for a second before Gabriel diverted his gaze to the ground, surprised at how intimidated he felt.

Ezana squeezed Gabriel's shoulder with a strength befitting his prowess. "What you have done here, I have never seen. I don't know who you are, white stranger, but you have a gift. You have the power of healing."

Gabriel couldn't find the words. His heart raced, chasing all thought out of his brain. He just stood there, nodding nervously.

Ezana took Gabriel's bearded chin in his palm and, with a strong grip, turned his face to and fro. "Do you come from Rome? Who are your people?"

Gabriel spoke in a hushed tone, self-conscious and aware that every eye in the room was upon him. "I come from the West, my lord. But I have not lived there for a very long time. My life was in the Rub' al Khali . . . with Bedouin nomads."

"What is your name?"

"Gabriel, my lord."

"Do you believe in God, Gabriel?"

"I do, my lord."

"That is good." He nodded and turned to the gathered masses. "God has worked his miracle here today. God has spoken to us through this man." He pointed to Gabriel. "Remember the name Gabriel. From this day forward, I, Ezana, son of Ella Amida, servant of God and the Lord Jesus, conqueror of all empires, and king of kings, hereby proclaim Gabriel of Arabia my personal doctor and advisor."

Gabriel was stunned at the proclamation. "But, my lord—"

Ezana silenced him with a raise of his massive paw. "Laloum. See that Gabriel has the proper armor. He will ride with us to Meroë and serve as the medicine man of our military regimen. With him at our side, no enemy can defeat us." He waved his fist in the air. "The might of Aksum will crush all who stand against us."

The king's men stomped with a ceremonial cadence to show their approval of the king's sentiments and their readiness to take on any enemy. Ezana dismissed everyone and stayed with his wife at Aria's side.

Gabriel wrapped his robes around his neck and head and threw his blanket over his shoulders. The bitter winter wind hissed through the bare trees and over the rooftops. Unsure of what had just happened and what it would ultimately mean to him, he sank into deep thought as he rode toward his cave.

By the time he arrived, he was shivering with a chill that penetrated his bones. He stacked dry kindling and rubbed two stones together to make a spark. The kindling crackled with the first flame. He blew into his cupped hands to warm them, then placed a juniper log atop the smoking pile.

His thoughts turned to war, the hand of anxiety churning his insides like a well handle. He imagined fire and destruction, spears bending, men wailing, and blood spilling. He lowered his head into his hands. "Let it be swift."

Gabriel inhaled the sweet scent of the burning wood. He reached for the flint, the same one Da'ud had given him in the caves of Qumran so long ago, the only thing that remained from his desert sojourn, and used it to scratch at the granite walls of the cave's inner chamber. Hairan's parting words echoed in his memory: *What you carry inside you, you must take to the great kingdom. And there you shall leave it.*

And so he did.

Twenty

Sarah felt the nerves in her stomach as she mentally reviewed her presentation. The UNESCO crowd was never an easy one to please. From her corner of the cavernous hall she surveyed the amphitheatre in which the audience of scientists and academics sat, their faces stern and unyielding under the fluorescent lights. She knew their kind well. Each one was a skeptic, a predator ready to pounce at the slightest misstep.

She picked out her toughest critic. Stan Simon looked sour as usual stuffed into a battered gray tweed jacket whose sleeves stopped a good two inches above his wrists, his neck bound by a navy blue paisley bow tie: the uniform. With pursed lips, he looked at Sarah. His eyes, narrowed in concentration or maybe contempt, looked like buttonholes behind his round eyeglasses. She read a warning in his gaze: *Don't screw this up. Don't embarrass Cambridge. Don't make waves.*

She anxiously looked at her watch. In twenty minutes, it would be their turn at the podium.

As if reading her mind, Daniel bent to whisper in Sarah's ear. "I want you to own this room. You can do it."

Something about the honeyed tone of his voice set her instantly at ease. She slipped her hand into the crook of his arm. He wore a navy Brooks Brothers blazer, slim jeans, and a yellow silk tie he'd bought at a thrift store. His shoulder-length hair was pulled back into a ponytail, a few errant tendrils framing his bronze face. He was at once professional and defiant, very much his own man.

It seemed an eternity before the chairman called Sarah to the podium. Adrenaline flushed her face as she regarded the austere expressions before her. She began with the requisite verbal genuflecting that funding bodies liked to hear, opened her laptop to begin the visual presentation, and delivered the words she had chosen ever so carefully.

"As some of you may know, the Aksum expedition has been both stellar and harrowing. You learned from our reports that the initial months of the project yielded only clues to the massive royal necropolis that we are convinced lies beneath the ground. We have found tools, coins, pottery shards, and ammunition dating to the fourth century.

"As important as these artifacts are, however, it is

another unexpected and most unusual find that captured our attention. On the fifth of August, I happened upon a cave carved into the mountains above the high plateau of Aksum. Inside that cave, which came to be known as Cave I, was a coffin, a simple acacia box containing what may be the most intriguing and important find of this century.

"The man buried in this coffin was at first a mystery: a tall Caucasian male with teeth as perfectly straight and well cared for as yours and mine, if not more so. When we had the bone tested, we confirmed it dated to the fourth century, very near the time during which the Aksum necropolis was erected. But the stature of this man, his sheer size and the fact that he was Caucasian, to say nothing of his perfect dentition, suggested otherwise.

"When we had a thin section of the teeth tested, we discovered something even more intriguing: a filling substance found in the mandibular second molar on the left side tested negative for any known dental material. The polymer used in this tooth was a hard, organic molded plastic, a substance never used in any dental procedures, past or present. What's more, the molecular composition of this material did not match the composition of any plastic known thus far to science. Could the dentists of the fourth century have known something we don't? It's possible but not likely, particularly since plastic itself was not invented until the nineteenth century. I stress this point deliberately and respectfully ask the distinguished panel to take note of it, as it is an important clue to what is shaping up as one of late antiquity's greatest enigmas and one that very much affects us to this day.

"But there is another component of equal consequence. Inside the tomb was a chamber whose walls were inscribed in an obscure language that was neither spoken nor written in Aksum or elsewhere in Abyssinia. This gave us further proof the man was not an Aksumite but rather a pilgrim from another region who had traveled to the remote mountain kingdom for reasons that perhaps would be explained by the inscriptions.

"After exhaustive testing and consultations with linguists, we discovered the text was written in an ancient dialect spoken by tribal peoples of the Syro-Arabian peninsula from the third century BCE to about the fourth century CE. These estimates are just that, however, because this language was of extremely limited scope and so few examples of it exist.

"So why would these texts be written in a tribal dialect? Who was this man? And, more importantly, what did the inscriptions say? These are all questions to which we found astonishing answers. Answers that almost cost the lives of my colleague, Daniel Madigan, and myself and have indeed cost the lives of several innocent Ethiopians who fell while defending an ancient secret whose time had come.

"Now I would like to turn the floor over to Dr. Madigan, who will outline this expedition's findings as relates to the Cave I Tomb."

Daniel walked to the center of the stage, eschewing the microphone and the Plexiglas podium. Sarah knew his reputation for making himself accessible to audiences and his talent for distilling complex concepts to their most relevant essence. It was his trademark quality and a brilliant one. It had won over both intransigent scientists and the mass public. She was counting on that very quality to get the attention of this panel.

"Thank you," Daniel began. "Incidentally, Dr. Weston is one of the finest scientists I have ever worked with. The tenacity she displayed during the Aksum expedition and, more specifically, while decoding the Cave I Tomb mystery is something of an endangered species in our business."

Sarah was taken aback. She hadn't expected any sort of validation, but the fact that it had come from Daniel was significant.

"When Dr. Weston and I were researching the content of the tablets, we called on a renowned linguist in Addis Ababa who specialized in South and West Semitic and East African languages. Rada Kabede, an Ethiopian man, recognized the dialect used to inscribe the tablets but did not have the knowledge to decipher it. He did say, however, that it was one of seven depicted on a monument called the Sheba Stone.

"While the Sheba Stone has been in existence since the first century, there are very few known references to it. Apparently, this ten-foot-high monolith was inscribed during the time of the Queen of Sheba in what is present-day Yemen to recount the queen's life and heroic deeds. The stone, Mr. Kabede told us, was said to reside in a remote monastery outside the town of Lalibela and was known only to the monks assigned to guard it.

"That was one of the last things Mr. Kabede said to us or to anybody, for that matter. He was found dead in his office a few days later, apparently the victim of a shooting by assailants who to this day remain at large.

"That was the first murder associated with the Cave I Tomb, though at the time we were not fully aware of the motives. The second wave of killings came on the night of October twelfth, when a group of assailants entered the monastery of Yemrehana Krestos, killed innocent monks, and destroyed the Sheba Stone.

"If you read the *International Herald Tribune*, you may have seen a two column-inch article on page six. Hardly headline news. And yet, in the sleepy town of Lalibela, such senseless carnage had never been known. Dr. Weston was there that night." Daniel paused at that critical point.

Daniel let the weight of his words sink in. The audience was silent, riveted. He went on.

"The guardian of the Sheba Stone died in Dr. Weston's arms as a result of a fatal wound by one of the attackers. As he uttered his last words, he told her of a secret document, a codex that contained the information we were seeking. That document, he said, was hidden within the catacombs of the church in a chamber known only to the chosen.

"It took my colleague's considerable investigative powers to discover the passageway that led us into the catacombs and the remarkable library of scrolls and lighted manuscripts contained therein, a library known to no one except a handful of religious scholars.

"Without going into too much detail, let me just say that we found the codex to which the monk was referring and, to our astonishment, it was a translation in ancient Greek of the Cave I Tomb inscriptions. I will explain later who this monk was and his connection to the inscriptions, but before I do I want you to be the first to hear the words written by the mysterious man in the Cave I Tomb."

Daniel read the English translation and projected the photos of the codex that they had managed to smuggle out of Ethiopia. The room was quieter than the death chambers of antiquity. With the urgent tone of an evangelist, he read the final lines: "And thus the race of men will become extinct. Take heed, children of God, for if you can read this, it is not too late."

His theatrical delivery did not go unrewarded. The room came alive with whispers and commotion. The chairman, sitting in the center of the assembly's first row, stood and banged his gavel to call for order.

Daniel continued. "The man I referred to earlier, a lifelong monk named Apostolos, was more than the guardian of the Sheba Stone. He was chosen to guard the secret of the tenth saint on behalf of Apocryphon, a brotherhood dating back to the sixth century and the time of Ethiopia's Tsadkan: the nine saints of Christianity. Apostolos was the direct descendant of Abba Aregawi, the saint who discovered the tomb of Gabriel and translated the inscriptions. Apostolos was the only person in the world who knew where the translations were and, rather than let that knowledge die with him, he entrusted Sarah Weston with it.

"That is how we came upon the tenth saint's sanctification cross and the codex detailing his final warning to the people of this earth. Relics that we no longer possess because they have since fallen into the hands of criminals."

After recounting the ordeal, first at Matakala's house and later on the remote reaches of the Simien Mountains, Daniel wrapped up his presentation like a star lawyer delivering his closing arguments.

"Let us weigh the facts: The man inside the Cave I Tomb was dated to the fourth century, yet neither his stature nor his characteristics fit the profile of a fourth-century man. The dental material found in his teeth is a substance as of yet unknown to science. The inscriptions speak of an apocalyptic event that this man supposedly witnessed.

"But who was this Gabriel? Was he, as the Ethiopian legend would have it, the tenth saint of Abyssinia? Was he a prophet? Were these insights dealt to him by a divine force? And who were the other two to whom he refers?

"The Cave I Tomb mystery is not wholly revealed to us. Science can only give us part of the answer. The rest, we may never know. But we cannot ignore what has been laid before us. It is not only a piece of history, but it may well be a piece of history in the making, a history we have yet to witness.

"This expedition may be temporarily shuttered by the Ethiopians, but we cannot drop our claim on a find this promising. As a consultant to this esteemed body, I hereby recommend that the funding of the Aksum expedition continue and be expanded to encompass more research on the Cave I Tomb and the true identity of the tenth saint. Thank you very much."

Almost immediately the barrage of questions

came from both the panelists and the press. After a period that seemed endless to Sarah, the conference broke.

"Let's get out of here," she said to Daniel, taking his arm and leading him out of the room. "Where are you staying?"

He smiled. "In a hotel about an hour out of the city. What about you?" He held the door open for her as they exited the building.

"I'm at the Plaza Athénée," she said as she hailed a taxi. "It's nice and quiet there. I'm desperate to get away from this circus."

The taxi delivered them to the Plaza, and they headed up the elevator to her suite. It was an apartment-sized room with nineteenth-century-style furnishings and lavish red accents. One of the windows framed a view of the Eiffel Tower, illuminated against the dusky sky.

He scanned the room. "Nice place you have here. Is that champagne in that bucket?"

Sarah raised an eyebrow. "Quite right. I was hoping we'd have reason to celebrate. Care to do the honors?"

Daniel poured two glasses of Dom Pérignon Rosé and raised his glass in a toast. "To the lady of the hour."

She pointed her glass to him. "No. To you. You were amazing back there. To tell the truth, I'm a little nervous about how the press will present this. You know I'm not on the best of terms with reporters. But whatever happens in the end, I am content for having done the right thing." She touched her glass to his, the vibrating crystal chiming. "I couldn't have gone down that road without you, Danny."

Daniel put his glass down and stood close enough to her that she could feel the warmth of his breath. He placed his hands on her neck and slowly moved the tips of his fingers across her collarbone and down to her décolleté.

She trembled with the sensation.

"Don't you think we've talked enough for one day? The only thing on my mind right now is you." His gaze locked with hers, and she parted her lips to say something. No words came out. He slowly unbuttoned her blouse.

Her heart pounded. In Africa, she had not allowed herself to acknowledge her attraction to him. Any emotional involvement would only have complicated things. But now that he stood before her, confessing his desire, she could no longer deny her own. In his arms, Sarah felt perfectly present and at peace. No one had ever made love to her like this, nor had she ever returned the favor.

Breathless, Daniel rolled onto his back. "Lady, you are a hellcat."

She laughed. "Hey, you reap what you sow. And

it gets better. Wait till you see what tomorrow brings." Smiling, she kissed his shoulder.

He propped himself on his elbow and stroked her hair, gazing into her eyes. "Sarah, when you asked me earlier where I was staying, I didn't want to tell you my hotel is by the airport. I leave for Riyadh first thing tomorrow. I have no idea when I'll be back."

Sarah had taken for granted that they would have more time together. The notion of his departure stung her more deeply than she would have expected. "Of course. I knew that. It's just that I . . ."

"Yes?"

She hesitated, unsure if she should put it out there.

"What's this? The great Sarah Weston at a loss for words?" Daniel grabbed his phone from the night-stand and punched away at the keys. "I must text everyone I know."

"I've come to think of us as a team. In fact, I don't know that I would have survived if not for you."

"Sure you would have. You're a tough little lady. You don't give yourself enough credit. You may be a product of the upper class, but you're nothing like them. You don't do what you do to keep up appearances or because the establishment expects it. You do it because your conscience compels you to. Your father, your people—they don't have soul like you do."

She stroked his chest with her fingertips. "Danny, you do see me."

"Yes, I do, Sarah. And I like what I see. So much so that I'm willing to take a gamble on you."

She tilted her head. "What do you mean?"

"I'm looking for an archaeologist to join me in the Empty Quarter. Remember I told you one of my head guys just quit? So . . . the post is open. And it's yours if you want it."

The proposition caught her unawares. "I don't know what to say." Her face warmed. "What about Cambridge?"

"You mark my words: those guys will sell you out before it's over." He ran the back of his fingers down her rosy cheek. "Think about it. You don't have to give me an answer today. But don't wait too long. You know, people are lining up to work in hundred and twenty–degree heat and swallow sand for a living."

She wanted to keep up the volley of conversation, but words escaped her. She pulled him close for a kiss. They made love until both their bodies gave out as a lavender dawn rose above the rooftops of Paris.

The sound of a persistent buzz woke her. It took her a while to figure out it was the phone and to remember where she was. By the time she found the phone, it had stopped ringing. She stared vacantly at the flashing red light indicating waiting messages. The clock showed one o'clock. She rubbed her eyes and started to reconstruct the evening. Could he have left without saying good-bye?

In the bathroom, she found a note atop her cosmetics case that confirmed her suspicions.

You own my heart, Sarah Weston.

She had no doubt he was en route to Saudi Arabia. Surprisingly, she didn't feel disappointed. She knew she would see him again.

Over a pot of strong black coffee, she read the *International Herald Tribune*, the *Times*, and *Le Monde*. The headline in the *Herald Tribune*'s page-four article read, "Message from the Grave." The deck: "Cambridge team uncovers fourth-century prophecy." The *Times* featured the piece at the bottom of page one: "Ethiopia's Tenth Saint: Could an Anglo-Saxon prophet have changed the course of a nation's faith?" The article described Sarah, "the only daughter of Sir Richard Weston," and Daniel, "the legendary American anthropologist," less like scientists and more like Indiana Jones types willing to risk life and limb to uncover hidden treasure.

Sarah cringed. She had always abhorred British journalists' flair for the dramatic. Still, the piece was effective in that it could capture the attention of the public and make them read further, tricking them into actually learning something. The author obviously had gotten a hold of the inscriptions of King Ezana, including the one Matakala had shown her on their first encounter, and had further interviewed Ethiopian cultural and theological experts, raising the question that Gabriel was indeed the country's tenth saint, the one who had delivered a message from God about the apocalypse. Sarah marveled at how much research the guy was able to do in such short time.

The phone rang.

"Sarah Weston," she answered.

"Darling, it's about time." Her father's voice came across urgent and impatient. "Where on earth have you been? Why haven't you picked up your phones or messages?"

"Sorry, Daddy. I had a long night. Slept in a little. What's the bloody emergency?"

"I have news."

"Good news or bad?"

"A bit of both, really. The police just found Matakala at his house in the highlands."

Sarah's mood soared. "That's brilliant. So he's under arrest?"

"Not so fast, darling. They found him at the bottom of the well in the back of the house."

Sarah dropped the newspaper.

"He'd been dead several days. It was a nasty scene, from what I'm told."

"What? How?"

"Police are investigating with the help of our agents. Seems like an inside job. He had a wound to the head that preceded the fall. Someone must have knocked him unconscious and dragged him into the well."

"Surely Brehan knows something. Can't you ask him?"

"Brehan is the one who tipped us off to start with. Apparently he went to the house to deliver something and saw Matakala struggling with a white man. Says he got frightened and didn't stick around to see what happened. Our deal, of course, was that if he led us to Matakala, we would let him go free. So we held up our end of the bargain and put him on a plane to the UK day before yesterday. Only he hasn't been at his flat since we dropped him off there. Hasn't touched his bank account either."

"What do you make of that?"

"Probably doesn't know what to do with himself in a civilized country, poor chap. Probably wandering around somewhere, lost and unable to communicate. But don't worry, darling. All dogs return to their lair sooner or later."

"Sure." She felt that familiar metallic taste rise in her throat. Her mind was suddenly crowded with thoughts of dread. "Do let me know if you hear anything. Cheers then, Daddy."

She hung up. Matakala's killer was at large. Could

he have been silenced by his so-called benefactor because he knew too much? Could Apocryphon have sought revenge because the inscriptions were brought to light?

And Brehan . . . She didn't buy the lost dog scenario for a minute. He knew more than he'd let on to Scotland Yard; she was sure of it. He likely had gone missing because he had something to hide.

There was a heavy knock on her door.

The panicked thumping of her heart resounded in her ears.

A second, more furious knock followed.

She frantically looked around the room. A heavy glass ashtray, the spent bottle of Dom Pérignon—either could cause damage if called upon.

An envelope appeared under the door, and she heard footsteps, which grew fainter.

Slumping to the floor, she cursed her paranoia. After a few deep breaths, she mustered the courage to open the envelope.

It was from the concierge desk.

Mlle Weston,

I have something that belongs with you. Meet me
at 65 Quai d'Orsay, 22:00 sharp.

Marie-Laure Olivier

Sarah ignored the directive, certain it was a trap, until the second missive came.

The prophecies said, "I was one of three." I know who the second was.

M-L. O.

Twenty-One

The church at 65 Quai d'Orsay was cold and eerie in the ghost light of the streetlamps. The sanctuary, a towering masonry structure on the left bank of the Seine, was framed by a tangle of leafless branches, harbingers of the Paris autumn. A gothic spire, enveloped in the patina of the ages, stood like a beacon to the faithful. A small sign at the entrance marked The American Church in Paris welcomed her.

Sarah ascended the steps to the breezeway connecting the church's two cloisters and stood behind a massive stone column to survey the surroundings. In the utter silence, her head buzzed with the rush of adrenaline, whether from the fear of walking into a trap or the anticipation of unlocking another piece of this puzzle, she did not know. She looked over her shoulder, checking once again if she was followed. She saw no one, not even the woman she was supposedly meeting.

She stepped lightly toward the courtyard garden and stopped beneath a jasmine vine hanging over a stone bench. She closed her eyes and inhaled the intense perfume.

"Sarah Weston?" A French female voice cracked the silence.

With a start, Sarah turned to face a slim woman gazing intently at her.

Madame Olivier was dressed in a fitted grey wool crepe dress with a black manteau draped over it. Her glossy black hair, twisted into a chignon held by a tortoise clip, framed her narrow face and fine features. Except for the creases around her eyes, her face was unlined and serene, as though she had not worried a day in her life. She extended a delicate hand. "I am Marie-Laure Olivier."

She sat on the bench and shot a few furtive glances around the courtyard. "We are alone." She pulled out a silver case and offered a cigarette to Sarah.

Sarah gladly accepted. She lit up and inhaled the menthol smoke. "Forgive my rudeness, but I am eager to learn the purpose of this meeting."

Marie-Laure nodded and exhaled a puff of smoke. "Before I tell you, I must give you a little background. It will help you understand."

Sarah gestured for her to continue.

"My family has been in France since the twelfth century. My ancestors on my mother's side lived in Paris for the most part. Some hailed from the south.

My paternal ancestors are French and English. Myself, I've spent time in both countries. I went to boarding school in England. Kent College. Do you know it?"

"Yes, of course. Some of my friends went there. Did you continue your studies in England?"

"Actually, I studied all over. Art history in Florence, classical studies in Athens. I did the requisite couple of terms at the Sorbonne. I was more interested in travel and adventure than I was in a strict education. When I met my husband, I tossed it all aside to follow him. He was an historian working in West Africa. I could think of nothing more romantic. We lived in Cameroon and Mali for fifteen years, but then I got very ill and had to return to Europe. I have been in Paris since."

"Your family. What was their business?"

Marie-Laure spoke openly. "They were landowners in the Middle Ages. As such, they amassed a great deal of wealth and were members of the aristocracy. Later, in the Renaissance years, some of my ancestors were scholars and literary figures. Men of letters. And in modern times, they have been industrialists, mostly in transportation. They had the first automobile factories in France and later got into manufacturing airplanes."

"It must be wonderful to know so much about your forebears. I wish I knew half as much about mine. How have you managed to learn all this?"

"My family kept meticulous records from very

early on. But over the years, they were scattered and some were even lost. As the wife of an historian and a student of history myself, I took great interest in recovering and restoring these records and organizing them into an archive, not only for the benefit of my family but also for the greater good. You see, Sarah, some of my ancestors were very important to French history." Marie-Laure assumed an enigmatic tone. "And others were deliberately erased from the history books."

Sarah was intrigued. "Was this deletion . . . just?"

"I have my opinion." She took a final drag and extinguished her cigarette in a flowerpot. "But you can be your own judge."

"I'm listening."

Marie-Laure took a book out of her black leather Birkin. Inside was a family tree. "My husband and I had produced this just before he died." She ran her finger down the document and stopped in the year 1318. "Bernard de Bontecou," she read. "Maternal ancestor, born 1318, died 1348. He was a shipping merchant in Marseilles who later moved to Paris, where he died during the Black Death. He opened trade routes between France and some of the Italian city-states and moved foodstuffs overseas. Apart from that, we don't know much about him other than the fact that he moved to Paris in the thirteen forties and apparently let his brothers run the shipping empire he built. Those final years of his life were spent essentially in isolation. No one is sure why. What we do know is that he wrote several manuscripts."

She retrieved a spiral-bound notebook from her handbag and gave it to Sarah.

Sarah read the title on the cover page. "Divination. By Bernard de Bontecou."

"Naturally, this is a copy," Marie-Laure said. "The original was found in the Manoir de Vincennes, a family estate in the outskirts of Paris that has since been razed. In the late fourteen hundreds, a relative by the name of Lady Antoinette Colbert inherited the manor and set about restoring it. In the process, she found these handwritten manuscripts hidden behind the bricks of a fireplace. She was struck by their contents and proceeded to have them published at her own expense. The book circulated briefly until the church found out about it and deemed it heresy. They tracked down and burned every copy except the one Antoinette managed to smuggle out of the country to London. It is now in our family archives." She again reached inside her handbag.

Sarah looked around the courtyard. Nothing stirred. The building was illuminated with the faint pewter light of the waxing moon. A light breeze whistled over the rooftops. Marie-Laure handed her a small reading light, and she looked through the pages carefully. The first chapter was an entry about the Black Death, written in the future tense and titled "Man's Divine Judgment."

The time is drawing near when
The sky will turn black and
The Almighty will appear from the heavens
To deliver his wrath upon France.

And he will say: Men have become greedy and gluttonous
And disregard the earth.
They think they can find salvation in gold
And in satisfying their banal appetites.

But no treasure nor pleasure
Can save men's souls.
It can only bring destruction
So terrible that the paper nation will be torn asunder.

It will rain rats
And these rats will hold in their blood
A powerful curse
That will spread among mankind.

Balls of poison will grow under men's skin,
And their bodies will turn black.
Fire will rage behind their eyes

And they will speak in tongues, like the Devil.

Brothers and sisters will abandon each other,
And there will be days of darkness
As the cities fall to chaos
Without laws or scriptures.

And then will come Death
Swiftly and with great pain,
And he will raise his iron sickle
And take the heads of the wicked.

Not sated with the blood of France,
Death will descend upon other nations
And without mercy
Attack men, women, and children.

He will claim one in every three souls.
Houses will be empty,
Blood will taint the soil,
And the rivers will swell with the dead.

Quiet will befall the great continent,
And the righteous will arise
To rebuild the nations
Ravaged by divine judgment.

Sarah felt a chill rake her skin. "I don't understand. When was this written?"

"In 1345. Three years before the plague struck France."

"How could he have known?"

"At first I thought he had witnessed something like the plague during his trips to Italy and perhaps had guessed the disease would inevitably reach France. But as I read more of his writings, it became clear he had a different kind of foresight. Turn to page one hundred forty-six."

Sarah did. The chapter titled "The Great Power" was an account of modern America. She read, stunned at the degree of accuracy, especially in this passage:

MEN WILL FASHION A GREAT EAGLE MADE OF METAL
AND SEND IT FLYING INTO THE DARK DEPTHS OF SKY
WHERE THE ONLY INHABITANTS ARE STARS AND DUST
AND THERE IS NO GROUND TO STAND UPON

Marie-Laure showed her other chapters—"War" about the Holocaust and the Second World War and "The Two Towers" about the September eleventh attacks.

Either this guy was truly prescient, or all of this was a forgery.

"I realize you are a scientist," the Frenchwoman said, "and as such you require proof. Our family archives will be opened to you should you wish it."

Sarah was flattered but puzzled. "Why would I want access? What is all this supposed to mean to me?"

Marie-Laure turned to a page near the end of the book. "I thought you might find this interesting."

Sarah read the final and untitled passage, which described great fires and all-consuming smoke.

The sea will be covered in grasses
So that it will be a vast expanse of green
Through which no eye, neither human nor marine, can see.
The oceans will appear as meadows,
So much so that men will attempt to walk upon them
Until they realize man cannot walk on water.

"Does it sound familiar?" Marie-Laure asked.

Sarah shook her head, stunned at the similarity between these writings and the words of Gabriel. Then she recalled Marie-Laure's message: *I know who the second was.* "Are you saying Bernard was one of the three prophets?"

"No. But I believe his lover was."

"His lover."

"All we know of her is her name: Calcedony. Bernard never spoke of her in his writings. The church has no record of a marriage. There were no children, apparently. It's as if she never existed."

"Then how can you be sure she did?"

"We have a letter, written by Calcedony to Bernard as she awaited her execution. She was apparently arrested as a heretic and imprisoned under the authority of King Philippe VI and was hanged forty-eight hours later. She must have written this letter when she knew there was no hope for her, for what it contains . . ." Marie-Laure fell silent. "Sarah, no living person except me knows about this letter. It has been a dark secret in our family for centuries. Only one person at a time has been burdened with the knowledge of it, passing the torch only at the time of death. No one has really known what to make of it. Some have believed; others, no. For my part, I thought it was the desperate attempt of a tragic woman to save her hide by claiming she was someone she could not possibly have been. Or maybe it was merely a hallucination brought on by the lack of food and water, torture, or perhaps the early stages of plague. Anything but the truth. But now, after reading about your discovery . . . I fear the truth is exactly what this letter contains."

"Why fear the truth?"

"When you read the letter, you will know. I will say no more. You must judge for yourself whether this is truth or rubbish. Whether there is any connection between your Gabriel and Calcedony."

Marie-Laure reached inside her manteau and pulled out a bundle of papers rolled into a scroll. "I hope it is the puzzle piece you have been seeking—for the sake of all of us."

Twenty-Two

It was the eve of the twenty-third day of battle. A moonless night had fallen swiftly on the barren lands of Meroë, blanketing the sandy wasteland with darkness. The acrid scent of stagnant blood and rotting flesh choked Gabriel's throat, and he fought back the instinct to gag. Death was everywhere, not least of all in the infirmary tent, more akin to a slaughterhouse than a place of healing. He made his way past the bloodied bodies that lay moaning in the darkness. He knew many wouldn't make it through the night.

A soldier moaned like a woman in childbirth and pleaded, "Let me die."

Gabriel checked his abdomen, where the sword had ripped the flesh from the sternum to the navel, to see if the bleeding had stopped. Two days earlier he had sewn the laceration with cotton thread spun by the elder women of the court and an iron needle, which he had designed and Hallas had forged before he rode to Meroë. That had stopped the bleeding, but now the wound was suppurating, the skin swollen like a milking goat's udder. The infection was too advanced.

"It will be better in the morning, friend," Gabriel lied to comfort the soldier in his last hours. "Get some sleep."

He moved on to another victim, a stoic boy who was too young to be drafted into battle but had insisted on volunteering. He was thirteen, fourteen at most, but had the serene countenance of a man who had lived many lifetimes.

"How's that arm?" Gabriel removed the blood-soaked bandage to find exposed, weeping flesh. The boy's forearm had been sliced off by a particularly sinister blade, and the bleeding would not relent in spite of the stitches Gabriel had put in earlier. He smeared the wound with fresh horse manure, which he'd used before to curb hemorrhage. It was risky—the bacteria in the manure could do more harm than good—so he gave the young soldier a myrrh broth to prevent infection.

"Tomorrow I'll be ready to fight," the boy said, "with thanks to you."

"I haven't done anything. I am only a simple man trying to help."

"That's not what the men say. They say you are a healer with divine powers. A holy man sent by the

Lord of heaven to protect us from evil. They say you came down from the heavens to help us win this war and unify the lands of the Nile into one great, impenetrable empire."

Gabriel smiled and squeezed the boy's hand. "You should rest. Big day tomorrow."

A few sleepless hours later, the dawn washed the sky in streaks of scarlet and saffron. It was an ominous beauty, heralding the advent of fresh bloodshed. Outside the tent, the troops were moving at a panicked pace, as if some malevolent force lurked beneath the sands. Gabriel approached a lieutenant readying his horse for battle.

"Why are the men so restless, friend?"

The soldier, a compact and muscular African with skin the color of tar, bowed his head: the standard greeting toward men of God. "This day will bring evil that we have never known. The men fear for their lives."

"Why is today different from any other day?"

"Today we will be challenged by a regiment fiercer than any we have met thus far. Meroë has called for aid, and thousands of Nobatae are riding south as we speak. The horse and camel warriors. The Meroan military elite. Some are here already, fighting our troops at the northern edge of the battlefield."

"Who are these Nobatae? Why fear them so?"

"These warriors know not God nor king nor country. The Romans themselves trained the Nobatae and bestowed upon them a cache of weapons far more advanced than our own. But the Nobatae were not to be trusted. They turned against the Romans and proclaimed their independence. They rode in the tribal lands, unchecked and untamed. Soon they forged a partnership with the most wretched and ruthless tribe in all the Nile. The headless warriors we know as the Blemmyes."

Gabriel could see the men feared the legend more than the enemy itself. "Headless warriors exist only in myth. Surely this foe is not as bad as you think it to be."

The soldier shuddered. "They are heathens. They kill everything and everyone crossing their path: men, women, children, horses, livestock. They are said to be undefeated in battle."

An Aksumite foot soldier stumbled toward them. Blood trickled from his forehead into his eyes, and his armor was split at the shoulder as if by an axe.

As the soldier's knees buckled, Gabriel held him up. "Quick. Into the infirmary."

"No." Blood sputtered from the soldier's mouth. "I bring a message from the king."

"What's happened?"

"They have closed in. The king is wounded. He calls for you. You must ride now to the river."

Gabriel calmly wrapped his sword belt around his

waist and secured his helmet. In his deepest meditations, he had foreseen being called upon to fight. Though he knew nothing of the ways of the sword, he trusted his instinct, his best weapon. He mounted his horse.

On the way to the northern front, his horse trampled hundreds of corpses, both Meroan and Aksumite. The battlefield was a graveyard, and the sands were stained crimson with the blood of the fallen. All around him was carnage. One young Aksumite who couldn't have been more than sixteen was beheaded directly before him. Gabriel felt the warm blood spray on his lips.

In the distance appeared the king's first regiment, Ezana included, encircled by a swarm of Blemmyes. These creatures of legend were not headless, as their reputation promised, but their shoulders were raised so high that their heads seemed to be tucked into their chests. They were almost apelike. Gabriel had never seen people like these. It was as if evolution had skipped over them.

Their war tactics were as ugly as they were. They had a taste for blood and were not beyond biting off chunks of their enemy in hand-to-hand combat. They clearly placed little value on life, others' or their own. Their purpose was singular: to kill.

Even from a distance, he could see that Ezana's sword arm was weakened from an injury. At the command of one of the lieutenants accompanying him, Gabriel spurred his horse to a gallop. The strategy was to ride into the thick of battle, remove the king from danger, and deliver him to safety where he could be treated.

It was a mission for the brave, but for Gabriel it was not a question of courage. It was his duty as a man to serve his fellow, be he king or slave. His deepest, most basic instinct sustained him as he rode against the wind to the riverbanks.

The Blemmye who clashed swords with the king struck another blow where the armor was weak, piercing Ezana's left side and sending him tumbling from his horse. The king got to his knees and continued to wield his sword with fierce determination despite his injuries. But the Blemmyes, not unlike hyenas, waited for their prey to be debilitated and then went in for the kill. The monster-warrior raised his sword with both arms to deliver a final blow to the stunned king's head.

Gabriel, riding past, drove his sword through the center of the Blemmye's rib cage.

The apeman growled in agony and fell from his horse, expiring in convulsions on the bloodied earth.

Gabriel met Ezana's raven eyes for a single moment: a king and a man on equal ground.

"Gabriel . . . behind you," Ezana muttered.

A spear penetrated Gabriel's armor and left rib, sending violent spasms through his entire abdomen. A white light overpowered his vision, and he felt himself sailing through the air before he hit the ground.

Twenty-Three

My dearest Bernard,

The king has signed the papers for my execution. It will be only hours before I face the gallows. The other prisoners spit on me and call me a witch, yelling the foulest profanities day and night, saying I deserve to burn for my heresies. But I am neither tormented by their insults nor afraid of feeling Death's savage grip. You see, I died a long time ago. And now I must speak the truth and hope the wise man in you will understand and forgive me.

I am not who you think me to be.

When we met in the year of our Lord 1340, you knew I was not of this place. Night after night you asked if I was an angel sent to guard you. How I longed to tell you then. But I could not. I feared you would flee when I confronted you with the truth. This I could not risk. I needed you. I need you still, even though I am in the grave as you read this. But now, as I face the end, the time has come to reveal what I have longed to tell you since that cold winter day when you took me in and showed me kindness even though you had every right to despise and fear me.

I am not a witch. I am not a prophet. I am not even wise to the world. The truth is I have seen with my own eyes the destruction men can cause, for I have lived in another place and time. As difficult as this may be to believe, I have traveled to your France from a country that does not yet exist and a day that has not yet been lived.

I was happy once, a wife and a mother. And then the world collapsed. It shouldn't have surprised me. Things had been in a fragile state for some time. But the truth is you don't think such days will actually come, at least not on your watch.

It started with smoke. I thought nothing of it at first, but the fumes became thicker, more pervasive. I looked outside my window and froze, my senses violently seized by the furious dragon before me. Flames were boiling with urgent, terrible rage. A wall of fire engulfed the pines and turned the forest of my youth into a graveyard. As the tongues of the flames licked my own house, I knew soon every wall of my ancestral home, every memory, would crumble into a pile of ash.

I ran through the house, calling for my son. Smoke seeped through the cracks, gripping my throat so that I could not scream. I found him lying facedown on the floor, and I knew. At that moment and forevermore, grace left me.

It is impossible, until it happens, to know what it feels like to hold your lifeless child in your arms. You feel as if your luck has just run out, that no matter what good may come, the scales will never be tipped in your favor again. I died at that moment. And I thought: Why not finish it? Why not incinerate these bones and liberate the soul to the beyond lands where it can drift in a place devoid of sorrow and ambition and the longings of the greedy flesh? I lunged toward the belly of the beast, offering whatever remained of my feeble presence on this earth. But it was not to be. I felt a hand pulling me back. It was my husband, saying that what we had feared most had come to pass. The fires were advancing like predators from north, south, east, and west, devouring all that stood in their path. We knew this day would come. We had prepared for it.

It was time to activate the escape plan. I gazed one last time at the place I'd always known as home and saw nothing of it but the ashen effigies of trees and the charred ground stripped of all life. In the gathering smoke, we wrapped our son in his favorite blanket and laid him, along with all of our dreams, to rest in his tiny bed. We were ghosts, the walking dead. There was only one thing left, a final act of decency: to tell whoever would listen what had befallen us. And that is how I came to be here.

My country lay to the west of France, beyond the great ocean. Decades before I was even born, the land was in a state of collapse. For centuries, men had been multiplying at dizzying rates. During my lifetime, I saw the number swell to eleven billion. What place would not buckle under so much weight? Weather changes began to take place. Temperatures rose. Storms came with a greater speed and fury. Crops scorched, causing famine. Shorelines were engulfed by rising water as ice melted in the Viking lands. And yet men continued to rape the land and hasten our annihilation.

When I was a young girl, the wild forests had vanished, burned to make space for more dwellings and farms and places of commerce. The solution did not come until many years later. A plant was dispersed into the oceans to breathe in place of the trees. For some years it worked, and men congratulated themselves for being more clever than Nature. But catastrophe was a single event away.

A powerful machine broke down, and its waste spilled into the oceans and caused the plants to multiply in great numbers. Men's attempts to stop the beast were futile. In a matter of months, it had spread to all the seas and grown so thick it blocked the sun from entering the water, thus killing all sea life. But the worst was still to come.

Great fires erupted on all the land. Eternal fires burned, consuming houses and farms and bridges. Nothing and no one was safe from their wrath. We saw our brothers and friends die in the inferno, howling as their skin separated from their bones and turned to ash.

This was the end of ends. The last moments of the lands we knew as home. That horrible autumn day, three of us escaped in a ship designed to transport men to other realms. The future melted into the past, and we were deposited in unknown places and times with nothing but our mission: to stop men from forging their own destruction.

Think me mad if you wish, but I promise I speak the truth. I said earlier that I needed you still. What I must ask of you is a leap of faith. Believe my words, for all that I write in this letter is true. Finish the book you started, and safeguard the manuscripts for future generations. The people will see them as prophecies. Only you and I need know they are the truths, spoken by me to you, of a history yet to be written. Mention nothing of me. I am insignificant, a mere whisper in your ear. It is your talent for the written word, your good standing in society, and your erudition that will cause men to take notice—perhaps now, perhaps long after your time here has expired. I pray you will hear the pleas of this dead woman who cared for you, so that time may vindicate me.

If you think me mad, then so be it. But know this: you have been the only source of light in a world I lost faith in long ago. I cannot tell you how many nights I awoke from a terrible nightmare, only to be consoled by your warmth. You have made me believe again in the goodness of men.

Do not lament my fate. I am where I belong, in the realm of grace, at last touching the peace that eluded me in life.

Yours eternally,
Calcedony

Sarah was numb. Everything was suddenly clear. Gabriel's escape from a destroyed world to which he could never return, the "beast" that would cover the sea with a blanket of darkness, the air that gives not life but takes it away. She finally understood the enigma of the intact dentition: the plastic polymer in Gabriel's teeth could not be identified because it had not yet been invented.

She asked Marie-Laure for another cigarette. The sweet menthol tobacco was like a lace veil over her racing thoughts, and she inhaled deeply again and again, lost in a surreal world becoming indistinguishable from her own. If everything in the letter was true, if Calcedony and Gabriel were indeed partners separated in a doomed world, then the discovery would take on a far deeper dimension. This wasn't a prophetic foretelling of the apocalypse but an eyewitness account by not one but two who had been there.

The thought chilled her. *This is what's coming, then. This is our future.* She knew the gravity of the proof she beheld; she also knew the Calcedony letter wasn't the final puzzle piece. Both Gabriel and Calcedony had mentioned a third time traveler. This person was still unaccounted for.

No one in the scientific world would take this

seriously. A set of prophecies inscribed on a cave in Ethiopia and a letter, supposedly written in the fourteenth century and kept under wraps all these years, conveniently released in tandem with the Gabriel prophecies. An alleged third party whose identity remained elusive. Who would believe any of it?

And yet she did.

She had no doubt she was meant to come into this knowledge. But what to do with it?

The church clock delivered its deep, resonant chime twelve times. "I should be going. Early flight tomorrow. This has been most illuminating." She took Marie-Laure's right hand in both of hers. "Thank you. For trusting me, I mean."

"I would rather this remain between us . . . for now."

"You have my word."

"Before you go, I must give you something." Marie-Laure pulled a newspaper clipping from her handbag. "I cut this from the *New York Times* about a year ago. I had a feeling it would be relevant one day."

Sarah unfolded it carefully and scanned the headline: "Environmental Firm Unveils Global Warming Plan."

Twenty-Four

Sarah tucked the article and the letter in her backpack and walked with Marie-Laure beneath the church's arches. A blast of cold wind swept across the river from the east. Sarah shuddered. She bade Marie-Laure adieu, with a promise: "I don't intend to let this go. I will find the truth."

Marie-Laure turned to leave but froze. Into the shadows, she spoke firmly, fearlessly. "Who are you? What do you want?"

A man swatted Marie-Laure out of his way with a heavy paw and sent her headlong toward the ground, where she lay in a motionless heap.

The blood coursing through Sarah's veins turned ice-cold. She had been followed from the Plaza Athénée. How much had he seen or heard?

The man reached for her shoulder bag with his

bear grip. "Let it go," he bellowed. "Let it go or die."

Sarah refused, but her strength was no match for his.

He grabbed her shoulder and squeezed on her collarbone with a force that could crush it into shards. She screamed and bit his hand.

He pulled back. "Stupid bitch," he yelled, and his giant mitts came with fury toward her neck.

Instinctively, she swung the bag toward his head. With a single swipe of his arm, he tossed her to the ground. As she scrambled to her feet, his guffaws echoed in the stillness of the night.

Sarah tried to run, but the giant grabbed her arm. Her hair whipped wildly as she tried to break free. She swung around and drove her thumb into his eye, eliciting a howl, but the pain didn't bring the three hundred pounds of her attacker to his knees; instead, it made him bear down harder on the arm he held captive.

Sarah buckled.

Saliva dripped from the corners of his mouth onto her face as he lifted Sarah and carried her like a bag of trash toward the river. She kicked wildly, but his grip around her waist was so tight she could barely breathe.

A siren blared.

The man stopped and dropped Sarah by the riverbank. Running along Quai d'Orsay, he disappeared into a dark alley.

Sarah looked up and saw Marie-Laure standing

ten feet away, waving her mobile phone at the police. The Frenchwoman, her face bruised and clothes disheveled, called out, “Run, Sarah. They must not see you.”

Sarah mouthed a breathless thank-you and propped herself up. On shaky legs, she ran toward the Pont de l’Alma and the bright embrace of the Rive Droite.

Twenty-Five

On the plane en route to London, Sarah could not sit still. Her entire body ached from the encounter outside the church. The bruises on her shoulder were so severe she could barely move it. She took two Paracetamol and tried to take her mind off the pain by reading and rereading the *Times* article Marie-Laure had handed her.

HOUSTON, TEXAS—The environmental research firm Donovan Geodynamics has announced the success of preliminary trials of its Poseidon program. The program, which has been tested since 2008 in an undisclosed area of Texas, is an experiment involving plankton-like microorganisms that theoretically consume carbon dioxide.

During the first phase of its Poseidon research, Donovan's aquatic microbial ecology researchers reportedly discovered that the phytoplankton manufactured in the company's labs was able to survive in a controlled environment for three hundred twenty days, well beyond the lifespan of a typical marine microorganism. In the second phase, scientists will attempt to lengthen that lifespan and to propagate the organisms via assisted reproduction. The objective is to create a self-sufficient form of plankton that can survive on sunlight and atmospheric gases.

"The rising carbon dioxide levels in the atmosphere are not going away," said Donovan CEO Wallace Cage in a statement. "Poseidon is a viable solution to the global warming anathema that faces our planet. If our trials continue to go as well as they have thus far, we will actually have a life form that absorbs carbon dioxide and converts it into oxygen, thereby producing cleaner air. By reducing carbon dioxide in the atmosphere, we can actually retard the effects of global warming."

According to sources familiar with the project, Donovan aims to seek backing from the Alliance of Nations to End Global Warming, a fifteen-nation coalition with considerable political influence, for testing Poseidon in seven ocean sites worldwide. Alliance representatives declined to comment.

The similarities were uncanny. It was entirely plausible that this project and the *beast* of Calcedony and Gabriel's writings were one and the same. Eager to research further, she was pleased when the landing announcement came from the cockpit.

As soon as the taxi deposited her in front of her Chelsea flat, Sarah rushed to her computer and pulled up the Cambridge articles database. She conducted searches with various combinations of *Donovan Geodynamics*, *Poseidon*, and *Alliance of Nations to End Global Warming*. Besides the *Times* article and a lengthier piece in the *Houston Chronicle*, the search of mass media outlets yielded surprisingly little.

She went through every issue of the trade journal *Nature* from the past two years and came upon an article titled "The Poseidon Paradox." In that piece, several scientists were quoted as saying any organism that self-propagates presents an inherent danger of multiplying out of control, particularly when introduced to warm waters, and Donovan's marine scientists had not yet adequately addressed that fact. Too much phytoplankton, they claimed, eventually would die and sink to the sea bottom. Their subsequent decomposition could harm the overall health of the oceans by releasing methane and depleting waters of dissolved oxygen, which other organisms needed to survive. Further, the opponents claimed the phytoplankton could be harmful to fish, which fed on exactly such substances. Because of its genetically engineered nature, the organism could lead to a massive loss of marine life, including endangered species of fish and sea mammals.

The sidebar was devoted to the view of the New York–based clean ocean initiative Oceanus. The president, Stuart Ericsson, cautioned:

"The consequences of Poseidon could be catastrophic. If the ocean temperatures rise by even five degrees, which is entirely plausible given the current rate of climate change, algae—whether naturally occurring or engineered in a lab—has the potential to grow and metamorphose. We saw this happen in the eighties in the Mediterranean, when the Caulerpa taxifolia algae grew out of control and threatened the sea's delicate ecosystem."

Caulerpa taxifolia, a type of phytoplankton commonly referred to as killer algae and alien algae, was accidentally released into Mediterranean waters in 1984 from the Oceanographic Museum in Monaco. Commonly used as a decorative material in aquariums, C. taxifolia was transformed into an invasive species when it came in contact with the Mediterranean Sea. The algae, which reportedly grew to cover some seven thousand four hundred acres of the sea and threatened the region's seaweed and fish populations, has been the subject of worldwide controversy. Some scientists believe reports of outsized growth are exaggerated, while others maintain that more than half the species of fish have been eradicated in areas of the C. taxifolia infestation.

If she had never seen Gabriel's prophecies or Calcedony's letter, Sarah would have dismissed all the controversy as rubbish. She would have never doubted that carbon dioxide–consuming algae would be a good thing for the environment. But the questions jabbed at her mind like barbed wire.

Her phone vibrated. The caller ID announced Dr. Simon. She answered, fearing he would tell her she no longer had a job or would be confined to a teaching post, the kiss of death for an archaeologist.

"I had a call from my counterpart at Rutgers." The professor's tone was graver than she'd ever heard it. "It appears Daniel Madigan never made it to Riyadh."

She sat up. "What did you say?"

"It appears he checked in at Charles de Gaulle but never got on the plane. I must know what you know about this. You were the last person to see him."

Sarah felt numb. "I . . . know nothing, I promise you. I mean . . . we were together the night before, but he left in the morning in a hurry, didn't even say good-bye. I haven't heard from him since."

"Apparently, no one else has either. Now, Sarah, I want you to keep your wits about you. We don't know what this is. He could be AWOL, or he could be in trouble. Trouble seems to follow you two."

Sarah hung up abruptly and checked her text messages.

A text had been sent from Daniel's phone at four in the morning.

You have something we want. We have something you want. We suggest an even exchange. Instructions to follow. Don't botch this.

Twenty-Six

"Call for the king. He is waking."

Gabriel heard the female voice and slowly opened his eyes. It took him a few seconds to realize where he was and to recall what had happened. He lay in a hard bed, covered with fine cotton sheets and sheepskin blankets. The windows were draped with great lengths of purple and gold silk tied back to admit the moonlight. Above his head hung an iron lantern casting flecks of golden light on the lion and zebra skin rugs. Women cloaked in white circled his bed, some preparing wet compresses while others sat in the corner muttering prayers and thumbing their rosaries. The palace.

His last recollection was of taking a life. Remembering the death squeal of the Blemmye who had met his sword, he felt ill. What had happened after that he did not know. Aware he was breathing shallowly, he attempted a deep breath and felt a stabbing pain in his left side. As more of the veils of confusion were lifted, he realized he was hot with fever and his bones ached mightily. He tried to move and could not. He had never known such intense pain or malaise. It was no ordinary infection, he knew. He closed his eyes and let his consciousness melt away in meditation, hoping to enter the elusive realm where comfort and peace dwelled.

Gabriel was semiconscious when Ezana entered the room. He could feel the monarch's presence and hear the voices around him, but the words were warped and without edges, like images in a surrealist painting.

"I am . . . sorry . . . King," he muttered.

Ezana's bellowing voice reverberated in Gabriel's ears. "You have nothing to be sorry for. You saved my life by risking your own. You served your king like an honorable man. Everyone in the kingdom will know of this."

He opened his eyes and tried to focus on the massive figure before him. Ezana was dressed in gilded robes encrusted with rubies and embroidered with gold thread, a garment usually reserved for ceremony. "What was the outcome?"

"We were victorious, God be praised. Meroë was a worthy enemy, but she fell to the might of our armies. The Aksumite empire grows as the Lord God has predicted. Soon all the lands of the Nile will be ours and the might of Aksum will reach from sea to sea. Glory be to God."

Gabriel gasped. The words came out without his willing them. "So many bodies . . . so much pain . . ."

"It was a necessary sacrifice. Those men were martyrs fighting not only for the kingdom of Aksum but for the kingdom of God. They rest in a place of plenty, eating and drinking and dancing with angels. It was their destiny. Do not mourn them."

Hot sweat trickled down Gabriel's forehead. His skull throbbed, the pain in his side immobilizing. "I feel life leaving me," he whispered.

"You cannot die. I need you in my army. Tell the women how to make you better. I have ordered them to do as you ask."

"No. It is too late for me. Leave me be."

Ezana looked at the head nurse who monitored the patient silently from across the room. She nodded her agreement with Gabriel's proclamation. The king stood abruptly.

"Incompetent, every one of you." He pointed to Gabriel. "This man was sent to me by God himself, and you just stand there and let him die? You must see to his recovery at once."

The king stormed out of the room, his long, jeweled robes undulating behind him.

That night, Gabriel was restless. Delirious with fever, he mumbled a stream of nonsense. He would fall asleep for a few minutes only to be jarred awake by convulsions. His breathing had become more labored. During one of his fits of coughing, blood splattered across his pillow. Even in his compromised mental state, he knew he was hemorrhaging internally.

The night attendant cried, "We must get the king—and Abuna."

Within moments, Ezana entered accompanied by Abuna Salama, the bishop of the kingdom, and a coterie of his lieutenants. The bishop, a diminutive, ancient figure draped with embroidered sashes and carrying a ceremonial silver cross, approached Gabriel's bedside. He sprinkled the patient with holy water and, with hands clasped, chanted a string of prayers. He placed his hand on Gabriel's brow and announced, "This servant of God is hereby baptized in the name of the Father, the Son, and the Holy Spirit. O Lord, let Gabriel ascend to your kingdom, forgive him his trespasses, and grant him peace. Amen."

Gabriel's thoughts swirled with no pattern or boundaries. He struggled to remain conscious and regain control of his mind, for he had left something unsaid.

Ezana announced, "Let it be known that Gabriel

of Arabia has sacrificed his life to protect his king and the Aksumite people and has proven himself to be an instrument of God. His faith did not waver, even in the face of his own death. That is a symbol of his holiness." Ezana removed the heavy golden cross that hung around his neck and slipped it over Gabriel's head. "For this reason and by the power granted me by God, I proclaim Gabriel a saint of the Aksumite kingdom and pledge to bury him with the highest honors alongside the great fathers of this land."

"My king." Gabriel gasped for air, unsure he would get the words out. "I have one last wish."

"Then it will be granted," Ezana roared.

"I wish to be buried as a humble man, for that is what I am. I make my home on the foothills of Dabra Damo, high up the cliffs." Gabriel choked on the words and succumbed to another coughing fit. Blood dripped from the corner of his mouth and from his nose, but he pressed on. "Bury me inside the cave where I have inscribed my story in the stone." He tried to utter more but could not.

"Very well, then. So be it." Ezana turned to his lieutenants. "See that Saint Gabriel's body is laid in an acacia coffin and interred in Dabra Damo. Find the cave he speaks of and let him be buried there for all eternity."

As Abuna Salama chanted the psalm of the

dying, Gabriel closed his eyes and drifted to a realm unknown to him until that moment. He regarded the visions silently and without judgment, for nothing could torment him now. There was his father teaching him how to swim in the river behind the family farm. The two of them on long walks across the fields, talking with reverence about the land. The overwhelming joy of holding his son for the first time. The boy's bumbling first steps to him. The pride he felt at beating his professor and mentor at chess that one and only time. The tall columns of flame on the last day he saw his family. The integrity in the deep furrows of Hairan's face. The Bedouins dancing with abandon by the fire. His own trembling hands as he cast in stone the message he hoped would be found by a worthy emissary. Calcedony. The way her lower lip trembled when she laughed. Her eyes that shone with the intensity of a thousand ancient stars. Her long locks falling around his neck as they made love. In the pure white brilliance of his mind's eye, a hand reached toward him, and he grasped it.

Twenty-Seven

For the next twenty-four hours, Sarah did not sleep. She was glued to her phone, checking every few minutes for word from Daniel's abductors. Nothing came. She was so fraught with nervousness that her stomach seemed to be crushed in a vise and her mouth tasted of acid. *You have something we want. Calcedony's letter.* Someone was determined to erase every mention of the impending doom. The questions swirled in her sleepless mind, making her crazy. She had to clear her head.

She walked out of her flat and breathed in the cool night air, laced with bus exhaust, soot, and urine emanating from the bowels of the Tube. The smell of London. She had come to love it. Though long ago she had chosen the life of a nomad, the familiar scent was as close to home as she would allow herself to feel.

Constantly glancing over her shoulder, she walked north toward a familiar destination: Hyde Park. The spooky outline of the beech trees in the dark, the moonlight reflecting on the Serpentine, the benches full of lovers on clandestine rendezvous—all were icons from her youth. Before the divorce and their move to America, Sarah and her mother used to walk there and talk endlessly about adventures and books, ideas and ideals.

But tonight, nothing could bring her comfort. She walked the entire width of the park from Knightsbridge to Bayswater Road, then turned west toward Kensington Gardens. On the way back, she took the Kensington High Street route to Knightsbridge, walking past storefronts displaying cacophonous getups in what seemed to her a conspiracy to make a woman look ridiculous. In that way, she did not mirror her mother at all. Whereas her mother had been a slave to fashion and looked the part of the Hollywood star even when having cocktails at home alone, Sarah eschewed fancy frocks and good manicures. She didn't see the point in it. To avoid the spectacle of wanton consumerism, she took a turn on Sloane Street and cut through quiet residential streets on her way to the embankment.

By the time she returned to her own address, she was tired but her thoughts were in focus. She took the stairs to the first floor and slowly walked the length of the corridor to the southernmost tip of the building, the side facing the Thames. She entered the flat, put her bag down, and stood in the darkness by the sliding glass door, taking in the river and city lights across the water in Battersea.

Her thoughts traveled to Daniel. Damn her ambition for leading them here. She had never felt so powerless.

In the inky water, she saw movement, but no boats went by at that hour. She focused on the spot. With a skipped heartbeat, she realized the movement wasn't on the water at all. Reflected on the glass was something stirring behind her.

She dared not move.

She could open the glass door and jump down the one floor, or she could grab the heavy marble lamp on the table behind her and swing at the intruder's head. She scanned the glass again for signs of motion. The figure emerged from the dark hallway.

The door, she decided, but suddenly her fingers weren't working. She tried to open the door, and in that blurred moment the intruder was upon her.

Instinctively she swung around and jabbed her elbow hard toward his chest. He intercepted and twisted her arm behind her back, pinning her to the glass.

Sarah wailed with pain.

"Don't scream. Don't scream," he ordered as she tried to break free, her protests overpowered by the full strength of his body.

"What do you want?" she said, her voice strained from the pain and shock.

"Listen to me very carefully. I will let you go, but you must not fear me. Understand?"

She nodded tentatively. He released her, and she slowly turned to face him.

He wore a hood, his face shrouded in darkness. He stepped toward the window, and the city lights illuminated the insignia on his hooded fleece: IEHO—the International Ethiopian Help Organization, a charity based in London. Then she saw his face.

"Dear God," she whispered as the sight of his charred and tortured flesh came into full view.

His visage, no longer covered by a mask, was horrific. One eye was sealed shut with swollen eggplant-colored flesh; the other practically floated in its socket with no eyelid to protect it. Streaks of skin on his cheeks and forehead were still raw and pink against his black skin. His hair had been singed away save for a few errant wisps that clung like parasites to his scarred scalp.

She winced in disgust, and he stepped away from the light, hiding his face.

"Brehan. What are you doing here?" She tried to appear calm, though fear gripped her.

"The English let me go. I gave them what they wanted, and they said I was free." Though his accent was thick, he obviously had been educated in English.

"But what are you doing here? In my apartment."

He put his hands together in the universal sign of prayer. "There are things you don't know. I am not the assassin you believe me to be. True, I have done things that can never be forgiven." He looked in the direction of the water, bitterness in his gaze. "I had to kill Apostolos to gain their trust. If I did not, the mission of the brotherhood would have been jeopardized."

Sarah lashed out. "How could the brotherhood be more important than a man's life? The life of your own flesh and blood?"

"Apostolos denounced his own flesh in service to Apocryphon. But he never knew that I did the same. Some years ago, when the brothers suspected Matakala was after the tomb of the tenth saint, the high priest of Apocryphon asked me to leave the church to become a spy in Matakala's organization. I was sworn to secrecy. No one else knew. Not even Apostolos. He thought I had betrayed Apocryphon and that was the way we wanted it. If he knew the truth, he would have tried to protect me, for that was his nature, and everything we worked for would have been for naught."

Sarah heard him out. Too many unresolved questions remained—questions perhaps this man, whatever his true identity, could answer.

"Right. And who killed Matakala, then?"

He did not flinch. "I did. After I left you on the mountain, I went to his house and told him I had killed you and your partner. Matakala said, 'Your work here is done,' and pointed his handgun at me. I ran. He shot me in the leg as I slipped outside, then shot at me again but missed. I kept running, but my leg was bleeding a lot, and I grew weak. I collapsed by the well. He jumped on top of me, and we struggled." He stopped short. "It was self-defense."

Sarah stood there stone-faced, piecing it all together. Brehan's story was plausible. If he was who he claimed to be, it would explain why he had let her and Daniel go free in the Simien Mountains. And why he had helped her father's emissaries find them.

"You don't believe me. Perhaps this will convince you."

He reached inside his jacket and pulled out a package wrapped in dirty white sailcloth. He unwrapped it carefully to reveal another package, this one swaddled in a bloodred textile embroidered with gold thread. He handed it to her.

She looked at him, baffled. "What is this?"

"Open it."

She pulled back the corners of the textile and laid the contents of the package bare. The golden cross gleamed with a light seemingly of its own. With trembling hands, she cradled the cross and bowed in reverence. An intensity she had never felt before filled her, moving through her like an electric current. She placed the cross down carefully, afraid of its power.

Brehan reached into the sailcloth and handed her another package wrapped in silk. She didn't have to open it to know it was the codex. She clutched it to her chest like a friend reunited after long years and looked at Brehan.

"Apostolos gave you the key and some instructions. You know what you must do."

Sarah did indeed know what to do with the relics, but would she get the chance? Being in possession of the tenth saint's cross and the codex and Calcedony's letter set her in the power seat—and in the path of peril.

"Look, my partner is in danger, and I am running out of time to help him. Do you know where he is?"

"I don't know. That is the truth."

She exhaled in frustration. "What do you know about these people? Who was paying Matakala?"

He nodded. "He is an American. A businessman, I think. He wants to erase every trace of the saint. I do not know his motives."

"You have met this man?"

"Never. But I heard Matakala speaking to him more than once. He was very careful not to reveal his identity, but he did call him doctor and one time referred to something called . . . a Wolf Prize?"

A promising lead. The Wolf Prize had been

awarded to mathematicians and physicists since 1978. With a bit of research, she could narrow the field down considerably.

"Do you have a name? A place of residence? Anything."

He took a paper out of his pocket and gave it to her. "This is all I know."

"Warehouse A, 701 Marlin Road, Port Mansfield, Texas. Whose address is this?"

"When I went to Matakala's house after depositing you in the highlands, I walked in on him as he was packing the codex and cross in a box marked with this address. He was going to send them there. This was information he didn't want anyone to have, which is why he tried to kill me."

"Port Mansfield is a small fishing town on the edge of the Laguna Madre." She recalled Apostolos' enigmatic note while she'd toiled over the translations at Yemrehana Krestos. "Mother Sea. That's it. That's the place Apostolos tried to tell me about. Things are starting to make sense."

"I have done what I came here to do. I will take my leave."

Before she had a chance to stop him, he opened the sliding glass door and with an agile jump landed on the shrubbery below. Sarah didn't try to call after him; he would be long gone anyway. Instead, she went to her laptop and looked up all the American winners of the Wolf Prize, hoping their respective disciplines would give her a clue. She scanned the list.

Theory of numbers . . . algebraic topology . . . combinatorics . . . Euclidean Fourier analysis . . .

Some of it didn't even make sense to her. She had vowed to forget complex mathematics after her requisite course of study at university. She continued searching.

Homogeneous complex domains . . . Hamiltonian mechanics . . . Hodge structures . . .

"Think, Sarah," she said aloud. What field of math could have anything to do with environmental destruction?

Quasiconformal mappings . . . holonomic quantum field theory . . . Riemann-Hilbert correspondence . . .

Nothing was clicking. She looked up each winner since 1978. Perhaps something in their curricula vitae would point to a nugget of useful information.

Eventually she stumbled upon this:

Sandor Hughes, 1987 prize in quantum mechanics, founder and chairman of the board, Donovan Geodynamics.

Her heart galloped like a Thoroughbred out of the gate.

She knew exactly what she would find in Laguna Madre.

Twenty-Eight

The residents of Port Mansfield, mostly older folks who'd come down to the edge of Texas to enjoy the fishing during their golden years, were idle and friendly. They were more than happy to oblige a young woman, especially when she played the part of the sweet but clueless British tourist so well. She had taken care to look harmless and blend into the background. The last thing she wanted them to know was that she was a rich girl who'd arrived on her father's jet, which was waiting for her at a remote airstrip on the outskirts of town for what she hoped would be a quick escape.

She wore a tight, black T-shirt and black skinny jeans with her favorite Puma track shoes. She'd tucked her hair into a black baseball cap, letting the ponytail of blonde curls spill out. Her backpack was slung across her shoulder, making her look like a tourist, though in reality it held all manner of tools for her mission.

Marlin Road was a long, dusty thoroughfare without much traffic, especially at that time of morning. It was lined with warehouses, many of which were shuttered, with eighteen-wheeler trailers parked outside. The coolness of fall had not yet set in here, and the late afternoon air was warm and heavy with humidity, like London in the dead of summer. Sea brine and fish scented the air. Sarah was grateful for the scant activity as she made her way to her destination; the fewer eyes on her, the better.

Number 701 was a complex of gray concrete buildings at the end of a cul-de-sac facing a parking lot empty but for a massive flagpole with the Stars and Stripes whipping in a brisk breeze. The place looked deserted and, with its dearth of windows, tomb-like. And it was far larger than she expected, likely the size of a power plant. *What is this place?* Daniel was likely captive in there.

She hid behind a trailer at a neighboring building and scanned the area around the doors. She could see surveillance cameras but very few exterior lights. It was as if the principals wanted the structure to be invisible. If she were going to slip inside undetected, she would have to wait for night, only a couple of hours away. Even then, her approach would have to be stealthy.

She pondered her strategy until the light in the sky waned and a moonless night cloaked Port Mansfield. When darkness was complete, she approached the building from the north side, where there were no doors or windows and therefore no cameras.

She walked along the edge of the building, stepping carefully so she would not be seen or heard and stopped beneath the camera at the rear entrance on the west side, which pointed toward a parking lot. She was outside its range.

Breaking and entering had never been part of her repertoire, but this time something grave was at stake. If she had to bargain for Daniel's life, she was prepared. Given the opportunity, she would use Calcedony's letter.

By its position next to a smaller parking lot, Sarah deduced that the rear door was used as an employee exit. Eventually, someone would come out and claim one of the few cars parked there. She was right. It wasn't long before the opportunity to enter the building presented itself.

An employee exited for a cigarette break and left the door cracked open. Engrossed in a conversation on his cell phone, the man paced and puffed. When his back was turned, she slipped inside.

She stood at the doorway for a moment to collect

her thoughts. She inhaled and took a look around, her senses on high alert. It was dark, compromising her vision. She faintly heard voices and footsteps. It sounded like two men, but she couldn't be sure. They could be security guards.

Overhead, she saw the shadowy outline of a catwalk, an exposed steel truss holding up the roof. With her back to the wall, she inched toward the corner nearest her and crouched in the dark.

Hearing no more voices or footsteps, she took out a length of climbing rope and a handful of cams and carabiners from her backpack. She knew it was dangerous to climb alone, but she had done it often enough to feel comfortable with her technique. She anchored the first cam into the exposed concrete wall, tugging on it to make sure it was secure. She tied the rope around her waist and groin like a makeshift harness and hooked into her wall anchor and repeated the process until she reached the catwalk a good thirty feet above the floor.

She collected her rope and wrapped it around one shoulder to use later for the descent. The space below was a long, wide corridor acting as a central spine to a network of pods. As far as she could tell by the limited light, the pods were sealed off from the main artery by big metal doors.

She had no idea what the pods held, nor did she

have any way of entering to find out. Her only hope was the guard returning from his smoking break. With a little luck, he could be her entree to the concealed portions of the facility. She waited until he came back. His footsteps echoed on the marble floor and created a slight vibration on the metal catwalk. She stood stone still until he was past her hiding place.

Using her rope, she quickly rappelled down. With catlike agility, she landed on the floor and followed the guard as he turned left toward another section of the building. She was confident she hadn't been seen because no alarm had sounded, but she didn't know how long her luck would hold.

The guard came to a set of solid steel double doors, where a sign announced Restricted Area. He slid a card down a reader and punched a code into a panel on the wall. The doors pneumatically slid open, and he entered.

With her heart in her throat, Sarah hurried inside just as the doors were closing.

Inside the pod, she was assaulted by bright light. She turned her head away and covered her eyes with the back of her hand until they adjusted. She crouched behind an unmanned security desk separating the entry from the work area and peered around the corner.

The guard went to his station and sat behind a desk with three computer screens displaying grids that appeared to be monitoring something. Each grid contained cells with individual color maps, a thermal measurement of some sort.

Sarah tried to understand her surroundings. Glass walls separated the guard's desk from a cavernous room the size of an automotive factory, which held thousands of panels suspended vertically from the ceiling. They were coated in a bluish film and hung about two feet off the floor, with troughs of water underneath. From the bottom edges of the panels, water dripped into the troughs. Around the room's perimeter were massive structures of round lamps, similar to those in a baseball stadium.

She knew what it was: a light-fed bioreactor holding potentially thousands of acres of algae converting carbon dioxide into oxygen. The artificial lights simulated sunlight, which made the algae grow and reproduce. Theoretically, there could be an endless supply of algae. It could grow as quickly as they wanted it to—or too quickly.

So this was Donovan's infamous plant, the place where all the experiments were being conducted prior to releasing the organisms into the sea for the next phase of research. Sarah wondered what else she would find if she snooped around, but her instincts told her not to push her luck.

Besides, finding Daniel was the core of her mission.

He was there; she was certain of it. But locating him in this vast network of restricted areas and top secret facilities was going to require all her strength and ingenuity.

The guard took a telephone call and called up a series of screens on his computer, explaining a procedure to the caller. Confident that his attention was elsewhere, she turned toward the pneumatic double doors and spotted the wall-mounted button that would open them from the inside. She pressed it, and the doors opened almost silently. She stepped onto the dimly lit corridor and tiptoed toward a dark corner where she could reassemble her gear and get back onto the catwalk. She would wait there and watch as she contemplated her next move. She roped up quickly; there was no time to waste.

As she reached for the cam to fasten her carabiner, a hand gripped her wrist.

A guard shone his flashlight on her, and she shut her eyes reflexively. "Well, well," the man said in a thick Texas accent. "Just the lady we wanted to see."

Twenty-Nine

As the two guards led Sarah through the corridor, she catalogued every detail in her memory. They passed through one set of sliding metal doors and then another. One area looked like an executive suite complex. Several closed doors were arranged in a semicircle around a receptionist desk, which held nothing but a phone.

"Wait here," one of the guards said. He and his partner exited through one of the doors, and she heard the lock click.

With the guards out of the room, she had an opportunity to look around, though she was certain she was being watched.

The room itself gave nothing away. Plain white walls stretched thirteen feet high, and the oversized doors were white with brushed metal handles. On the desk were no papers, no computer. Other than the phone, not a single item identified this as a working office.

After what felt like about thirty minutes, one of the guards reappeared, and she got a better look at him. He was a giant of a middle-aged man with big, beefy shoulders and a disproportionately small head. His legs were slightly bowed. His feet, clad in black alligator cowboy boots, pointed in a V. His uniform consisted of a light blue, short-sleeved shirt that stretched too tightly across his beach ball–sized belly and navy pants cinched with a belt and holster. He worked a wad of chewing tobacco, his thin lips snarling, then spat the brown filth into a spittoon on his belt. “Come with me.”

“Where are you taking me?”

“Don’t be impatient, little lady. You’ll know soon enough.” He led her through one of the locked doors down another corridor to a maze of rooms. Stopping at one of the doors, he knocked. “Hey, got a visitor for ya.” He swung the door open and pulled Sarah inside.

She caught her breath.

Daniel. Blood had formed a crust over his left eye, and his T-shirt was ripped at the neck. He was sitting on the floor, back to the wall.

Sarah bit her lip to contain her emotion.

“Sarah?” He stood abruptly. “What are you doing here?”

"Well, she came looking for you, of course," the guard interjected. "And to hand something over." He turned to Sarah. "Ain't that right?"

"Yes," she said, her eyes fixed on Daniel. "That's right."

"Sarah, no." Daniel's tone was firm. "Don't give them a thing. They already have—"

"You shut up." The guard drove the butt of his handgun between Daniel's shoulder blades, driving him to his knees. "Now, little lady, you got a letter for me?"

She crossed her arms. "Maybe I do, but I have some conditions."

The guard laughed. "Do you, now?"

"You bring me your boss. I want him to look me in the eye and tell me why he wants this so badly."

"Lady, you're crazy. You are in no position to call the shots." He yanked her backpack so forcefully she stumbled. "Let's see what we've got in here."

Methodically, the guard opened all zippered compartments and picked her gear apart. The letter was nowhere. "So where do you have it stashed?" His eyes traveled down her body. "You can tell me now, or I can strip-search you. What's it going to be?"

A single, hard knock sounded and the door flew open.

A second guard entered. His jaws smacked as he chewed gum. "Boss wants to see you, Nate."

The guard unhooked the small pewter vessel from his belt and spat into it. He stuffed everything into the backpack and carried it to the door. "I suggest you and Pretty Boy here think long and hard about it. I'll be back in five minutes, and you better be ready to bargain 'cause I'm in no mood for your British antics. You hear?"

She shot him a fiery look.

He slammed the door and locked it from the outside.

Daniel touched his cheek to hers, whispering into her ear so they would not be overheard. "Listen to me, Sarah. These guys mean business. Have you seen anything that looks like an exit?"

"I snuck into the bioreactor. But I don't think . . ." She paused to recall the details of the room. One element in particular stood out in her mind. "These panels they're growing the algae on—they were hanging above big troughs of water. Those have to drain somewhere."

Daniel snapped his fingers. "That's it. When they first brought me here, they held me in a room somewhere under this complex. I could hear pipes draining day and night. It was quite loud, like a lot of material was passing through."

"So the water beneath the algae panels—"

"Is actually the waste product. Algae sludge spiked with carbon dioxide is being carried out of here."

"Do you remember how to get there?"

"Yes. But it'll be next to impossible. What's this letter he was talking about?"

"It's a medieval document corroborating Gabriel's warning. Long story."

"Where is it?"

"I can't tell you." She couldn't risk being heard.

Footsteps approached.

"I've got an idea," Daniel whispered. "Follow my lead."

The door swung open, and two guards stood in the entry, arms crossed.

Nate spoke. "Well? What's it going to be? Speak quickly 'cause I ain't got all day."

"If we give you what you want," Daniel said, "what's in it for us?"

"Hand over the letter, and you're free to go."

"How do I know you're not bluffing?"

"If we have this letter and a package en route from Ethiopia, we have no more need for you."

They still think the package is coming. They don't know the cross and codex have been intercepted. She decided to keep that card hidden, even from Daniel.

"We have your word on that?"

"Scout's honor."

Daniel looked at Sarah. "Tell him where you dropped it."

Sarah understood what Daniel was doing and

played along. "It's somewhere in the basement. I can take you there."

"Well, all right. Let's go." He waved an open palm. "Ladies first."

Sarah led the two armed men into a basement she knew nothing about, trying to look confident but in tatters inside. She didn't know if she could pull this off. She glanced furtively at Daniel, who raised an eyebrow almost imperceptibly. She felt reassured just knowing he was there.

As they stepped out into the corridor, Daniel signaled Sarah to turn left. After two more left turns and a long walk, they came to the entrance of another pod and took a staircase down. There must have been a thousand steps leading to this basement. The tomb chambers she had entered before seemed like shallow graves by comparison. The underground structure obviously housed something elaborate. She couldn't shake the thought that there was a second bioreactor conducting separate experiments, hidden for a reason.

At the bottom of the stairs, they came to a doorway to a large space partitioned in mazelike fashion. Fluorescent lights hung in rows down the center, illuminating the center of the room and leaving the corners dim. She glanced at Daniel and got no signal in return. She could tell by his crumpled brow he was struggling to remember which way to go from here. She swallowed hard.

Nate broke the silence. "We've got to keep moving, lady. Let's go; let's go."

"Just a minute," she snapped. "I'm thinking."

"Maybe this will remind you." He drove his elbow into Daniel's midsection, causing him to double over.

Sarah clenched her fists but didn't lose her cool. She nodded toward the partitioned area. "This way."

Though he didn't question her, it was evident by his wide eyes that Daniel feared the worst.

Sarah didn't have a plan but felt secure in her ability to negotiate twists and turns and remember where she was in relationship to the exit. It was a gamble, but it was all they had.

She led the way, with Daniel behind her and the two guards in tight formation bringing up the rear.

Daniel's breath brushed the back of her neck. One long breath, followed by two short ones.

It was another code.

A pause, then three long breaths. Again. Then a short breath, a long one, and another short one.

Morse code.

Door.

At the opposite end of the maze was a big metal slab like the entrance to a vault. Before she could compute the meaning behind his message, he sent another. Short breath, long breath, short breath. Two short breaths and a long one. Long breath, short breath.

Run.

With a swift knee to the groin, Daniel incapacitated one guard.

Sarah launched into a sprint. Behind her, she could hear the men grappling. A gunshot sounded. Alarmed, she looked back.

Daniel struggled with the young guard, wrestling the weapon away from him. He pointed the revolver at the guard's face. "Stay right there." He turned to Nate. "You. Kick your weapon over to me."

She exited the maze with relative ease and tried to find a way to open the massive portal.

Daniel emerged with his two captives.

"I think this is the place, Danny. Listen."

A faint murmur could be heard through the thick concrete walls.

Daniel smiled. "All right, gents, what do you say you open that door for us?" He held the men's own guns to their heads. "And don't try anything funny."

Nate punched the code into the keypad on the wall. A soft click indicated the door was unlocked. The other guard pulled the heavy metal handle until the door cracked open.

"Assholes first," Daniel said. "I insist."

Sarah and Daniel followed the guards inside and onto a metal platform above a sheer drop. The murmur they'd heard from the other side of the door was now a rhythmic drone as loud as a helicopter at full power.

A spiral staircase with metal treads wound around a pole, leading to a floor so far down they could not even see it. In the cavernous space below was an elaborate network of pipes, twisting in several directions and crossing above each other like the ramps of a major urban freeway. The pipeline appeared to be carrying its cargo deep underground.

Sarah shouted above the roar, "What is this place?"

Nate spat toward her feet and scowled. "You'll get nothing from me."

Daniel pointed one of the guns between the eyes of Nate's young partner, whose frightened expression betrayed his trepidation. "And what about you, son? You ready to sing?"

The guard stuttered incomprehensibly. His eyes were closed, sweat forming on his brow.

"Open your eyes," Daniel shouted. "Look at me."

The guard did, slightly, and inched toward the door. Daniel threw one of the guns to Sarah and grabbed the young guard with his free hand, dragging him toward the edge of the platform.

"All right," the guard shouted. "All right. This is the sewer. Let me go. For God's sake, please let me go."

"Sewer? What kind of sewer? What's going through these pipes?"

"Al-al-al-al—"

"Algae?"

"Yes." His voice was panicked. "Let me go."

Daniel released his arm.

That was all it took for the fear-crazed young guard to attack. He wrapped his hands around Daniel's throat and squeezed.

Daniel dropped the gun, grabbing the guard's wrists to break his grip.

Sarah aimed to fire but couldn't risk hitting Daniel. Instinctively, she reached for the gun he'd dropped.

A forceful kick to her side sent her tumbling across the platform and onto her back. She jammed both heels toward Nate, but he intercepted them and turned her facedown. His knee dug into the small of her back, pinning her to the perforated metal floor. Through the holes, she could clearly see the network of pipes a hundred feet below. She would not survive a fall. Adrenaline surging, she rolled and dislodged the guard from her back. Her biceps burned as she tried in vain to hold him back.

Daniel had broken free of the other guard's grip and held him over the platform rail. The young man, obviously overtaken by fear, wailed and vomited, collapsing on the floor.

Daniel ran to Sarah's aid and grabbed Nate in a choke hold. "Sarah, run!"

She wasn't going anywhere without him. The noise was overwhelming. She saw his mouth form the words, "Get out now."

Sarah darted out of the room and into the maze, looking behind her as she ran. Thoughts of the carnage in the maze at Yemrehana Krestos crossed her mind, adding to her terror. Her mouth was dry, and sweat drenched her shirt. She had been afraid many times but never like this.

There was no sign of Daniel.

She couldn't lose him.

When she looked back again, he was there but not alone. "Danny, behind you!"

Nate was in pursuit, but Daniel was too swift for the lumbering, overweight guard. Daniel gained ground, leaving Nate well behind.

Nearing the exit, he yelled, "There's a short cut. The freight elevator. Down that corridor to your right."

Sarah nodded and ran in that direction. By the time she called the elevator down, Daniel was at her side. The two stepped inside and pressed the up button, embracing tightly the entire time it took to travel from the basement to the ground floor.

Her father's Dassault Falcon 900 was the only jet parked at the airstrip outside of town. Sleek and more expensive than the fanciest house in town, it was the kind of plane folks didn't see much in these parts, where turbo props were considered high-tech aviation.

Sarah had never been so relieved to get on a plane.

She collapsed on a leather seat and buried her face in an ice-cold towel.

Daniel motioned to the flight attendant and asked for a double bourbon, up. Branford Spencer, the Westons' private pilot for more than twenty years, approached. Removing his cap to reveal a head full of white hair, he spoke in a gentle voice Sarah had come to associate with stability and safety. "Good evening, miss, sir. Shall I set a course for Heathrow, then?"

"Not quite yet, Branford," she said. "We're going to make a detour to New York."

"Very well, miss. Shall I phone ahead to the Plaza and see if your apartment is available?"

"Yes, that would be lovely."

Daniel turned to her. "You have an apartment at the Plaza? You are just full of surprises, aren't you?"

She laughed. "You have no idea."

He took a big gulp of his bourbon. "So what's next?"

"Next, we beat them at their own game."

Thirty

The Oceanus headquarters was on the first floor of an anonymous glass building in downtown Manhattan. The lobby was clean, sterile almost. Sarah sat in one of the four sleek black leather and chrome chairs. Daniel, now shaven and wearing the respectable clothes procured for him by the Plaza's concierge, walked to the front desk.

The young receptionist recognized him right away. "Oh my God, you're that anthropologist from TV. Daniel Madigan, right?"

The plan was working. He put on his most charming southern drawl. "Now, how'd you know that?"

She blushed and pushed a lock of hair behind one ear. "Well, I watch you all the time. I loved your show about the Queen of Sheba. That part about her being a temptress? I could listen to you all day long."

"Yes, this is a fascinating business. I'll tell you all about it sometime. But, hey, darlin', I'm actually here to see Mr. Stuart Ericsson. I'd love to talk to him about participating in one of my shows."

Sarah knew Daniel was as tightly wound as she was, and she admired his ability to lay it on thick regardless.

The receptionist took the bait. "Really? I'm sure he'd be delighted. Wait just a minute."

He took a seat next to Sarah.

The receptionist returned to the desk and announced Stuart Ericsson would be glad to see them.

Daniel winked at Sarah. "When you're good, you're good."

Stuart Ericsson was finishing a phone call and waved to them to sit down. He was fortysomething, Sarah calculated based on his career history, though his boyish Scandinavian features and fine blond hair combed to the side in the manner of a Ken doll made him look like he was in his twenties. Dressed in a navy suit and red tie, he didn't fit the tree hugger profile Sarah had expected. His immaculate desk was a gleaming expanse of glossy cherry wood interrupted only by two neat stacks of papers.

He hung up and greeted Daniel like he'd known him for years, when in reality they were meeting for the first time. For once, Sarah was grateful for Daniel's high profile and the doors it could open.

"Dr. Madigan," Stuart said. "This is an unexpected honor. What brings you to New York?"

"Pleasure's mine. This is my colleague Sarah Weston. She's an archaeologist. We've been following your work. In particular, your efforts to sway the Alliance of Nations to End Global Warming against a project called Poseidon. We'd love to learn more about that."

Stuart gave them the well-rehearsed company line. "Our goal at Oceanus is to maintain the marine environment in as natural a state as possible and to minimize the human footprint on our oceans. Our conservation practices include funding projects that support marine life and clean water and fighting initiatives that could threaten the delicate balance of our oceans. We believe Poseidon is such a threat."

"I've been reading up on your organization," Sarah interjected. "I hadn't realized it was your program that saved the western North Pacific gray whale from extinction a couple of years ago. That was quite a triumph. How did you manage it?"

"We are well connected politically. Our board, and funding base, is an international who's who of powerful and influential people. Let's just say we use that to our advantage."

"Influential enough to bring down a giant like Donovan Geodynamics?"

Stuart shook his head. "Donovan has been our biggest challenge to date. They have the support of special interest groups in every industry from energy to automotive. They are the darlings of Washington right now. Their technologies are the most promising alternatives to the prohibitive cost of changing our oil-based economy."

"So they say."

"Yes, but they've built a pretty solid case for themselves. They have scientists from the world's top institutions on their board, on their staff, and in advisory capacities. The chairman, Sandor Hughes, has sunk hundreds of millions of his own considerable fortune into funding this thing. His big pitch is that water treated with Poseidon is as effective as the rainforest in its ability to remove carbon dioxide from the atmosphere. The governments of key nations have bought right into this rhetoric and are expected to give Donovan the green light to go to the next phase of their research, which involves testing the algae in an ocean environment. Which is precisely what we don't want."

"So it's been an uphill battle."

"To say the least. I spent the better part of last year trying to convince Alliance member nations to vote against Poseidon, with only marginal success. Our biggest ally is Lars Pedersen, minister of the environment for Denmark. He's an outspoken opponent of any protocol involving the oceans and most notably Poseidon. He plans to vote against it. He has been meeting with ministers from other Scandinavian countries and tells us they are at least sympathetic, if not completely on board. All except Norway, which is bafflingly immovable. Then there are a couple of nations on the fence—namely, France and Australia. Australia actually had an outbreak of Caulerpa a few years ago in some lakes in New South Wales. They're extremely squeamish about anything involving algae, and I think they can be convinced to vote no. If we get all of those delegates on our side, we have a chance. Otherwise, we're looking at a runaway victory for Donovan." He cocked his head. "Tell me, why are you so interested?"

"Our own findings indicate such a victory could have a fateful outcome." Sarah placed on his desk a binder containing their research from the beginning of the Aksum expedition to the most recent revelations in France. "We believe there are clear parallels between these ancient writings and the Poseidon project."

Stuart put on his reading glasses and took his time examining the pages. A wrinkle formed between his brows, and he looked at the two of them.

Sarah recognized it as her cue to explain. "When we first found these inscriptions, we weren't sure what the author—the man Ethiopians call their tenth saint—was trying to tell us, because the language obviously has evolved over seventeen hundred years. We have been working around the clock to translate these cryptic phrases into something that is relevant today—very similar to how the Nostradamus prophecies were interpreted. Let me give you an example. The tenth saint wrote, 'He will rape her and dig into her core, sucking out the black blood that runs through her veins and using it to sate the hunger of his machines.' By 'black blood,' we believe he meant oil, which was dug from the core of the 'Mother'—the earth. A little later, he referred to the air 'fouled by gases.' The logical explanation for this is greenhouse emissions into the atmosphere and the high levels of carbon dioxide.

"But what we find most interesting is the verse that tells us 'Man will beget a child, a terrible creation he will unleash on the seas, and order it to return the life force to the feeble air.' It is plausible that this is a reference to a man-made substance whose aim is to restore the oxygen—the life force—into a feeble, or polluted, atmosphere. Are you with me so far?"

Stuart leaned forward, his aquamarine eyes sparkling with curiosity. "Continue."

"In my opinion, there are uncanny similarities between what I've just described and the Poseidon experiment. Now consider his next statement: 'And the child will obey until the day will come when it must answer only to its own will.' A man-made substance growing out of control, perhaps? We know that such a thing is possible given the right conditions: thermal hydrovents, possibly, or rising sea temperatures, which we are witnessing already." She paused for emphasis. "Or a nuclear accident."

"He refers to a foul enemy that joins with the child to become 'the Beast.' I'll grant that this sounds apocalyptic, but think about it. Is it so far-fetched that Donovan's phytoplankton and some other force of nature, or of man, could merge and create a mutant substance that will destroy the seas? The tenth saint's words were, 'The monster will cover the sea with a blanket of darkness and bury the fish in watery graves, and the air will not give life but take it away.'

"The air's very chemistry would change. It could be something as simple as algal bloom, or it could be far more heinous than we could imagine. It is entirely plausible that an organism such as Poseidon can, under extreme conditions, grow so rapidly it will cover the sea."

Daniel leaned forward. "Now, Stuart, you of all people know that without healthy oceans, the world will be subject to all kinds of ills, including extreme climate change, which could bring serious destruction. The last words in the inscriptions were: 'Great tongues of fire will cover the land. The tainted air will feed the flames. Smoke will rise to the heavens with a terrible fury until all life is devoured and there is nothing but the eternal silence.' What's that sound like to you? 'Cause to me it sounds like an end-times scenario. The end of the world by fire."

"Sure, it is plausible," Stuart said. "When marine life dies and falls to the ocean floor, it releases methane gas. Methane is combustible—"

Daniel finished his sentence. "And oxygen, released by these carbon-consuming algae, feeds the flames."

"This is no fantasy," Sarah added. "This man was there. He saw the end with his own eyes. He and two others." She flipped through her papers and stopped at Calcedony's letter. "This is a copy of a letter written by a woman in France. We have authenticated the original document to the fourteenth century, around the time of the Black Death. It describes the same events in plain English. Coincidence? I don't think so."

Stuart read the letter, then removed his glasses and frowned. "This is all very fascinating business. But it isn't going to be enough to convince a group of politically motivated delegates, some of whom have very complicated special interests. I will need some harder evidence than a bunch of prophets and a nebulous time travel scenario."

Sarah locked eyes with Stuart. "Then how about this? We have reason to believe Donovan are diverting the carbon they are capturing. There is a maze of piping beneath their facility in Texas."

Stuart sat up. "Are you sure about this?"

"Oh, we're sure," Daniel said. "We were there; we saw it. And let's just say it's not part of the tour. Whatever this underground system is, it's not meant to be found. We sort of stumbled upon it on our . . . way out."

Stuart bit the tip of his reading glasses and looked away. "If what you are saying is true, it may just be the missing link in a chain of events that has baffled us for years. There is an Inuit tribe on the western coast of Greenland whose population has been diminishing mysteriously. The Kalaallit, they're called. We've only recently found that the marine life in the region, which the Kalaallit depend on for food, has been severely depleted, and what's left is compromised, tainted. When we had the waters tested, we found remnants of non-native algae. No one has been able to explain how the algae got there."

"And you think this could be related?" Daniel asked.

"Maybe. The Donovan pipeline has to lead somewhere. If there is any relationship between the algae they are testing and the algae that has been killing the fish in the Arctic regions, we could be on to something. Problem is . . ."

Sarah nodded. "We're running out of time."

"The Alliance meeting is in less than two weeks," Stuart said. "Even if we were able to gain access to Donovan's facility, which they would certainly try to block, there is not enough time to do the proper testing."

"Perhaps the mere raising of the issue can stall the Alliance vote," Sarah said. "Perhaps you can convince the delegates something evil is afoot and they can demand this testing before authorizing phase two. We can help you."

"Why is this so important to you?"

"Mr. Ericsson, I am an archaeologist. I study the past, not the future. But for the first time in my career, I am faced with the prospect that the two are inextricably linked. We already know our past and our present have an impact on our future. Decisions we make now will either venerate us or haunt us through the ages. And while we don't have the gift of foresight to know what the future holds, we have, for the first time in history, clear and undisputable evidence that persons who have witnessed the future have left an account for our benefit—our redemption, if you will. It is my professional duty and my human responsibility, as the person who has come to possess this evidence, to make it known to mankind."

"It's a rather noble view, and I don't disagree with what you're saying," Stuart said. "But you have no idea what you're getting into. This is a formidable enemy. They will not hesitate to crush you."

"I know exactly what I'm up against," she said, at last fully aware. "But I have an idea."

Thirty-One

On the eve of the Alliance vote, Sarah could not sleep. Outside the window of her hotel room, the streets of Brussels were steeped in ghostly lamplight. In the distance, the gothic spire of city hall pierced the black velvet sky like a gilded needle, the sole beacon of light in the thick darkness. She looked at the clock—three in the morning—and then at Daniel, who tossed restlessly beside her. They had just completed their fourth day of nonstop meetings with Alliance delegates and were both exhausted. But Sarah couldn't rest.

The confrontation with her father earlier that evening had left her rattled. As a member of the Alliance panel, he was in Brussels for the conference and had taken the opportunity to give her a piece of his mind. The conversation had been haunting Sarah's thoughts since.

Sir Richard had said, "My sources inform me you have been . . . lobbying. They say that you have joined forces with those New Age loonies at Oceanus and gone before various and sundry environmental ministers to convince them to vote against Donovan's Poseidon project. And worse yet, that you plan to speak before the assembly tomorrow. I've had to explain to them that this is preposterous, that my daughter is a respected scientist and she would never do any such thing."

She still shuddered at the steeliness of his glare.

"It is preposterous, isn't it, Sarah?"

Though trembling inside, she had delivered her answer without flinching. "It's true, actually. Stuart Ericsson did ask for my help in delivering the message that Poseidon isn't the savior you all think it is. So, yes. We met with ministers. He did the lobbying, and I merely told them what my research has yielded: two eyewitness accounts that a program just like this one was once responsible for destruction on a vast scale. Do these ministers have the capability to swing the vote? Yes, they do. Will they? I do hope so."

With calmness like the eye of a tempest, he said, "Darling, why do you insist on humiliating me? Everyone knows I am a staunch proponent of Poseidon. Why, Her Majesty herself has spoken out in favor of it. The whole of the Western world believes this is our answer to global warming, but my own daughter publicly and blatantly disregards my position and indeed that of the crown. How dare you defy me in this manner?"

"I'm not defying you. I'm simply doing what my heart tells me is right."

"Your heart? Oh, grow up, Sarah. When will you give up your childish idealism? When it costs you everything? You do know that if you stand up before the Alliance and deliver your ridiculous hocus-pocus, your career with Cambridge is over. I will make sure of it."

"Professor Simon answers to the board of regents, not to you."

"Does he, indeed? Remember this, Sarah: what I have the power to do, I have the power to undo."

"What does that mean?"

"Remember that little gift I made to the school for the new engineering arts building? Let's just say it came with a few strings attached."

She shook her head. "What are you saying? You bought my way into the Aksum expedition?"

Sir Richard's blue eyes had all the warmth of a glacier as he delivered the final blow. "Come now, darling. Surely you don't think these things are done on merit. It's all about who owes what to whom."

The words still clung to her mind like remnants of a bad dream. That's what she was to him: the collection of a debt. The realization stung. There was no place for her in her father's elitist world.

Sarah tried to shift her thoughts to her plan,

which she'd put into motion before leaving for Brussels. It was a long shot and so fraught with danger that she questioned whether she'd done the right thing. Too many people had been hurt already; she didn't want to add to the toll. But the consequences of doing nothing were far too great.

She knew she needed to calm her mind and nerves before the Alliance meeting. There was no margin for error.

But there was no rest for her this night. After another hour of lying in bed, grappling with her doubts and demons, she finally gave up on sleep and decided to go down to the business center, which thankfully was open round the clock. She would read the news over a cup of tea.

She changed into a pair of jeans and a zip-up hoodie, then closed the door quietly behind her.

She launched down the long corridor to the elevator. Everything was still at that hour. The slight creak of the floor beneath her feet assaulted her ears like thunder. In the eerie hush she noticed things she never would have, like the stale smell of these old halls or the ambitious names of the suites—Lotus, Orchid, and Bird of Paradise, they were called, as if the names alone could transport one away from the reality of the fading European grandeur that imbued the place.

She thought she saw a shadow and quickly turned

around, but the hallway was devoid of any movement or sound. She blamed her paranoia on her sleepless state.

At last she arrived in front of the antique brass elevator doors and pressed the down button. As the elevator began its slow labor, she shifted her weight nervously from one leg to the other. She was full of anxiety over the day ahead, the confrontation with her father, and the looming menace that still haunted her consciousness.

She heard the dull sound of footsteps on the carpet. Before she had a chance to turn around, she felt firm pressure and the coldness of metal on the small of her back.

"It's loaded."

Sarah heard the gun's safety being released.

"Now come quietly. There's someone who's been dying to meet you."

Thirty-Two

The fingers of sunrise were barely touching the sky when Sarah's captor pulled up to the Gulfstream G-550 parked on the private aviation tarmac at Brussels Airport. Two dark-suited men with coiled wires extending from their ears to the inside of their collars stood at the base of the stairway. One spoke into a microphone on his wrist, announcing the car's arrival. The other opened the door and helped Sarah out of the backseat. She shivered as the icy predawn air hit her face. Neither of the guards said anything while they escorted her up the stairs to the cabin of the Gulfstream.

Sarah knew these jets well, but this one was an extraordinary specimen. The interior had been customized to the hilt. Instead of a traditional configuration, it was arranged like a living room with a modern, almost futuristic, sensibility. An elliptical white leather sectional faced a grouping of Lucite tables in various freeform shapes. Abstract art was mounted on the walls dividing the main cabin and the galley. The floor was made of a glossy, ebony stained wood composite, with an intarsia-style inlay of a familiar logo at the center. Before the black leather Eames lounge chair swiveled around, Sarah knew whom she was about to meet.

Sandor Hughes was an elderly man, ruddy faced and wearing a barbed grin. His white hair was thicker and wavier than a man his age should have been entitled to. His blue eyes were dulled from cataracts but surveyed her with an alertness betraying his intellect. The chairman of Donovan Geodynamics waved his guards away with a pink, puffy hand and spoke in a raspy voice, not with the Texas accent she was expecting but rather with the familiar diction of a northeasterner. "It's a pleasure to finally meet you, Sarah. Please, sit."

She sat tentatively on the edge of the sofa and waited for him to start the conversation. Her senses were on high alert as she faced the man responsible for so many deaths on her path here, a man capable of anything.

Hughes got right to the point. "I know you think you know who I am. The truth is, you're right. And very, very wrong."

She looked out the window. A drizzly morning

was dawning, and in the gloom the Belgian capital looked older and more tired than usual. She kept quiet.

"Andrew Matakala was a brilliant young man with an education, a Western sensibility, and a whole lot of connections. I hired him to find the tomb and keep the prophecies hidden, nothing more. I had no way of knowing he would become more and more corrupt with every ounce of power he tasted. People have been hurt . . . killed. I never asked for that, never sanctioned it. I am many things, but I am not a murderer. Yet every drop of blood he spilled, I have on my hands." He closed his eyes and lowered his head.

"Did you bring me all the way here for a confession?" Sarah snapped. "Or are you just trying to get me out of your way?"

"You know, you and I are more alike than you might want to believe." His hands shook as he took a sip of his morning scotch. "When I was your age, before I saw the worst in human nature, I was much more of an idealist. I believed I could change the world . . . just as you do."

"Don't presume to know what I believe." Her tone carried more emotion than she wanted to betray.

"How can I not? You've made it amply clear by taking on this quest to vindicate the tenth saint, even if it means gambling everything—your job, your reputation, the respect of your own kin. I admire that kind of conviction. I do. But there are things you don't understand. You have no idea what's at stake here. Not everything is as it appears."

Sarah looked squarely into his opaque blue eyes, bloodshot to match his ruddy complexion. "Oh, I know what's at stake. I've known men like you all my life. Everything is a pawn in your game. You need the Alliance's support to advance Poseidon. And you need Poseidon to make Donovan the biggest provider of alternative energy in the world. So what if there are a few pesky thorns in your side? Just banish them, like all the others." Her face was hot with rage. "Where is your conscience, Mr. Hughes? Are you willing to put the earth's future in jeopardy for your corporate profits?"

He rested his left hand on the arm of his chair and leaned forward. "Is that what you think? That I'm doing this for material gain? Because if that's the case, you're not as astute as I thought."

"Then why are you trying to silence the messages of two people who saw with their own eyes an end brought on by exactly such a manipulation of the planet? The beast they spoke of and your Poseidon are one and the same. And yet you simply refuse to allow for such a possibility. It is the height of arrogance."

He rose with great effort and leaned into a cane. He shuffled over to the bar and poured himself another two fingers of scotch over a single ice cube. "If you believe the world could be destroyed by an errant algae, you're absolutely right."

The last thing she had expected was for him to agree with her.

"Only that algae won't be Poseidon. What if I were to tell you that forty years from now, the world will be suffering so much from greenhouse gases that a company named Aurora Technologies will introduce a similar product far more aggressive and volatile? And that nations, anxious to counter the insidious effects of global warming in the face of vast deforestation, will not scrutinize or test it adequately? That our leaders, desperate and out of time, will regard that program as the savior and hastily approve it without bothering to verify its stability? And that it will gradually bring about destruction, just as your prophets predicted?"

She was perplexed. Was this a theory? Or a declaration?

"If we continue on our current trajectory of manipulating the earth, Sarah, planetary conditions will deteriorate so rapidly that leaders will be forced to assume great risk to mitigate the damage. That's why it's important to go forward with Poseidon before things reach that breaking point. Our years of research have been focused on controlling the growth of the algae so that it does not spread or multiply out of control. We have foreseen every possible scenario—toxic substances, nuclear waste, extreme temperatures, changes in the atmosphere—and have been testing Poseidon against all of them. Our facility is so advanced that we are simulating true oceanic conditions. We are not the bad guys here. We want the same things you want: to save the planet from certain ruin. If Poseidon gets voted down, we will hasten that ruin rather than curtail it."

"So you say. But it's not enough to change my mind. Anyway, it doesn't matter what I think. The decision rests with the Alliance. It's in their hands now."

He coughed nervously, and his face turned an ugly shade of magenta. He loosened his shirt collar to catch his breath. "Let me be candid here. I know you know things that could be very . . . damaging. I need your cooperation."

Sarah stood. She stared him down, her teeth clenched but thoughts clear. She wasn't playing his game, damn the consequences. "Why would I want to cooperate with you, after all you've done?"

"Because I'm on your side, Goddamn it," he thundered. "Yes, there will be a nuclear accident. It will be the most horrific, deadliest meltdown in the history of mankind. The runoff will spill into the oceans, and Aurora's algae will mutate and grow exponentially. There will be nothing anyone can do to stop it. With every additional square foot it occupies, it will consume more carbon dioxide. Before long, it will crowd the oceans and cause marine life to die, sinking to the ocean floor and leaving behind a cloud of methane. The algae will eventually sap the carbon dioxide from the atmosphere, leaving it with dangerously high levels of oxygen. The intense concentrations of methane will cause fires to erupt, and oxygen will feed their flames. One fire will beget another. And another. And another, until fires rage all over the earth, leaving destruction and death in their wake. And all will be lost." He looked out the window with misty eyes. "Your prophets are right."

Sarah froze, a chill raking her skin, the fine hairs on her arms standing on end. "Who *are* you?" she asked, though she already knew the answer.

Thirty-Three

Sarah didn't need to hear Hughes' story to know the truth. She could feel it in her gut with a clarity she had known only in rare moments of grace. Just as she needed no proof of Gabriel's words, just as she harbored no doubts about Apostolos' divinity, as surely as she trusted the mystical force that had moved her through a minefield of setbacks since the discovery of the tomb, she knew who Sandor Hughes was. As she listened to his version of events, she felt she was witnessing the unfolding of a story to which she already knew the ending.

"Gabriel and Calcedony were my students at Caltech," he said. "Brilliant physicists, both of them. When they were doing their postdoctoral work, I handpicked them to assist me on a project that would shatter all previous conceptions about time travel. Together we built the Chronopod, an experimental device that could warp space-time into a loop where everything—past, present, and future—exists in a continuum. The idea was that you could travel backward and forward in time, but you just couldn't know where exactly in the loop you were going to land."

Sarah struggled to wrap her mind around the concept. Even for a scientist who believed in the infinite possibilities of the human mind, she could not fathom time travel. There was much she wanted to understand.

"Judging by the messages left behind by Calcedony and Gabriel, there was no way to get back. Is that true?"

"Well, this was not like the time machines of the old science fiction writers, where you could dial in a year and a destination and be magically transported there, then get back into your ship when things got tough and safely travel home." He chuckled. "No, even science cannot catch up to the imagination of men. The truth is, we had no way of getting back. It was, in effect, a one-way trip. That's why we had never before sent a live chrononaut."

"So the pod wasn't ready for human travel yet. You could just as easily have perished."

"Yes, and we knew that. It was the risk we took. Miraculously, we all lived. That had weighed on my mind since 1963, the year I landed as a chrononaut in Philadelphia." He grinned absently at the recollection. "That was quite something."

"Surely you had nothing . . . not even an identity."

"Right again. My identity could not travel with me. My name actually is Amur St. John. My father was a zoologist, and he named me after a long-extinct leopard."

"So who's Sandor Hughes?"

"He was a homeless man I befriended in Philadelphia. He was an alcoholic who was dying of end-stage liver disease. He had no next of kin, no friends to speak of. I was homeless too, technically. I would go to the back doors of restaurants and beg for food and share it with him. He'd tell me stories about his life, and we kind of bonded. When he died, I took his papers and assumed his identity. Back in the sixties, there was no such thing as identity theft. No one monitored such things. It was too easy."

"And how did you build a fortune?"

"Well, I happened to have some insider information." He winked. "I struggled, to tell the truth. I had no résumé or job experience to report, so I worked odd jobs: washing dishes, working on construction sites, that sort of thing. I lived like a pauper, collecting every dime to invest later in the stock market, in companies like Berkshire Hathaway and Microsoft. That was back when they were trading for a mere pittance. I got in on the ground floor and made huge money, which I then invested in my own scientific research. I knew what I had to do, and I devoted my entire life to it. I had been given a chance to right the wrongs of my contemporaries."

"I want to know exactly what happened."

"In the year 2056, the world around us crumbled in flames . . . an utterly hellish scenario I never thought I would witness in my days. Aurora had unleashed its 'miracle algae' into the oceans some ten years prior. For a while, it seemed like it was actually working. We all took for granted that it was keeping carbon dioxide in check and that global warming was an affliction of the past. But Gabriel was not convinced. He had predicted this scenario from the very beginning. We just didn't want to believe him. But then the nuclear accident happened and the algae started to multiply. The governments of developed nations assured the masses it was all under control, but we knew better. At one point, we three decided that if the annihilation we feared came to pass, we would use the Chronopod to escape. Any fate that awaited us on the other end of the space-time continuum would be no worse than certain death. It was an all-or-nothing bet."

"Didn't you ever wonder what happened to those two?"

"Every day of my life. That's why I became so interested in prophets and apocryphal writings, scanning them for clues that could have been left behind by my friends. Eventually I found out about Gabriel.

I first heard about the legend of Ethiopia's tenth saint from a friend of mine, a German collector. When I visited him in Frankfurt, he showed me a stele he kept in his basement. He said it came from Aksum and told me the story of a Caucasian male who lived in the fourth century and became sanctified by King Ezana for his heroics in Meroë. Ethiopian legend said the saint was also a prophet and had been buried with cautionary writings detailing the earth's final hours. But the location of his tomb was unknown to all but a band of mystics. I was intrigued. I decided to look further into the mystery of the tenth saint and personally went to the monastery of Dabra Damo. It was there I was first told the saint's name was Gabriel."

Hughes crumpled into his chair. He looked exhausted. "Before we left on the Chronopod, we made a pact. We agreed to use our knowledge to throw the past off-course, thereby changing the future. So I knew Gabriel's writings detailed what we'd witnessed. They were a warning to mankind. But their discovery would be catastrophic to my plans. I was so close to a real solution that I could not let anything interfere. That's what Gabriel himself would have wanted."

Sarah shook her head. "No. I don't believe that's true. The essence of Calcedony and Gabriel's message was that man is not meant to interfere with nature.

And that's where you and they differ."

"Don't be so naïve, Sarah. We all wanted the same thing. I am only trying, through whatever means available to me, to stop the annihilation I know is coming. Gabriel left some inscriptions on a cave wall. Calcedony left a letter to her lover. I am the only one who had the advantage of landing in modern times. I actually had the perfect opportunity to change things. They didn't."

"I don't believe they would have changed anything even if they'd had the opportunity. They were wise enough to know the only way to make a change is to help people understand the consequences of their actions. Especially actions that are motivated by greed or fear. Those have the most disastrous outcome of all. You, of all people, should realize that. The real solution is to live honorably so we don't get to the point where we have to interfere."

Hughes looked pale, and his breathing was labored. He reached in his pocket for a pillbox. With a trembling hand, he took out a handful of capsules and swallowed them with his last swig of scotch. "Sarah, I know you have a lot to think about, but we don't have the luxury of time. Despise me if you want to. I did what I had to, just as Gabriel and Calcedony did in their own way. Things happened that I'm not proud of. Things I can never atone for. But I don't want to regret the ultimate mistake: letting the future unfold in the way I witnessed so long ago. I am eighty-two years old and have multiple sclerosis. There is not much time left for me. This is my final attempt to change the course of a doomed future. If I fail at this, we all fail. This may be our final chance to derail the locomotive, to be the shield in the path of an onslaught of arrows. Whatever you think of me, do what is in your conscience. I beg you. Remember why you set off on this crusade in the first place."

"I remember. Trouble is, I don't think you do. What you're doing is as misguided as the follies that led to the planet's demise in the first place. Don't you get it? You are championing what you purport to be fighting."

"If you are referring to the pipeline, I can explain. It's not what you think."

It was her perfect opportunity to call his bluff and get the confession she needed. "Isn't it? I suppose you are going to tell me that the pipeline doesn't lead to the Arctic Circle and isn't killing off marine life by the ton. That it has nothing to do with the demise of the Inuit, whose tribes are on the brink of extinction."

"You are a clever girl," Hughes said. "But not clever enough, or perhaps not experienced enough, to realize that nothing comes without sacrifice."

"So you admit it, then?"

"In wartime, a few fall for the benefit of many. If

you don't think we are fighting a silent war, my girl, you are sadly mistaken. What is happening to our environment, what *could* happen, is the biggest conflict of our lifetime. Bigger than Hitler, bigger than bioterrorism, bigger than the bloodiest jihad. This is the battle for the survival of our planet. The average Joe just doesn't realize it because he still has food on his table and doesn't have to worry about his house being bombed to ruin. The thinking is, if it doesn't affect me, then it isn't happening. The shortsightedness of people is astonishing."

"I don't disagree with some of what you're saying, but to turn the other way as people are dying, all in the name of advancing your cause? That's criminal."

Hughes swatted off her accusations and looked at his watch. "If you are smart, you will work with me, not against me. I can offer you an opportunity of a lifetime, something no one else will have access to. This is your chance to make a name for yourself without Cambridge, without your father, without Daniel Madigan. A project that's purely yours."

Sarah looked at him without emotion. She was not interested in anything he had to offer but had to let him think she was. Perhaps by talking, he would dig his own grave. "Go on."

"You said earlier that some Inuit tribes are on the brink of extinction. This is true. The Kalaallit of

Greenland now number fewer than ten thousand. Soon they will perish completely, leaving behind only legend—and some extraordinary manuscripts buried deep inside the ice sheets. If you know your Inuit history, you probably already know the Kalaallit elders have long been known as healers with untold powers. It is generally believed that their healing traditions and teachings were only spoken. But we know different. We have found fragments of seal skins inscribed with ancient spiritual writings."

Clearly, Hughes knew which buttons to push. Surely he hadn't come this far without knowing his enemy. Normally, Sarah would have been intrigued at such a revelation, but there was nothing about Hughes that she trusted. Fully aware she would probably not get a straight answer to her question, she asked anyway. "What interest does a company like Donovan have in the Kalaallit or their traditions?"

He laughed loudly. "We have no interest in the Kalaallit, my girl. We found the seal skins quite by chance. Greenland is a country rich in geothermal resources, though they haven't been exploited nearly enough. We have been funding a Norwegian research team there for the past six years. The deal is, we help them build a plant to harness geothermal energy that can be funneled to the Western world, and they let us run our, shall we say, experiments offshore. Our researchers found the manuscript fragments while examining different sites for boring feasibility. Does that answer your question?"

That was exactly the answer she needed. Donovan did have interests in Greenland, just as Stuart Ericsson suspected. On top of that, Donovan and the Norwegians were in bed together, which explained Norway's vehement opposition to Oceanus.

Sarah stayed her course. "Say I do accept your offer. What would be in it for you?"

"Your loyalty. I would fund your operation completely and give you carte blanche to run your dog-and-pony show any way you please. In return, you would pledge to me your full loyalty. No questioning. No interfering. You do your job, and you let me do mine. Do you need me to spell it out further?"

"No, sir. I understand completely."

He extended his puffy, trembling hand. "So we have a deal, Dr. Weston?"

Sarah did not offer her hand but stood motionless for several seconds, looking into the chairman's opaque eyes with more determination than she had ever felt before. She had what she needed. Now she just had to finish it. She adjusted her watch face and looked at the time. The Alliance would be meeting in less than two hours.

She looked up at Hughes. "You've given me a lot to think about. Now let me give you something to think about. Your offer holds no interest for me, not because of the subject matter but because I will not sell my soul the way you have. I still have morals, Dr. Hughes—something you clearly don't. You are so blinded by your ambition, by your grandiose plans to play God, that you don't even see the ruin you are leaving in your wake. Gabriel warned against the impudence of men like you. *Man, in his infinite narcissism, will assume the role of Creator.*" A calm washed over her, like she had been set free. For Sarah, this was a victory in more ways than one, regardless of what happened next. "I will not take part in your wicked game."

Hughes regarded Sarah with the cold stare of an assassin. "You are making a big mistake, young lady. But I will not let you ruin my life's work." He pressed a button on his seat, and within seconds the two guards reappeared. He signaled to them to approach. "It's unfortunate that you don't share my vision. I didn't want to do this, but you leave me no choice."

The two men gripped Sarah by the elbows, their crushing grasp sending her to her knees.

"Let me go." She struggled to break free and turned to Hughes with savage eyes. "This is kidnapping. You will not get away with this, you bastard."

The next thing she felt was a current going through her body and a heaviness overtaking her eyelids as she crumpled to the floor.

Thirty-Four

Sarah came to, slumped on the leather sectional, with no recollection of what had happened. Her head felt heavy and foreign, like a bowling ball attached to her shoulders, and she barely had enough control of her tingling fingers to make a fist. With great effort, she focused on an etched glass sliding door and the exotic wood paneling framing small, rectangular windows. She was still inside Hughes' plane. Her attempts to lift herself to a sitting position were futile. As much as she wanted to find a way out, she had no choice but to lie still and let her body recover.

"Okay, we got clearance. We should be off the ground in ten minutes."

"How long a flight?"

The two male voices came from the cockpit.

"About forty-eight minutes once we're airborne."

Sarah knew enough about jets to recognize forty-eight minutes as the flight time between Brussels and London. It was obvious they were flying her away from Belgium and the Alliance conference, and London seemed like the logical place to deposit her. The realization sent a rush of adrenaline through her. Suddenly fully alert, she sat up with great difficulty and looked around. The only people in the plane were the pilot, copilot, and one of the guards who had subdued her. The pilot was pushing buttons and clicking levers to ready for taxi, and the guard was hovering at the doorway of the cockpit with his back to Sarah. *It's now or never.* She stood and tiptoed toward the lavatory in the back of the plane.

The guard saw her. "Hey, where do you think you're going?"

"Look, it's an emergency, all right?" she shouted back. "I won't be a moment."

"We're about to take off. When we're in the air . . ."

"No way. This can't wait. Do you want a mess on your hands?"

"Fine. You have one minute. Any more than that, and I'm coming inside and pulling you out myself. Understand?"

Sarah nodded and locked herself inside the lavatory, grateful for the stupidity of her captor. Had he been more astute, he would have realized that the G-550 had a door that led from the lavatory to the baggage compartment. Obviously he was hired for his brawn, not his brains. His folly was her gain, for she knew this plane well. Her father had owned a G-550 until last year, when he'd traded it in for the Falcon. At her insistence, the pilot, Branford, had given her the full technical tour. She even knew how to unlock the door. Though a member of the crew had the main key, there was always a spare behind the paper towel panel, in case of emergency. She swung open the burled walnut panel that held the towels and reached inside for the familiar key holder. She pulled out the tiny box and slid the top back to reveal the very thing she was looking for. Calmly, she tried the key, which yielded a satisfying click.

The plane began to move. They were taxiing, which meant she'd have five minutes max to make her move.

An urgent knock, and the guard's furious voice came from the other side of the lavatory door. "Lady, I don't know what you're doing in there, but you gotta come out now." He knocked so hard she thought the door would come off its hinges. "You hear me? I mean *now*."

She slipped inside the baggage compartment and locked the door behind her, then looked around for the threshold plate leading to the outside. It was on the far end of the compartment beyond the baggage webbing and electrical equipment boxes.

The plane turned right. She had a minute or two

at most before the wheels would rise above the tarmac. Holding on to the walls of the compartment, she made her way carefully to the door that stood between her and freedom. Aware a light would soon go off in the cockpit, alerting the pilot that a door was ajar, she knew she had to act swiftly and decisively. She turned the latch and swung the door open.

The tarmac was a good fifteen feet below, a gray blur speeding past. She stepped out onto the threshold, her hair whipping in the wind. The cold gust lashed at her face, and she braced for what would come next. To jump now would be suicide; she had to wait for the plane to come to a momentary halt before the final full-throttle assault down the takeoff runway. It was a narrow window of opportunity, but it was her only window.

The plane stopped at the foot of the runway to ready for takeoff. She inhaled the cold air heavy with the sharp odor of jet fuel. If ever there was a leap of faith, this was it.

She quickly shut the door behind her, hoping it would buy her some time before the pilot realized it had been compromised, and jumped just as the plane started to pick up speed.

Before landing on the unforgiving blacktop she curled herself into a ball, tucking her head to her chest, to prevent massive injury. It was a trick she had learned while skydiving into the remote jungles of Guatemala during her first Mayan dig. She rolled, feeling a brutal sting as the asphalt punished her body over and over. It seemed a lifetime before she stopped moving.

She lay on her back, every square inch of her flesh in agony. Her bones felt like they had been crushed in a vise. But she was free.

She trained her eyes on the steely gray horizon and watched the wheels of Hughes' G-550 leave the tarmac.

Thirty-Five

Half an hour into the Alliance meeting, Daniel was pacing the lobby of the assembly building, checking his cell phone every thirty seconds for word from his partner. Finally, it vibrated. The text was from a Brussels number, but it was exactly what he was hoping for.

Ran into trouble. OK now. Activate plan. SW

He exhaled in relief and texted.

Get here safely. I'll handle the rest.

Daniel knew what he had to do.

Before arriving in Brussels to help Stuart Ericsson with his campaign, Sarah and Daniel had made a stop in London. It was Sarah's idea to find Brehan and solicit his help. It was a shot in the dark, but they were running out of time and options. The mere exercise of finding the elusive monk proved to be complicated.

Sarah remembered the IEMO logo on Brehan's jacket on the night he broke in to her apartment and thought that would be a logical place to start. She and Daniel went to the International Ethiopian Men's Organization center on the East End and found a building not unlike the bullet-riddled hovels of Addis Ababa. Inside, it reeked of dust and mildew, as if no one had cleaned in a decade. There was no one at the desk downstairs, so Sarah and Daniel proceeded to the TV lounge, where a young man with bloodshot eyes was staring vacantly at a Japanese cartoon.

"We are looking for a man," Sarah said in Amharic. "His face is burnt very badly. Have you seen him?"

The young man looked at her suspiciously and didn't say a word. Daniel motioned to her to try the upstairs. They climbed creaky steps to the second level, where they found a handful of bedrooms and a shared bath from which emanated a fetid odor.

Sarah knocked.

A man cracked the door open but didn't even let her finish her sentence before slamming it in her face.

It was Daniel who finally found Brehan. He figured, quite accurately, that the monk would hide out during the day and surface only after dark, when his charred visage could be obscured by the shadows of the night. It was well after ten in the evening when Daniel saw him picking through the trash behind the soup kitchen, looking for something to eat.

“I come as a friend,” Daniel said, offering the startled monk a bag of dried meat he had procured earlier at the corner grocer.

Sarah came around the corner. When Brehan saw the two of them standing before him, he froze. It was obvious by his look of surprise that they were the last people he’d expected to see there.

“Brehan,” Sarah said softly, “we need your help. Are you on our side?”

He nodded.

“Good. Then I must ask you to deliver this to Port Mansfield, Texas.” She handed him the small bundle wrapped in red silk.

“The codex,” he whispered. “No . . . We had a deal.”

“You must trust me, Brehan. Now listen carefully. This is what I need you to do.”

Daniel slipped quietly into the assembly room while the presentations were under way. Though the room was filled to capacity, his entrance went undetected, as all eyes were on Sandor Hughes, who was delivering his closing arguments on behalf of Donovan. He was in a wheelchair next to the podium, speaking into a wireless mic. In front of him was a three-tiered amphitheater, where Alliance delegates from all over the world were seated. He spoke eloquently and with conviction to a rapt audience.

“Let us weigh the facts. The earth is sick. It is dying of harmful pollutants that are breeding storms and pestilence. Lands are going barren, and crops are dying. Men are fiercely competing for what few resources remain on this overpopulated planet, and this feeds hatred and brings about war. And this scenario gets worse with every year that passes. We need to act now. Poseidon, ladies and gentlemen, is the solution, not the problem. It is the most promising research that has ever been done on carbon dioxide reduction, and we have the track record to prove it. The scientific community recognizes it as a breakthrough. We have scientists from the world's top institutions on our board, on our staff, and in advisory capacities. I have personally invested my own fortune into this project, not because of potential profit but because I believe in it.

"Poseidon is many years in the making, with vast amounts of research and development behind it. We have already demonstrated that an acre of water treated with Poseidon is equivalent to a quarter acre of rainforest in its ability to remove carbon dioxide from the atmosphere. We cannot go back on the rampant deforestation our species has caused. But we can do something to mitigate the damage. It is no secret that we have been criticized by our foes in the media and in various other forums. They have stated, without knowing all the facts, that such a product could actually be harmful to the planet should it come into contact with other substances and mutate. Is this a possible scenario? Yes, it is. Have we thought of such a scenario and then some? I assure you we have. We employ scientists who study nothing but this very thing. Poseidon is a highly stable product. We have made sure of it. We have put it in contact with high temperatures, adverse atmospheric and oceanic conditions, and even toxic waste, and its constitution has not changed.

"In our research facility in Texas, we are employing technology unlike anything in the world. In our patented bioreactors, we are growing algae in a revolutionary way that is extremely promising. We have been able to use photosynthesis to propagate this algae in vast proportions, and we are confident that with our current population of Poseidon product we can cover enough oceanic surface to make a one percent reduction in carbon dioxide levels. And that, esteemed delegates of the Alliance, is only the beginning. Poseidon is the best defense against global warming and the answer to a cleaner, healthier planet. It is the future. And today, you have the opportunity to forge that future for the betterment of our planet and the benefit of future generations. Thank you very much."

As the room roared with applause, Daniel whispered something in Stuart Ericsson's ear. Stuart nodded and turned his laptop toward Daniel.

He typed in the domain number of the Cambridge intranet, which Sarah had given him when they'd put her plan into play. "Just in case something happens to me," she had said, like she had a premonition.

Daniel logged in to the site with Sarah's password and then sent another text. He handed the computer back to Stuart, who was preparing to take the podium to deliver the Oceanus case statement. Daniel pointed to a dialogue window. "When you're ready, click here. I've alerted our contact to start transmitting."

The Alliance chairman, a silver-haired German with tortoise-rimmed round glasses, stood and pressed his palms down to quiet the room. "Thank you, Sandor Hughes, for that very thorough presentation. Ladies and gentlemen of the assembly, as you all know, our governing bylaws require us to allow every one of our proposals for action to be challenged by organizations who wish to make a formal statement of opposition. Today we will hear such a statement from Stuart Ericsson, president of the American clean oceans initiative Oceanus. We will then turn the floor over to the audience for comments and questions before convening to vote. Without further ado, I give you Mr. Ericsson."

Stuart took the podium and adjusted the microphone up. His hand shook slightly as he put on his reading glasses. He cleared his throat and nodded to the laptop operator.

The first image that flashed onto the projection

screen was a photo of a healthy coral reef just beneath the water's surface.

"The world's oceans. They cover seventy-one percent of our planet and are our single most important resource. Quite simply, oceans give life. They control climate and weather, hold ninety-seven percent of the earth's water supply, and provide nourishment for nearly half of the people of the world. In the United States alone, one in six jobs originates from marine-related industries. Humanity has always been intertwined with and dependent on the existence of the oceans. And yet we have a complex relationship with the bodies of water that support life on our planet. In fact, studies show that only four percent of the world's oceans have not, in some way, been impacted by man. Oceanus' mission is to help, through conservation practices, intervention, lobbying, and the dissemination of vital information, restore health and balance to our oceans and prevent further damage to the oceans from climate change. In realizing our mission, we do not hesitate to fight initiatives that could threaten the delicate balance of our oceans."

Stuart paused until the next image, a cluster of blue-green algae, was cued up. "Algae are critical to the existence and preservation of life within our oceans. They provide oxygen through photosynthesis and are a source of food for a variety of marine life. But algae, like many life forms, can only function and thrive if there is balance of their ecosystems. When that balance is thrown off, algae can multiply so rapidly that it can actually harm marine life and marine environments. We have seen this every time there is an algal bloom, whereas vast concentrations of algae in the water cover the surface and prevent light from entering the sea. In nature, this occurs infrequently enough that the damage is not permanent. But with human activity, the picture is entirely different."

The next image was of a German ship conducting algae research in the polar belt. "This is the *Polarlicht*, a German expedition vessel that has been conducting small-scale experiments in the Arctic Circle to determine whether the release of algae into the ocean can help sequester carbon dioxide from the atmosphere. The scientists on board the *Polarlicht* treated the seawater with iron to bolster algal populations, with disastrous results. The numbers expanded so rapidly the algae could not be consumed fast enough by the marine organisms that fed on them. When the dead algae sank to the ocean floor, they released methane and decreased oxygen concentrations, killing marine life by the ton. And remember, this was on a small scale, off one island in polar waters. Had this experiment been carried out in a larger area of ocean, I shudder to think how many resources we would have lost."

He waved toward the screen, which showed a photo of the Monaco Oceanographic Museum. "Now I would like to call your attention to an incident many of us are familiar with. In the eighties—1984, to be precise—a species of algae called *Caulerpa taxifolia* was accidentally released into waters off the coast of Monaco. When this algae came into contact with the Mediterranean Sea, it grew out of control and threatened the delicate ecosystem. It grew to cover some seventy-four hundred acres of the sea and choked or crowded out native plants, altering the ecological balance so much that many studies show more than half the species of fish have been eradicated in areas of the infestation.

"I share with you these facts, ladies and gentlemen, because they illustrate just how volatile algae can be under extreme conditions. This alone should be reason to give you pause about approving a project such as Poseidon. But let me take it a step further."

He nodded to the laptop operator to bring up a series of images from the Donovan plant in Texas. "You have already heard from Sandor Hughes that Donovan Geodynamics is growing algae in a bioreactor and that this algae has been genetically engineered to be hardier than its naturally occurring counterparts and able to withstand extreme temperatures and environmental toxins without blooming out of control. You also heard him say that the Poseidon algae has been propagated, and I quote, 'in vast proportions.' But there is something that Mr. Hughes did not tell you."

Stuart paused and took a sip of water. The room was quiet as a morgue.

"Beneath the Donovan bioreactor facility in Texas is a sophisticated maze of pipes we believe acts as a sewer of sorts, diverting captured carbon and algal waste to an unknown subterranean location. And the reason we believe so is this: last year, Oceanus conducted water tests off the western coast of Greenland in an effort to determine why so much marine life had been compromised and why the local population of Kalaallit peoples had for years been on the decline. What we found, ladies and gentlemen of the Alliance, was excessively high concentrations of carbon dioxide—more than twenty times the normal levels. *Twenty times*. But that's not all. We also found traces of decomposed algae that did not fit the biological profile of blue-green algae at all. According to our researchers, the algae we found in Baffin Bay had been genetically modified. A coincidence? Maybe. But maybe not."

Whispers erupted in the audience, and an air of agitation descended upon the assembly hall.

Hughes, sitting in a wheelchair in the front row

of the audience, stood and supported himself with his cane. His face was flushed, his breathing labored. "Lies," he bellowed as he pointed at Stuart, his arm shaking. "Mister Chairman, esteemed Alliance members, forgive this interruption, but I cannot allow such rubbish to be spoken in a venerated forum such as this. These are pie-in-the-sky theories that are one hundred percent unfounded. Mr. Ericsson is taking something that is a fact, which is the naturally rising levels of carbon dioxide in the seas of the Arctic Circle, and fabricating theories around it. What he is suggesting here is simply false, and I will not stand for it."

The chairman stood from his seat on the third level of the delegate amphitheater. He tapped his gavel thrice. "Mr. Hughes, you are out of line here. The floor belongs to Mr. Ericsson. You may reserve your comments for the end of the presentation, but such outbursts simply will not be allowed. Mr. Ericsson, please continue."

Stuart gave the double nod to the laptop operator, a signal to switch windows and call in to the Cambridge intranet.

"Mr. Hughes, if these statements are false, then how do you explain this?" He pointed to the projection screen, but nothing came up. The login had been authenticated, but there was no transmission. The screen was black, with only the words *Waiting for transmission* flashing in the lower left corner. "It appears we are having technical difficulty." Stuart turned to the operator again. "Try again."

The second attempt yielded the same result. Daniel shifted in his seat, his brow wrinkled with worry. He quickly sent another text: Transmit NOW.

There was no reply, and Daniel feared the worst.

Stuart turned to look at him, his eyes wide.

Daniel shook his head.

At that moment, the metal double doors of the assembly hall opened, and all heads turned to watch Sarah enter the room.

Thirty-Six

The left side of Sarah's forehead was scraped raw, and the palms of her hands were crusted with blood and asphalt. Her sleeve was ripped from the shoulder to the elbow, revealing a nasty purple contusion beneath. She was limping, her twisted knee sending sharp stabs into her thigh, but she felt strong. All eyes were upon her—including, she knew, her father's.

She imagined the old boy would be fuming over her unexpected entrance, the state of her appearance, and the public humiliation she had, once again, brought upon him. She did her best to avoid his eyes as she quickly scanned the room to locate Daniel in the crowd. What she couldn't avoid was Hughes' caustic glare. His usually flushed complexion turned the shallow gray of a marble statue. His eyes narrowed as he regarded her, and she could feel the fire of his wrath. She turned away from him and did what she had come there to do.

Standing in front of a mic near the audience seats, she spoke. "Mister Chairman, members of the assembly, please excuse my bold intrusion, but I am here to deliver something to Mr. Ericsson that is vital to his presentation." She was calm and composed. "Unfortunately, I had an unforeseen encounter and was delayed."

The chairman looked over his glasses at her and then at Stuart, who nodded his approval. "You may approach," he told her.

Sarah hobbled toward the front of the room, and Stuart immediately left the podium to meet her halfway. He shot her a baffled look, but there was no time for words. She leaned in and whispered some instructions, then handed him her watch. He squeezed her hand, and she mouthed, "Good luck."

Stuart looked down at the face of the watch, which indicated the record mode. He put his thumb on the play button and said, "If I may, Mister Chairman, I would like to submit a voice recording as evidence of Donovan's ill intent toward the environment and native peoples of Greenland."

He pressed the button, and the audience heard the dialogue between Hughes and Sarah:

"Greenland is a country rich in geothermal resources,

though they haven't been exploited nearly enough. We have been funding a Norwegian research team there for the past six years. The deal is, we help them build a plant to harness geothermal energy that can be funneled to the Western world, and they let us run our, shall we say, experiments offshore. Our researchers found the manuscript fragments while examining different sites for boring feasibility. Does that answer your question?"

"Say I do accept your offer. What would be in it for you?"

"Your loyalty. I would fund your operation completely and give you carte blanche to run your dog-and-pony show any way you please. In return, you would pledge to me your full loyalty. No questioning. No interfering. You do your job, and you let me do mine. Do you need me to spell it out further?"

"The voice you just heard," Stuart said, "is that of Sandor Hughes. And to borrow his words, do you need this to be spelled out further? I think not."

"This is nonsense. It proves nothing. This is taken completely out of context. Mister Chairman, please." Hughes, clearly agitated, choked on his words and succumbed to a violent coughing fit.

The assembly hall became a beehive of noise as everyone tried to make sense of what was going on.

The chairman pounded his gavel. "Order, order!"

The image flashed on the projection screen, and the room fell silent. The video camera panned across a dark catacomb of steel pipes. Naked blue light from a few wall-mounted fixtures cast a ghostly halo on the piping, so only their outlines were visible. The image was dark and silent but for a maze of bones.

Sarah's plan was working. Brehan had gained access to the Donovan facility by posing as a messenger of the deceased Matakala, there to hand deliver the package Matakala had intended to send just before his death. When inside, he snuck into the engine room and activated the video camera on Sarah's expedition cap.

As Sarah watched the images flash on the screen, she felt sick with regret for placing Brehan in the path of danger. He had gone willingly, prepared for the worst. For Brehan, it was retribution for his brother's death, the destruction of Ethiopian sacred ground, the defilement of holy relics. Being a martyr for upholding the message of the tenth saint was not only his duty; it was an honor. But for Sarah, it was one more life on the line in a battlefield that had already claimed so many. Brehan's presence in the Donovan pipeline facility could seal the fate of Poseidon. But at what price?

Have faith, she kept repeating to herself, her heart pounding in her throat. *Have faith*.

Brehan began descending a spiral staircase, following

the pipeline about a hundred feet. *What is he doing?* Sarah had specifically told him to record the image, then get out. Now he was taking the plan a step further. *This is suicidal*, she thought. *Get out, damn it. Get out now!*

As every eye in the assembly hall watched the image on the screen, Brehan suddenly stopped descending. He froze for a moment, then jerked his head upward. Sarah's body trembled involuntarily. Something was wrong. A faint voice could be heard in the background and then the downward descent resumed, this time faster and more frantic. The barrage of rapid footsteps on metal treads sounded across the room.

Brehan was being chased.

The voice came closer. "Stop right there."

An alarm sounded, signaling that there was an intruder. The camera registered nothing but a blur of metal. Sarah could hardly breathe as she watched the images with wide-eyed horror. What she feared most was coming to pass. When the shot thundered across the engine room, she fell to her knees. At the sight of the freefall of the monk's limp body fifty feet to the bottom of the pipeline, she dropped her head to her hands.

Sarah gasped for air. The room was in chaos, the verbal exchanges reaching a deafening pitch, but all she heard was her own inner voice repeating the words Hughes had spoken to her earlier that morning:

In wartime, a few fall for the benefit of many. Nothing comes without sacrifice.

She looked up and saw the final image flashing on the screen. It was a guard in a uniform bearing the Donovan logo, shining a flashlight on his victim. He called out to his partner. "Hey, Charlie, I have the body over here."

The screen went black.

The Alliance chairman stood, his glazed look indicating that he was numb with shock. He composed himself. "I think we have seen enough. Delegates of the Alliance, you have heard from both sides, and it is time now to cast your vote. We will convene in the assembly room and return to deliver the results. Audience, remain seated until the delegates return."

The delegates left the room single file. A hushed murmur fell over the audience.

Sarah exhaled. Everything felt like it was moving in slow motion as she tried to reconcile the events of the last twenty-four hours. She felt a gentle hand on her shoulder and turned around to see Daniel. Unable to utter a word, they embraced.

Ten minutes later, the Alliance members returned and reclaimed their seats in the amphitheater. The chairman remained standing as he made his announcement.

"Esteemed delegates of the Alliance, ladies and gentlemen of the assembly, we have tabulated the results. In the matter of funding and sanctioning Donovan Geodynamics' continued research for the Poseidon project, the vote is eleven delegates for, thirty-four against. Further to this decision, the Alliance will work with the appropriate enforcement entities to inspect the Donovan bioreactor plant for any evidence of transgression and will act accordingly." He gave two quick taps to his gavel. "Meeting adjourned."

In a matter of seconds, Sarah was surrounded by Stuart and his Oceanus board members, every one of them ebullient and giddy with victory. Their comments were a blur of congratulations and thanks, droning in her ears like bubbles underwater. She smiled graciously, but in her heart she wondered if this victory was worth the price.

Over the gray-suited shoulders, she caught a glimpse of her father. Sir Richard, who was obviously waiting to catch her eye, clenched his square jaw and shook his head. His eyes were hard, betraying the black hole that was his heart. He turned and walked out of the room, and she knew there was no going home again.

Sarah did not flinch. She straightened her shoulders and looked at Daniel. "Let's get out of here."

On their way out, they walked past Chairman Hughes. He clapped his hands aggressively. "Congratulations, young lady." His voice was stiff, his gaze vicious. "You've sealed our fate."

She took a deep breath and lifted her chin. "Fate, sir, is not mine to seal. Nor yours."

Daniel put his arm around her shoulder and led her outside. As he hailed a cab, she saw two swallows flying overhead in a perfect figure eight: the symbol of infinity. The tears in her eyes formed prisms that broke the sunlight into hundreds of tiny crystals, each one a microcosm of dancing color. She blinked, and the illusion was gone.

Epilogue

Sarah stood at the base of the rocky mound, contemplating the length of frayed cowhide oscillating like a doubt, a tenuous thread separating the earthly from the divine. Her eyes followed the rope a hundred feet up to the top of the vertical cliff face and looked upon the ancient church that stood atop it, a low-roofed edifice of jagged old stones held together by wood lintels. Dabra Damo was exactly as she'd imagined it: a treasure vault masquerading as a hovel, a king in pauper's clothes. She turned her gaze to the man beside her.

"Ready to go?" Daniel asked.

She gave him the thumbs-up.

"Good. Let's get one last look at you. Baggy pants . . . Loose Windbreaker . . . Hair tucked under cap . . . Okay, it's official. You look like a man."

She laughed loudly. His humor had a way of slicing through her anxiety and buoying her optimism.

"Wait. You need one more thing." He reached into his pocket and pulled out a string of ivory-colored prayer beads with a frayed tassel at the end. "A monk gave these to me when I was trekking in Ladakh years ago. They are yak bone. Supposed to bring luck. Way I figure it, a little luck couldn't hurt right now."

The beads felt substantial in her hand. She rolled them in her fingers, then wrapped the string around her wrist three times. "Thanks, Danny. I mean, thanks for coming here with me."

"Hey, I've been dying to come back to Ethiopia. Besides, you need someone to catch you if those sour old monks figure out you're a woman and decide to throw you over the edge."

She secured her backpack with its chest straps and slipped the noose end of the leather rope over her head. It slung loosely across the small of her back.

"Let's hope this baby holds," Daniel said as he tugged on the weathered hide.

"Really, Danny, this has been in use for hundreds of years."

"Yes, that's what worries me." He squeezed her shoulder. "Now you be careful. I mean that."

She held him for a long time and reveled in his musky scent. "Danny, I've been thinking about your offer. To work with you."

"It still holds."

"I may just . . . take you up on it."

His smile was broader than she had ever seen it. "Better get your sunscreen ready. It's a hundred twenty degrees in the desert this time of year."

"I can take the heat. In case you haven't noticed." She tugged twice on the rope, a signal to the monks above that someone was ascending.

A decade's work among the stones had taught Sarah the art of negotiating cliff faces even as steep as this one. Holding on to the rope, which was much stronger than its shabby appearance suggested, she climbed up the sheer rock like a pro.

At the top, she was greeted by an acolyte dressed in the familiar dingy white robes and white skullcap of the devout.

"Welcome, brother," he said in Amharic. "You have made long journey to worship here. The sanctuary of Dabra Damo will receive your prayers."

"I wish to see the abbot."

Her voice gave her away, and the monk stared at her in shock. When he realized he was looking at a woman, he went into hysterics, flailing his arms and cursing her foul presence on the sacred mountain.

The abbot heard him and rushed outside.

"A woman, a woman." The scandalized young acolyte pointed at Sarah as if she were a demon. "She must leave this instant."

Sarah removed her cap and sunglasses and gave the abbot a good look at her face. They instantly recognized each other. They had met long ago, outside the tenth saint's tomb. He was the old monk who had warned her about the wrath of God. Now that she had come full circle, she granted that he hadn't been altogether wrong. The journey had indeed been cursed at times, but it was one she would undertake again without hesitation.

"I bring word from Brother Apostolos."

The abbot looked at her serenely. "I have been expecting you." He turned and walked toward the sanctuary.

She followed him past the column of bewildered acolytes who had now gathered to see what the ruckus was. Inside, she felt the pious gaze of the nine saints, silent inhabitants of gilded icons and mosaic murals, as she walked across the narthex. She walked past niches in which were displayed illuminated manuscripts in Ge'ez, as magnificent now as on the day they had been rendered. The air was heavy with the scent of frankincense that burned eternally inside golden censers hanging from the walls. She felt light-headed.

The abbot stopped in front of the holy of holies and dropped to his knees.

She kneeled beside him and, after a long moment of silence, said, "I feel responsible for the brothers' deaths."

"Their fate was written, child. It is all written."

She wiped a single tear from the corner of her eye. "And what of the devastating future that awaits us? The destruction the tenth saint warned of? Is that written?"

"It will all unfold as it will. It is not for us to know."

"But knowledge informs our actions. And actions bring about change."

"Some change, yes. But we cannot know if our actions change the course of history or if we are merely instruments in fulfilling a predetermined future. That is the province of the divine, not of man." He turned to her and smiled. "Or even woman."

She let the weight of that statement settle on her shoulders. For all the schemes she had concocted and trials she had endured in the name of derailing the catastrophe she had been certain was coming, she still had no idea whether she had clinched the outcome. For the first time in her life, she had to allow that not every question had an answer. She inhaled deeply, then did what she had come there to do.

"Apostolos wanted me to bring these home." She took a carefully wrapped bundle out of her backpack.

The abbot accepted without unwrapping it and held it to his forehead. He was silent for a long time, obviously lost in prayer. When he rose, he offered Sarah his hand to kiss. Hanging loosely on his bony middle finger, the ring with the familiar golden seal of Apocryphon gleamed in the candlelight, betraying his status as the brotherhood's high priest. It was the same ring worn by Aregawi, used to mark the wax that sealed the codex some fifteen hundred years ago. She touched her lips to it in reverence and walked out of the church without looking back.

At the cliff's edge, Sarah surveyed the craggy highlands of Ethiopia, a place she could neither forgive nor forget. Somewhere in those hostile hills lay the tomb of the tenth saint with all its secrets and unrequited hopes.

She closed her eyes and tried to imagine Gabriel's face, to connect some image with the legend she had come to know so well. But there was nothing, only the stiff west wind. She slipped into the leather harness and slowly, deliberately stepped off the ledge.

Acknowledgments

The author wishes to thank the people of Ethiopia, Sunit Sanghrajka, Ethiopian Airlines, the priests of Lalibela, Suran Wijayawardana, Deborah Koepper, Mario Lioubin, Julian Wood, Yamit Wood, Michiko Kurisu, the excellent editors at Medallion Press, and the incomparable Peter Lioubin, who inspired and guided this story.

Want to know what's going on with
your favorite author or what new releases
are coming from Medallion Press?

Now you can receive breaking news,
updates, and more from Medallion Press
straight to your cell phone, e-mail, instant messenger, or Facebook!

twitter

Sign up now at www.twitter.com/MedallionPress to stay on top of all the happenings in and around Medallion Press.

For more information
about other great titles from
Medallion Press, visit

medallionpress.com